THE
RETURNING

**Center Point
Large Print**

Also by Ann Tatlock
and available from Center Point Large Print:

Every Secret Thing

**This Large Print Book carries the
Seal of Approval of N.A.V.H.**

THE
RETURNING

ANN TATLOCK

CENTER POINT PUBLISHING
THORNDIKE, MAINE

This Center Point Large Print edition
is published in the year 2010 by arrangement with
Bethany House Publishers,
a division of Baker Publishing Group.

The text of this Large Print edition is unabridged.
In other aspects, this book may vary
from the original edition.
Printed in the United States of America
on permanent paper.
Set in 16-point Times New Roman type.

ISBN: 978-1-60285-754-4

Library of Congress Cataloging-in-Publication Data

Tatlock, Ann.
  The returning / Ann Tatlock.
    p. cm.
  ISBN 978-1-60285-754-4 (library binding : alk. paper)
  1. Ex-convicts--Fiction. 2. Marriage--Fiction. 3. Families--Fiction.
   4. Large type books. I. Title.
  PS3570.A85R48 2010
  813'.54--dc22
  2009052568

For Viola Blake, *a kindred spirit*

ACKNOWLEDGMENTS

As always, I'm indebted to numerous folks who gave generously of their time and expertise to assist me in the research of this novel.

I'd like first of all to thank **Chris Burke**, who provided the inspiration for the character of Billy Sheldon. I've admired Chris since 1989, when millions came to know and love him as Corky Thacher on the hit ABC television series *Life Goes On*. Today he stays busy traveling with his band and serving as a spokesperson for the National Down Syndrome Society. Chris and his mother, **Marian Burke**, graciously agreed to read my manuscript and offer their feedback. Chris and Marian, for your help and for your kindness, I'm more grateful than I can say. God bless you.

A huge thank-you also to:

Roxann Colwell, for reading the manuscript and making numerous valuable suggestions. Roxann is program coordinator of the Family Support Network of WNC and Resource Center, and in that capacity she works collaboratively with the Western North Carolina Down Syndrome Alliance. She is the mother of a grown daughter with Down syndrome.

Carole Hawkinson, who sat with me on her front porch and talked about life with her son Jamie, a delightful young man with Down syndrome who was adopted from Korea.

Nancy Gossett, whose son D.J. participates in the Progressive Education Program at one of our local high schools. He has a great sense of humor and enjoys playing the PlayStation, watching *SpongeBob*, and listening to music. But it was the fact that he loves to swim and participates in the Special Olympics that gave me an "Aha!" moment. Because D.J. is a fish in the water, so is Billy Sheldon.

I'm also grateful to a number of people in Virginia who answered my questions about drug and alcohol abuse, the workings of the legal system, and the ins and outs of prison life, probation, and parole:

Martha J. Shurts, Norfolk Drug Court Counselor (as well as best sister imaginable), Commonwealth of Virginia

Julie Chavez, Senior Probation Officer, Norfolk Drug Court, Commonwealth of Virginia

Matthew Hahne, Assistant Commonwealth's Attorney, Commonwealth of Virginia

Timothy Mattson, Assistant Commonwealth's Attorney, Commonwealth of Virginia

Dawn Obliskey, Norfolk Drug Court Administrator, Commonwealth of Virginia

Marla Newby, Forensic Services Program Coordinator, Commonwealth of Virginia

And finally, a thousand thanks also to:

Julianne Presnell, daughter of fellow writer and friend Deborah Presnell, who read my manuscript with the eye of a sixteen-year-old to make sure Rebekah Sheldon was believable. Thank you for taking time out of your busy summer schedule to do that, Julianne!

Dimitrios (Jimmy) and **Constantine (Dino) Zourzoukis**, my neighbors and the owners of Three Brothers Restaurant in Asheville, North Carolina. Thanks for sitting down with me and giving me the inside scoop on running a restaurant. By the way, your spanakopita is the best.

Alice Denneville, town historian, Conesus Lake, New York, who took a telephone call from a stranger and yet kindly and patiently answered my questions about life at the lake today.

Sharon Asmus, my editor for more than a decade now. Sharon, you have unfailingly made every story better, and for that I'll always be grateful.

CHAPTER ONE

He would be here soon. The waiting was over. She'd had five long years of it, had felt every minute of it ticking by. At first his coming back had seemed impossibly far off, something that would never really happen. But here it was, the day she'd been waiting for, and now it was almost too much to believe.

Andrea glanced at her watch, then gazed back out over the lake. Another long winter had passed, and spring had thawed the water's thick covering of ice. Now, on the sixth of June, the surface of the lake was busy with motorboats, rowboats, and jet skis. A light breeze carried the sound of laughter over the water. Andrea breathed deeply and found herself smiling. The timing was right. Even nature, in turning again to life, seemed attuned to her hope.

This had been a good place to wait, this little cottage on the edge of Conesus Lake. While it was almost too small for the four of them, it was still as good a place as any, she supposed. Certainly better than that awful house they'd owned in Virginia Beach, with its beat-up aluminum siding and decades-old wall-to-wall carpeting. She'd always felt dirty there, as if she were living in a deserted strip mall. But worse than that was the fact that Virginia wasn't home.

New York was. At least she'd had the comfort of being home these past five years.

She checked her watch again, as she had done a dozen times already in the last half hour. How was it that the minute hand had scarcely moved since she'd last glanced at the time? She clenched her hands together tightly at her waist, squeezing until her fingers ached. Maybe there was such a thing as second chances. She didn't generally ask for much from life anymore, but a second chance would be nice. Heaven knew, she had waited long enough for this one.

"Mama?"

Phoebe's voice reached her from somewhere inside. Andrea sighed, smoothed her skirt, then turned away from what she thought of as her widow's walk. Not that the water out there was an ocean, and not that he would be coming back from a distant place on a sailing ship. No, it was a Greyhound bus that had made the trek up from Virginia. By now, Owen should have met him at the station, and they should be nearly home. Unless he got off at an earlier stop and disappeared. Would he do that? Maybe he didn't want to come back. Maybe—

"Mama!"

Andrea opened the screen door and stepped into the front room of the cottage. Phoebe sat cross-legged in the bay window, her coloring book and crayons and her game of Chinese checkers spread out in front of her. In one hand she loosely held a kaleidoscope. The child spent hours on that window seat, quietly entertaining herself. Of Andrea's three children, Phoebe was the shyest, the most withdrawn. Andrea would be glad when she started first grade and began socializing with other children.

"What's the matter, Phoebe?" Andrea asked.

"What time is Billy getting home?"

"You're in luck. He'll be home early today."

"How come?"

"It's a surprise. You'll see."

Phoebe smiled, though tentatively, as if she didn't quite understand her mother's words. "You look pretty, Mama," she said.

Andrea was surprised. "Do I?" She touched her hair, her fingers floating over the dark curls. She'd had Selene style and perm it and, for the first time, wash out the gray. She had wanted it to be just right.

The child nodded. "Are we having a party?"

"Not exactly."

"Then why are you wearing lipstick?"

"Well, I . . ." How to explain? "I don't know, Phoebe. I just thought I would for a change. Is it too much?"

A small line formed between Phoebe's brows. "Too much what?"

"Too much lipstick."

"I don't know." The child shrugged. "I guess not."

Andrea looked at her daughter. Of course she wouldn't know if it was too much lipstick. She was six years old.

"Do you want a snack to tide you over until dinner, honey?"

"No, I'm not hungry." She lifted the kaleidoscope to her eye and pointed it toward the window. "When Billy gets home can he play Chinese checkers with me?"

"Sure, I guess so. Maybe after supper."

Phoebe didn't respond. She was busy slowly turning the end of the kaleidoscope, making pictures of beads and glass and sunlight.

As she gazed at her child, Andrea felt something twine itself around her heart and squeeze. Everything was about to change. Their whole day-to-day life was about to shift in a way inconceivable to a six-year-old, and Andrea wondered what it would do to her youngest child. What it would do to all of them. Andrea wanted them all to be happy, and she hoped that somehow there would be something like happiness in their future. But she sensed—though she couldn't see it yet—she sensed the wave of disappointment beginning far off, past the horizon of the present moment, a wave that would swell and grow and crash over them sooner or later. That was how it always was, it seemed. Happiness thwarted in a thousand ways.

But maybe not this time, she thought. *Maybe this time it'll be different.*

One was allowed to dream, after all. And hope.

"Well, let me know if you change your mind," she said to Phoebe. "You can have some peanut butter and crackers if you want."

From the bay window came the small disinterested reply. "Okay."

Andrea went to the kitchen where she had a pork roast in the oven. It would soon be time to peel the potatoes. She reached for the apron that hung on a hook by the fridge and tied it around her waist. Even as her fingers worked, twenty years fell away, and she was a teenager again, nervous and breathless as she waited to be picked up by her date. Not that she had dated much—a couple of movies, a few school dances, and then, suddenly, marriage. The circumstances weren't the best, but that was all right; she'd married the man she wanted to marry. She had been in love, after all.

She opened a drawer and fished for the potato peeler, but before she could find it, a car pulled off the road and came to rest in the gravel drive. There they were, Owen behind the wheel, John in the passenger seat. Andrea quickly untied the apron and hung it back up on the hook.

So this was it. He was home now.

She watched from the window as the car doors opened in tandem and the men stepped out. One door slammed, then the other. Owen stretched, rising up on his toes and reaching for the sky.

John stood still, a black garbage bag clutched in his right hand. He seemed to be waiting for a cue from Owen, something to tell him it was time to walk on stage and get this show going.

Andrea raised a fist to her mouth and pressed it hard against her lips, if only to stop the tears that were threatening to rise. She wouldn't cry, wouldn't embarrass herself by crying. He wouldn't like it.

For one agonizing moment she felt the old rage rise up in her. She wanted to pound her fists against his chest and curse him for what he'd done. She hated him—hated him for his weaknesses and his lies, for the shame and hardship he'd brought on his family.

And yet, in spite of all reason, she couldn't deny the affection, the feelings of longing that washed over her even now. How would she ever untangle the knotted skein of emotions that wrapped itself around every corner of her heart?

The two men climbed up the slanted wooden walkway to the kitchen door. Owen knocked briefly. And then they were in the kitchen, all three of them occupying that cramped space, staring wordlessly, wondering what on earth this moment called for.

She would have to speak first, she knew. "Hello, John," she said.

His eyes, anxious and unsettled, came to rest on her face. "Hello, Andrea," he said quietly.

She thought she should kiss him, hug him at least, but the moment passed. "I'm glad you made it all right."

"Sorry we're late," Owen offered. "The traffic coming down from Rochester was heavier than I expected."

"That's all right," Andrea said, relieved to turn her attention to her brother. "Thank you for picking up John."

Owen nodded slightly. "Well, I've got to get back to the restaurant." He glanced at his watch. "Almost time for the dinner rush."

"Of course. You go ahead."

"Owen." John held out his hand. "Thanks for the lift."

Owen looked at John's hand, his face, his hand. He shook the proffered fingers briefly. "No problem."

Then he was gone, and Andrea and John were alone. Andrea pressed her sweaty palms against her thighs. The moment was too big and too small at the same time. Here was the hour she had walked toward these past five years. Now that she had reached it, she could see that it was smaller than it appeared from a distance. John was still John, after all, the man whose love seemed always beyond her reach.

She pointed at the bag. "Are those your things?"

"Yes." He nodded. "I guess they were out of Samsonites."

She tried to smile. "Well, why don't you just

drop it on a chair for now. Later you can unpack upstairs. But first . . ." Her voice trailed off. She moved from the kitchen to the front room, hoping he'd follow. He did.

Phoebe still sat at the window, her face turned toward the glass, her knees drawn up to her chin. Andrea knew the child didn't like to meet strangers, was trying to make herself small enough to be overlooked.

"Phoebe?"

No response.

"Phoebe, can you turn your attention this way for a minute?"

The child turned her head slowly. She chewed shyly on her lower lip.

Andrea lifted a hand toward John. "This is someone I've wanted you to know for a long time," she said. "Phoebe, this is your father."

Chapter Two

John flinched as the screen door banged shut, then watched in surprise as his daughter's blond curls disappeared down the steep bank by the lake. He hadn't even managed a good look at her face. He felt a burning in his cheeks, as though he had just been slapped.

After an awkward moment he heard Andrea say, "I haven't gotten around to fixing the spring on that door."

"No." John cleared his throat. "I can see that."

A few more seconds passed before she said, "I'm sorry, John."

He thought she was talking about the door. "It's all right, Andrea. I'll take care of it later."

"No. I mean, I'm sorry about Phoebe. She's so shy, it's hard for her to meet people. Don't take it personally."

"Maybe I should have allowed you to bring her when you visited. That way, she'd know who I am. It wouldn't be such a shock to meet me now."

"No." Andrea shook her head. "It was best not to take her into the prison. She was too young, not like Rebekah and Billy. Heaven knows, it was hard enough on them."

A muscle tightened in his jaw; he worked his mouth a bit to loosen it. "I guess you're right," he conceded. "But you did tell her I was coming, didn't you?"

He heard her sigh.

"No, I didn't. I thought—well, I thought I shouldn't."

He turned to her sharply. "But why not?"

"I don't know." Andrea looked up at him then with apologetic eyes. "I guess I didn't want her to spend days worrying about it." She looked away again, toward the door through which Phoebe had disappeared. "I'll go get her. She's just hiding under the dock, where she always hides."

She took a step forward, but John stopped her

with a hand on her shoulder. "Let her be for now. No doubt she needs to get used to the idea."

He felt Andrea stiffen under the weight of his hand. He withdrew it and suddenly didn't know what to do with it. He made a loose fist and stuffed it into the pocket of his trousers, the new pair of slacks Owen had given him at the bus station, along with a casual shirt and a pair of loafers. Andrea had sent them, wanting him to come home in something other than the telltale jeans, blue shirt, and brogans—the heavy work shoes—that prisoners were issued on release.

"She knew, didn't she, that I'd be coming home eventually?"

"Of course, John."

He hesitated, then said, "And she knew where I was."

"Yes, she knew. I don't think she really understands it all."

"No." He shook his head. "I wouldn't expect her to. But she's always known she had a father? You spoke of me?"

"Yes. I spoke of you often. You must know that, John."

He didn't respond. He pulled a handkerchief from the pocket of his pants, looked at it absently, tucked it away again. He was thinking of the child he had last seen as an infant, the child he had watched grow up only through photographs that came to him in letters already opened, courtesy of the Virginia Department of Corrections. Then he asked, "What about Billy and Rebekah? Where are they?"

"They're both at work, but they'll be home for supper. Billy usually stays through the dinner rush, but Owen is letting him off early today."

"That's good of Owen."

"Well, it's a special occasion, isn't it?"

Only after a moment did John realize his hands had become fists. He breathed deeply, stretching his fingers, trying to unleash his tension. "Do they know? Do Billy and Rebekah know I'm home?"

"Yes, of course they know."

"How are they taking it?"

John and Andrea didn't look at each other as they spoke. Instead, they both had their eyes fixed on the screen door, as though it were a third person in their conversation, a mediator of sorts, something that could keep them focused.

"It'll be all right, John," Andrea said. "You'll see. They've grown so much since last summer, you'll hardly recognize them."

That's what I'm afraid of, he thought. *I don't know my own kids anymore.* The children's annual trip from New York to Virginia was all they could afford, though Andrea made an additional solo trip each year, leaving the kids with Owen and Selene. Maybe, though, John should have had his family stay in Virginia instead of sending them up here. That way he might have watched the kids grow up. But, at the time, sending them to live in the cottage had seemed the right thing to do. Anyway, what was done was done.

"I'm making a pork roast and mashed potatoes," Andrea told him, her tone lighter now. "I know that's a hot meal for a summer night, but . . ."

He nodded, a small tilting of his head. Pork roast had always been his favorite, and Andrea had remembered. "That'll taste good. I haven't had a good home-cooked meal in—well, in a long time."

They ventured a glance at each other.

"Um," she said, "I'll get started on the potatoes, then. It'll be an hour before the kids are here. Why don't you just"—she looked around the room, waved a hand—"well, make yourself at home."

The irony of what she said wasn't lost on him. This cottage had been his home long before Andrea had ever set foot in the place. Now, in a strange twist of roles, she was the hostess, inviting the stranger in. He looked toward the screen door again. He heard rather than saw his wife leave the room.

He was alone now except for a voice in his head, the voice of a man he knew only as Roach. *"How many more days, Sheldon?"*

Roach had asked him that question as soon as

he had learned John was a short-termer. Without having to calculate, John had told him the number of days.

"*Yeah?*" A smirk crept over Roach's leathery face. "*Well, enjoy the taste of freedom while you can, because once it comes for real, it's not nearly as sweet as it's tasting right now.*"

"*Is that so, Roach?*"

"*Yeah. I ought to know.*"

"*You've been out?*"

"*Out and back. Out and back. It's a revolving door, Shel.*"

"*Not for me it's not.*"

"*That's what you say now. Wait and see.*"

"*I'm not coming back. Once I'm out, I'm out for good.*"

Roach had laughed, an infuriating little laugh. "*Sure, Sheldon. Good luck on that one. What you don't seem to know is once you're in the system, there's no way out again. Not for good, anyway. You might get out for a while, but you'll be back. Warden's got you on the end of a rubber band.*"

John shook away the thought of Roach. He moved to the screen door and opened it. He could do that now—just open a door and walk outside into the fresh air, the sunshine. He stood on the porch and breathed deeply. The air carried the scent of lake water mingled with something sweet, maybe honeysuckle. And freshly cut grass. Yes, that too. The breeze caressing his face swept over the lawn in front of the cottage and lifted the earthy aroma to him. Billy must have cut the grass just this morning. The pattern of the mower was still evident in the neat stripes falling back and forth across their narrow property.

At the edge of the yard was the bank and the wooden stairs, six steps down, leading to the dock. He and his brother, Jared, swam from that same dock all the summers of their childhood. Their folks brought them down to the cottage from Rochester every year as soon as school was out. This was where John and Jared passed the hot lazy days of vacation with their mother, their father joining them every weekend, driving down from the city on Friday afternoon after he got off work. To John, this was the greatest place in the world. His happiest memories had been made right here on Conesus Lake.

And now, finally, here he was again, back at the lake. How often in the past five years had he dreamed about standing right here and looking out over the water? Every day. Every single day of every single one of those years.

Roach was wrong; freedom was sweet. The late-afternoon sun hovered on the far side of the lake now as it journeyed westward, and it was sweet to stand here squinting against the blinding glare of the water's surface. It was sweet to feel the wind, to hear the tangled song of the birds, to know he could walk down off the porch and all the way to the far end of the dock, where he could dip one hand in the cool water if he wanted. It was sweet simply to gather to himself the memories of the place that had always been more home to him than the house thirty miles away in the city of Rochester.

He moved down the porch steps and stood on the freshly cut grass. He took off his shoes, stuffing his socks in the toes of each new loafer before tossing them back toward the porch. He could do that now too. He could stand with the warm grass beneath his bare feet for as long as he wanted, and there was no one to tell him otherwise. The regimented schedule was behind him now. The bars, the single-file lines, the inedible institutional food—all gone. He was free.

A motorboat sped by close to shore, sending a ripple of waves across the surface of the water. In another moment John heard the knocking of wood against wood, just the way he remembered. Two boats were moored on either side of the dock, one a rowboat, one a small motorboat, and as they rode the waves they bumped against the dock's sturdy posts. John loved that sound better than any song he'd ever heard. There was a time when he'd lie awake at night on a cot on the porch, hands under his head, listening to that rhythmic lullaby drifting up from the water.

The boat he remembered was an old rowboat, long ago retired. The two boats tied up now were new to John, though hardly new in actual fact. Both had been gifts from Owen to John's kids, in a left-handed sort of way. Owen had passed them along when he bought better boats for his own kids.

Billy was thrilled with the motorboat, according to Andrea. She'd written in a letter that while she didn't allow Billy to take the boat out alone, he felt very confident driving his mother and sisters around the lake. He also enjoyed it when his cousins Russ and Stuart came over and helped him tinker with the engine. John tried to imagine that. He never thought his son would be capable of working with any kind of machinery. Never thought he'd be able to do something as basic as cutting the grass. But here he was—tinkering with engines and cutting the grass and even holding a job as a busboy at Owen's restaurant.

At the same time that he marveled at the boy's accomplishments, John felt an unexpected shiver of dread at the thought of Billy. And Rebekah. And the little girl he didn't even know cowering down there under the dock.

"Phoebe," he said aloud, though he knew she couldn't hear him. He pressed his lips together, shut his eyes, opened them. Soon they would all be together, all five of them sitting around a table eating pork roast and mashed potatoes. If Phoebe's reaction to him was any indication of what was to come, it was going to be a difficult night.

"Phoebe," he called again, more loudly this time, but still he got no answer.

He thought of all the nights he had lain awake, not on a cot on an open porch but on a bunk in a stifling cell, listening to the cries in the dark. Tough men, hard as stone by day, reduced to pitiful creatures at night, like wounded animals. Not every night, but sometimes, especially when the new ones came in, the long corridors echoed with the unmistakable sound of weeping and men calling out the names of their children.

They were afraid their sons and daughters would forget them. Or worse, would never know who they were in the first place.

Now John knew that their cries were justified. The cottage, the dock, the lake—they were all here and hadn't changed. He could return to a place. But his children—they had all gone on without him, had grown into people he would not know. They would be little more than strangers to him, and he to them.

The sweetness of only moments before took on a bitter edge. He was free, but he realized he hadn't quite finished paying for what he'd done. He'd served the time, but the hardest part of the payback might be ahead.

And it would start in another hour or so, when they all gathered together as a family for dinner.

CHAPTER THREE

John carried a handful of flatware out to the table in the screened-in section of the porch. That was what his mother had most loved about this place—the wraparound porch, which was almost larger and roomier than the cottage itself. But that was the whole purpose of a lake house, wasn't it? Not to be indoors but to be outdoors, living right in the middle of nature rather than glancing at it occasionally through a window.

John let the flatware tumble out of his hand and onto the plastic tablecloth. The knives and forks clanged noisily as they toppled onto the pattern of red and white squares. The table covering was the typical picnic cloth, and its simple familiarity looked beautiful compared to the unadorned steel tables of the prison dining hall. John ran his fingertips over the plastic covering and almost marveled, as though it were white linen. Chuckling at himself, he lifted his head, breathed deeply of the fragrant air, felt his heart tighten with gratitude.

Lord God, he thought, *thank you.*

He took a step forward, squinted against the sun. His eyes swept over the lake again, this time settling on the massive stone structure that had been an object of intrigue around Conesus for decades. Once a private residence, the place was deserted now, left empty and crumbling after the untimely death of its owner, Arthur P. King. The man had been something of a wealthy scoundrel, as well as a womanizer and a drunk, and yet the locals had dubbed him King Arthur and looked with awe and envy on the mansion they called the Castle. In its heyday, during the years of Prohibition, the Castle had been the site of notorious parties for the residents of Conesus Lake. Large crowds of dandies and flappers drank home brew and danced by the water to the music of jazz bands, while every summer some drunken sod fell off the end of the dock and drowned. It got so that bets were placed as to who might be lost before the season was over. Oddly enough, in the summer of 1929, it was King Arthur himself who hurled headlong into the lake and didn't come out again—at least not on his own.

John assumed the property was still in the hands of the family, though they hadn't put in an appearance since the death of King Arthur, and nobody seemed to know who they were. Still, the parties went on without them, year after year, mostly for young underaged drinkers who brought their own booze. John and Jared had been among them once, years ago, when the brothers were teenagers. The Castle, rumored to be both cursed and haunted, was the perfect place for young men to display false bravado while dabbling in forbidden wonders. It was there John had his first drink while listening to a boom box blaring the music of Pink Floyd and the Grateful Dead. . . .

But he didn't want to think about that right now. That was another life. Things were different now. Everything.

He moved the knives and forks around to form five settings, then realized there weren't enough chairs around the table. Only four when there should be five. He'd have to find another.

In the kitchen Andrea stood over a boiling pot on the stove, poking at something inside with a fork. She looked up at John when he came in and smiled weakly. She laid the fork aside and rubbed her palms against the skirt of her bibbed apron. He noticed how, in spite of the oscillating fan on the kitchen table, her bangs were plastered to her forehead with sweat. He had almost told her earlier that her hair looked nice, but for whatever reason he hadn't moved the words from his mind to his tongue. Chiding himself, he decided it was too late now.

"The potatoes are almost ready to mash," she said, "so I hope the kids will be here soon."

John nodded, unsure of how to respond. Stepping to the table, he picked up a chair. "We need one more," he explained.

She looked stricken, her eyes moving from the chair to his face. "I meant to do that. I'm sorry—"

"It's all right. I've got it."

He carried the chair to the porch and made

room for it at the table. Andrea's mention of the kids had triggered a wave of fear somewhere inside of him. He took a deep breath, trying to calm himself, but even before he could exhale, a car pulled off the road and came to rest in the gravel drive. A young girl with long blond hair sat behind the wheel of a Volkswagen Jetta that was long past its prime.

Rebekah.

He took a step forward, stopped. He waited. She seemed to take forever to open the door and get out. When she did, he could see that her eyes were fixed on him.

He had loved her more than all of them. She was the one who had given him his greatest measure of joy. Ten years ago, when she was a golden-haired child just Phoebe's age, she had been a daddy's girl and had given him something to come home to at the end of the day. But over the years he had watched her grow not only older and less childlike but, to him, achingly more distant each time Andrea brought her and Billy down for their annual visit.

Now she was almost grown up; he could see that as she walked toward him, tall and lithe and confident. His little girl was a young woman now, coming into her beauty.

Andrea appeared in the kitchen doorway just as Rebekah moved up the slanted walkway to the porch. The girl stopped when she became level with her mother. For a moment the three of them looked at one another, saying nothing. John wondered whether anyone else could hear the pounding of his heart and the hollow sound of blood rushing through his ears.

"Your father's home," Andrea said quietly.

"Yeah," the girl responded. "I can see that."

John felt his daughter's eyes on him like burning coals. The heat of her stare left his mouth dry, his tongue like sandpaper. He tried to moisten his lips discreetly before saying, "Hello, Beka."

Andrea wiped her palms against her apron again. "Well, Rebekah," she said. "Aren't you going to say hello?"

"Hello."

The word was as lifeless as tumbleweed. John felt it roll through him, snagging his heart on the way.

He fumbled for something to say. In his nervousness, he found himself echoing Andrea's comment to him earlier. "You've grown so much since I saw you last summer, I hardly recognize you."

John watched the blue eyes narrow. "Yeah?" she said. "Well, it's hard to keep track of things when you're not around, isn't it?"

"Rebekah!"

"It's all right, Andrea. I—"

Mumbling something John couldn't hear,

Rebekah pushed past her mother. Ducking into her bedroom off the kitchen, she shut the door heavily.

John and Andrea avoided each other's gaze. At length John said, "Well, that didn't go very well, did it?"

"You'll have to give her time, John."

He nodded, drew in a deep breath.

Andrea went on, "It hasn't been easy for her these past few years, growing up without her father around."

"No, I suppose not."

"We'll have to be patient. But she'll come around."

He took a step backward, stopped again. "I've missed so much." He looked up at his wife. "I've missed too much. Maybe there's no way to come back now—"

"No," she said quickly. "No. It'll be all right. You'll see."

He wanted to believe her. Following her into the kitchen, he started to say, "Do you think Billy—"

But she interrupted him again. "He should be here in just a few minutes. Owen was going to have Maggie bring him home when she got off her shift."

That wasn't what he was going to ask. He was going to ask her if Billy might be glad to see him. Now he decided to let it drop.

Andrea opened the oven door and peeked inside, releasing the aroma of pork roasting. Andrea had always been a good cook. John suddenly realized how hungry he was, how his stomach felt like a huge empty valley inside of him.

She shut the door and, turning swiftly, almost bumped into John. He started and backed up. "I'm sorry," he said. "I didn't mean to be in the way."

"You're not in the way," she assured him. "I'm just not used to . . ."

She didn't finish, didn't seem to know what else to say. John looked around the kitchen, searching for a way to end the awkward moment. "Here," he said, "can I carry this trash out for you?"

"Yes. Thank you." She looked relieved. "You know where the cans are."

"Of course." He pulled the plastic bag out of the wastebasket, tied the top in a knot, and carried it outside. The garbage cans had always been around the back of the cottage so they couldn't be seen from the lake.

When he found them, he lifted the lid of one of the cans and dropped the bag inside. As he settled the lid back on, he heard a car slow down and pull over to the side of the narrow road that skirted the lake. He recognized neither the car nor the woman who drove it, but when the passenger-side door opened and a young man got out, John knew

Billy was home. He would have known his son anywhere—the small head sprouting like a stunted bud from a thick neck, the flat round face, wide nose, lipless mouth, the slanted eyes.

For just a moment the boy didn't move, but then, even from a distance, John could see the small eyes widen, the mouth draw back in a silent laugh, the chinless jaw point skyward. Then Billy moved around the car, and dropping his backpack on the gravel drive, he ran on short but powerful legs toward his father.

John stood breathless in his son's embrace while Billy cried out happily, "Dad! It's Daddy. Daddy's home!"

CHAPTER FOUR

Thank God for Billy, Andrea thought as she watched her son through the kitchen window. In throwing his arms around his father, he had done what neither of the others had done, maybe what neither of them *could* do—at least not yet. She kept her eyes on Billy and John as they moved toward the walkway together. Then Billy burst into the kitchen, grinning widely, sputtering as he announced, "Look, Mom! Dad's home!"

Andrea smiled lovingly at her son. "I know, Billy. Isn't it wonderful?"

"Dad's home!" he said again, as though he couldn't quite believe it.

"Yes."

"Home to stay!"

"Yes, Billy. He's home to stay."

"Does Phoebe know? Where is she?"

"Last we saw, she was heading for her hiding space under the dock."

"Again? What for?"

Andrea looked at John.

"I'm afraid she's hiding from me, Billy," he said.

"From you?" Billy laughed. "Why would she hide from you?"

"Well, I guess she's a little shy. Do you think you could coax her out?"

"Sure, Dad! Come with me." Billy smiled confidently, leading the way outside with a wave of his arm.

Andrea followed but stopped on the porch as her husband and son moved down to the edge of the bank. At the top of the steps leading down to the dock, Billy cupped his mouth with his hands and hollered, "Phoebe Sheldon, this is your brother Billy. Come up here! Come up here now! Say hi to Dad!"

He dropped his hands and waited. He seemed certain he would get the response he wanted. Soon the blond head bobbed slowly up the steps. Once she reached the top, Phoebe leaped toward her brother, her small arms circling his waist so that her hands met in the small of his back.

Billy hugged her tightly, then straightened up and pointed at their father. "Look, Phoebe, look. It's Daddy. Daddy's home. You got to say hi, okay? Or you'll make him feel bad."

Andrea held her breath as John bent down on one knee, down to the child's level. He held out an open hand. "Hello, Phoebe," he said tenderly. "I'm very happy to meet you."

He waited. Andrea waited. Phoebe looked up at her brother's face.

With an exaggerated sigh, Billy urged, "What are you waiting for, Phoeb? A gold-graved invitation?"

Andrea laughed quietly to herself. How many times had Billy heard her chide the children with that line: *Go on, do as I say! What are you waiting for, a golden-engraved invitation?*

Slowly Phoebe unlocked her hands and let go of Billy. She turned and looked at her father, then touched the palm of his hand briefly, the way a moth alights on a lily and flutters off. She might have said something, but Andrea couldn't hear.

Thank God for Billy, Andrea thought again. All hope was not lost. Though heaven knew that even hope had its limits.

Leaving the three of them to get acquainted, Andrea made her way to the room off the kitchen, Rebekah's room. The door was closed. Handwritten on a piece of notebook paper and newly taped to the door was the warning: No Adults Allowed.

Andrea knocked.

"Go away."

"Rebekah, it's Mom."

"I said, go away. Can't you read the sign?"

"Beka, please."

"What do you want?"

"To talk with you—just for a minute."

The door flew open and Rebekah stood there, her face a mask of defiance.

"Beka—"

"I know what you're going to say."

"Oh? And what's that?"

"Be nice to Dad."

"Well, yes—"

"I hate him."

"I don't believe that."

"Well, it's true."

For a moment Andrea didn't know how to respond. She studied her daughter's angry face. "There was a time," she said slowly, "when you didn't want anything more than just to sit on your father's lap—"

"Don't go sentimental on me, Mom. I was a kid. Well, I'm not a kid anymore."

No. No, she wasn't. She was a young lady now, and on the whole, Andrea was pleased with how her daughter was turning out. Rebekah was generally pleasant at home, willing to help out around the house without too much complaint. She was fairly responsible, did well at school, and rarely got into any real trouble. But she had a stubborn streak that lately was showing up as defiance toward all authority. Andrea blamed it on teenage angst and expected her daughter to outgrow it eventually. In the meantime, it had to be tamed.

"Okay, listen, Rebekah, your father's home whether you like it or not—"

"I don't like it."

"And we have a chance to make this family work. I won't have you ruining it for all of us."

For one brief moment Andrea thought Rebekah might back down. A certain calm crept over her face, as though she were suddenly remembering the father of years ago. But when she spoke, Andrea's hope faded.

"Everything was fine without him, Mom. Why did he have to come home?"

"Because this is where he belongs, Beka. Where else could he go?"

Rebekah's gaze turned cold then, like granite in winter. She pursed her lips, and her eyes froze over with angry unshed tears.

"I know it's been hard on you, honey . . ." Andrea began, but before she could finish, the bedroom door slammed, and the latch was snapped shut on the other side.

CHAPTER FIVE

Clutching a box of wooden matches, Rebekah ran one bulbous head along the lighting strip. The end of the match sizzled and flared, then settled into a tiny flame. A wisp of gray smoke, smelling of sulfur, drifted upward and disappeared.

She held the flame to the wick of the largest lavender candle on her nightstand. Lavender was the fragrance for peace. Rebekah had read that in one of the books Lena gave her. She now had a drawer full of lavender candles in the nightstand, as well as three candles of varying sizes in chipped stoneware saucers next to the digital clock.

Her mother didn't like her lighting candles indoors, but she didn't forbid it either. She simply told her to be careful. She trusted Rebekah. So far. Which was how Rebekah wanted it, because as long as her mother trusted her, she could do whatever she wanted to do and maybe even get away with it.

Of course, that all might change now. Now that there was another grown-up in the house. Another parent, supposedly.

Once the candle was lighted, Rebekah shook out the match with a flick of her wrist. She added the blackened stick to the pile in the saucer. Leaning toward the flame, she inhaled deeply. Lavender was a pretty scent, and upset as she was, maybe if she let her room fill up with it, the lavender would kick in and help calm her down.

After all, she needed something, now that *he* was back.

At the thought of him she flung herself down on the bed and beat the pillow with her fist. She had missed her father at first. She'd cried a lot, asked when he'd be coming home. Then, as month melted into month, she'd gotten used to his being gone. His absence became the norm. Some days she didn't even think about him. When other kids asked where her father was, she made up stories to fill in the blank. Finally she grew happy with the way things were. She had friends. She had a boyfriend. She was sixteen years old, and she was having fun. Now *he* had to come back and change everything.

"Be nice to your father, Rebekah."

Oh sure, and what had he done for her? He'd betrayed her, for starters. Or maybe he'd just been a phony all along, because the father she'd loved wouldn't have done what he did. She'd practically idolized him, thought he was a hero who could do no wrong. Then, in one night, his true colors came out, and the next thing she knew, he was locked up in prison. As far as she was concerned, *two* men had died in that accident, not just one. The man she'd known as her father was as good as dead. In fact, it'd be better for all of them if he really were—

You don't mean that.

Yeah, I do. I mean it.

How can you wish Dad was dead?

"I can't help it," she said aloud. "I—" She froze for several seconds and then hit the pillow with her fist again when she realized she was arguing with herself. Her friends would call her crazy. One head with two people inside who couldn't even get along with each other.

She wished she'd been born into a regular family, one where everyone was just a normal person. But right from the start something was wrong, because she went straight from the hospital into a house where there was already an older brother no one would call normal. From the time she was conscious, she'd had to deal with the embarrassment of that—the stares in public, the whispers, the muffled laughter, and later at school, the constant teasing by the other kids. Then, her father! Her father was a prisoner convicted of manslaughter. How many of her friends could claim that distinction? She didn't know anyone else whose father had spent time in the slammer.

She squeezed her eyes tight against the thought. Not that all her friends would care about where her dad had been. Her best friend, Lena, who already knew, didn't care at all. Lena

42

seemed to think families were better off without men around to mess things up. Her own dad had left years ago when the circus came through town and he discovered his high school sweetheart working as a member of the prop crew. When the circus pulled out, so did Mr. Barrett. What a lowlife. Lena's mom had married again after that, then divorced and married again. And divorced again. Now it was just Lena and her mom, which was how Lena liked it. She didn't want her mother dating anyone. She said it always ended up bad for her mom.

"So you think your mom should just spend the rest of her life alone?" Rebekah had once asked.

"She's not alone. She's got me."

"Yeah, sure, like that's going to keep her happy for the next thirty years. You know she's going to find herself another man someday. Then what?"

"Simple. I'll do what I did with the last one. I'll just get rid of him."

"How'd you do that?"

"I have ways of making things happen."

Lena was mysterious and strange and fun, and Rebekah knew she didn't have to worry about losing her friendship. But what about the others? And most important, what about David? What would he think? He was the best thing to happen to her in a long time. She couldn't stand the thought of losing him.

Someone tapped at the door. "Beka, supper's ready."

Rebekah sighed. "All right, Mom. Just a minute."

She heard Billy say something in the kitchen and then her father's reply.

Strange to hear his voice. Strange to think he was here.

"I've got a secret for you, Bekaboo."

Oh yeah, that was what he called her. Bekaboo. It used to make her laugh.

"What is it, Daddy?"

"Promise not to tell?"

She nodded.

He leaned down and tickled her ear with a whisper. *"You're the apple of my eye."*

"I'm an apple in your eye?" she squealed.

"Not in my eye, silly. Of my eye. You're the apple of my eye."

"But what does that mean, Daddy?"

"It means of all the people in the world, I love you the most."

She almost asked him if he loved her more than he loved Mama and Billy, but she didn't bother. Of course he did. That was easy to believe.

"Daddy?"

"Yeah, Beka?"

"You're the apple in my eye too."

Another tap on the door. "Beka, I don't want to

have to tell you again. Everybody's waiting on you."

Rebekah sat up and blew out the candle. The stupid thing wasn't doing any good anyway.

CHAPTER SIX

"Billy would like to say grace," Andrea said.

John glanced apologetically at his son and laid down the fork he had only just picked up. When had this family started saying grace?

Billy lowered his head, and John followed suit. Then he listened as his son prayed quietly over the food. "God is great. God is good. Lord, thank you for all the food. Amen."

When John opened his eyes, he smiled at the boy and said, "Thank you, Billy."

"Welcome, Dad."

"Where did you learn that?"

"From the Sunday school teacher. She's nice."

"They let Billy sit in on the little kids' class," Rebekah said smugly.

"I don't just sit in," Billy objected. "I'm a helper."

"Yeah, right."

"I am!"

"Listen, cut it out, you two."

"She started it, Mom."

"Let's drop it, Billy."

Billy and Rebekah glared at each other briefly before turning back to their food.

When the table was quiet again, John asked, "So you go to church, Billy?"

"Sure I do." He punctuated his sentence with an energetic nod.

John looked at Andrea for an explanation. "He walks up to Grace Chapel Sunday mornings," she said. "It's not far. When it's cold, I drive him."

John remembered the white frame church just up the road and around the bend. "Oh? Well, I'm glad you're going, Billy."

"Yeah, just think, Billy," Rebekah said, "you won't have to go to church alone anymore, since Dad found religion in prison."

"Rebekah!"

"Well, you said so yourself, Mom. You said he got that jailhouse religion." She thrust her chin up and looked toward the ceiling. " 'I'm saved by Jesus, so give me points for good behavior and get me out of here.' "

"That's enough, Beka."

"Of course, it only lasts till they *do* get out and then—"

"I said that's enough, Rebekah!"

"—they go right back to being jerks. It's all a farce. Just wait and see."

"Beka, I don't want to hear another word out of you."

John steeled himself against the conflict brewing across the table. He didn't want the meal ending up in angry words, maybe tears. An argument between men behind bars was one thing, but a confrontation between one's wife and daughter—that was a whole different playing field, far more unnerving. He knew he should step in, be the warden with the authority to subdue the riot. But before he could think of anything to say, Billy took over.

"Listen, Beka," Billy scolded, "stop fighting. If you can't be nice, you can . . . you can . . . go to your room!"

Rebekah shrieked with laughter. "Like you can tell me what to do!"

"I'm the older brother."

"And that makes you the boss of me? I don't think so."

"I'm not saying I'm your boss. I'm just saying, this is Dad's first night home. If you want to be ugly, go be ugly somewhere else."

Rebekah sneered, then shrugged Billy off and went back to eating. John looked around the table at the others. Andrea, red-faced, pushed her bangs off her forehead and reached for her glass of water. Phoebe rolled a pea around her plate with her fork. Billy munched happily on a dinner roll.

John swallowed, then cleared his throat. "So, Billy," he said, "how do you like working for Uncle Owen?"

Even as he spoke, he chided himself for side-stepping Rebekah's comments. He should have met them head on. He should have told her it was true, that he was different now, that he was not the man she'd seen being led out of the courtroom in handcuffs. That somewhere between that day and this he had found not religion, but something better, something real. He should have told her, but instead, he had veered back toward the ease of small talk.

John gradually became aware that Billy was answering his question. "It's great, Dad. It's really great. I make money and put it in the bank."

"Good for you, son." John nodded. "So you like working at the restaurant? You like bussing tables?"

"Yeah, Dad. It's fun. You'll like it too. It's going to be great, Dad, having you there."

John felt humiliation wiggle through him. He'd wanted to have a job waiting for him when he came home, and he'd asked Owen to help him find work. Owen told him he wasn't likely to find much in a town the size of Conesus, but he could have a position at the restaurant if he wanted. John agreed, hoping for something like assistant manager, but Owen said the only spot he could slip him into right now was cleaning tables.

"It's only temporary, you know, Billy," John said. "Maybe only a few weeks. Just until I can find something—" He almost said "better" but stopped himself. "Just until I can find something more in my line of work."

"And what would that be, Dad?" Rebekah asked, her eyes steely.

She was trying to goad him, John knew, though her question was valid. What line of work was he in? He'd been in life insurance, mortgages, real estate. He'd sold municipal bonds, cruise packages, vacuum cleaners. In Virginia Beach he'd been working as an ad rep for the small local magazine his brother owned. Jared had convinced him the position might lead to something better, which was why he'd pulled up roots in the first place and moved the family from Rochester, New York, to Virginia Beach, Virginia. But then there'd been the accident and the arrest and . . .

The piece of speared meat at the end of his fork stopped midway between the plate and his mouth. His stomach felt sour. His head spun to think of how his life had turned in all the wrong directions. What if he had never let Jared talk him into moving to Virginia? What if he had never driven that particular stretch of road on that particular night? And for that matter, to get right to the source of the mess, what if years ago he had been able to finish college instead of having to quit to get married?

"You know, Dad," Billy said, smiling brightly, "you might like the restaurant so much, you won't want to leave. You can stay there with me."

John nodded slowly. "Sure, son," he said. "Maybe."

He moved his gaze to the lake, saw the water shiver as the wind slid over its back. It was a beautiful sight, especially the way the sunlight danced in a chorus line on a watery stage. He certainly hadn't seen anything like that in a while. He was home and he was free and he wasn't going back—not to the prison of concrete and steel and not to the inner prison of soul-wrenching despair.

He turned to his wife. "So Owen's still making good with the restaurant business, huh?"

She answered him, but he wasn't really listening to what she said. And though they strove toward something like conversation until the meal was done, John was all the while tamping down memories of clanging bars and prison guards and the dull-eyed face of a lost young man peering into the window of his car.

CHAPTER SEVEN

John thought often about the man he'd killed. He wondered who the guy was, wondered even what his name was. No one knew. He'd had no identification on him, and afterward, as he lay in the morgue with a "John Doe" tag on his right big toe, no one claimed him. He'd been buried in a common grave without a soul to grieve for him. Except for John.

After all this time John had never quite stopped

grieving. He was saddened mostly by the fact that the man was young. The medical examiner thought he was somewhere around twenty-five, maybe thirty. He was an unkempt, bearded guy with a stench great enough to reach even John's rum-sodden brain and linger there so that John thought he could smell the unwashed flesh now. Even as he sat on the porch overlooking a star-pocked lake on his first night of freedom.

"You coming to bed?" Andrea asked. "It's nearly midnight, you know." She stood inside the screen door, as though she needed something—some protective barrier—between them.

John looked up at her from the glider where he sat. "I'm not tired. But you go on." He thought she looked relieved.

"All right."

"The kids asleep?" he asked.

She nodded. "For the time being. Phoebe usually wakes up in the night and moves over to Billy's room."

"How come?"

"She's scared."

John waited for more, but Andrea didn't go on.

"But he's only got that rollaway that's hardly big enough for him."

"She takes her pillow over and sleeps on the floor. So be careful to step around her if you go to the bathroom in the night."

Billy didn't have a room. Not really. Between

the front room and the bathroom was a hall wide enough to fit the rollaway bed on one side and a chest of drawers on the other. That was his space.

"Phoebe wouldn't rather sleep in the bed with Rebekah?"

"No. She's scared," Andrea repeated.

"Of her own sister?"

"No, of the room."

John frowned. "She think it's haunted or something?"

"She's a kid, John. Kids get funny ideas."

"I guess so."

They were quiet a moment. Andrea seemed to want to say something, so John waited.

Finally she spoke. "Beka has been having nightmares lately. Sometimes she wakes up screaming, so don't be alarmed if you hear her."

"Why is she having nightmares?"

"I don't know. Probably adolescent anxiety or something."

"Does she say what they're about?"

"She says she doesn't remember them once she wakes up."

"Oh. Okay."

"She'll outgrow them."

"Yeah, I hope so. Maybe that's why Phoebe moves to Billy's room. Hard to sleep with someone screaming in your ear."

Andrea smiled wanly. "I suppose. Well, good night."

"Good night."

She turned and climbed the stairs. John watched her disappear. He was afraid of the bedroom on the second floor, but not because of ghosts.

He turned back to the lake and to the memories that had been clawing at his mind since dinner. The man had been a drifter; he may have been on the road for years, looking for something. He'd never find it now. John had put an end to all that.

He had been at Jared's house that night, the two of them drinking together after work, as they did almost every Friday night. Neither of them drank during the week, but those first drinks together on the crest of the weekend were the kickoff for two days of boozing. They told themselves and they told each other that they weren't alcoholics. No, they didn't have to have it. But they wanted it. The weekends were what they lived for. It didn't matter that they both had wives, families, responsibilities. They spent five days a week being responsible. They deserved two days off.

They had sat on the porch of Jared's beach house, listening to the waves pound the shore till sometime after midnight. When John stood, unsteadily, and said he needed to get home, Jared had warned, *"Listen, bro, be careful driving. The last thing you need is another DUI."*

"I'm fine," John had said, and then he eased his way through the house and out to his car in the drive.

He might have made it home all right, but John was a happy drunk, and when he was tanked he was inclined to do random acts of kindness. On that long and little-traveled road, he caught a figure in the high beams of his headlights, moving along the side of the asphalt, weighed down by a backpack that looked heavier than the man himself.

John passed the guy, then pulled over to the side of the road and rolled down the passenger-side window. When a moment later a scruffy face peered into the car, John said, *"Hop in, buddy. Where you going?"*

Brown eyes peered out from beneath a swirling waterfall of dirty hair. The drifter leaned a little closer and said, *"Anywhere."*

"I can take you partway," John told him cheerfully, and the next thing he knew, the guy was seated beside him in the front seat while the pack rested on the floor behind them.

John had wondered briefly at the fact that they trusted each other right off, but he didn't have much time to think about it because just a few miles farther down the road a summer rain spat fury on the windshield, and the car was all of a sudden turning in ways it shouldn't be turning, and after that John Sheldon's life went veering off in the wrong direction. Again.

Later, John didn't remember much about the accident. He didn't remember much about that night other than the tangled hair and the stench and the rain. He wondered whether he had asked the man his name, and if he did, whether the man had replied.

The accident might have been blamed on the rain and the slippery road were it not for the fact that John's blood alcohol level was .21 percent. A good thirteen points over the legal limit for driving in the state of Virginia.

The judge decided John had killed the man. That, and his previous DUI, earned him five years. John didn't miss the irony of it. While he was simply trying to do someone a favor, he actually ended up snuffing out a life.

Since then John wondered if the young man might have found himself in the midst of his travels had he been able to keep traveling. Some young men who hit the road ended up finding their way home again. Maybe this guy would have too. Maybe he would have stopped looking and made peace with himself. Maybe he would have cut his hair and shaved his beard and settled down and had kids, if the journey hadn't been prematurely ended.

John hadn't had a drop of liquor since that night. Not even a sip of the underground supply flowing freely through the prison. He'd promised himself he'd never drink again, and then he'd promised God. Keeping that promise was the first thing he was going to do to make sure his life stayed on track now that he was out.

The moon hovered over the lake, a slim crescent hanging like an unclosed parenthesis in the sky. John couldn't remember ever having seen the moon from prison. There was plenty he'd have to get reacquainted with, plenty he'd have to get used to all over again. He wanted things to be good this time around. He didn't want to make the same mistakes he'd made too many times before.

"God, help me," he whispered. That was what Pastor Pete, the prison chaplain, had said to pray when you didn't know what else to pray.

Andrea was probably asleep by now. John hoped it was safe to go up. He stepped inside and climbed the stairs, careful not to let his shoes land too heavily on the uncarpeted steps. When he reached the garret room at the top, he discovered that Andrea had already been thinking ahead. No wonder the old queen bed was in Rebekah's room now. Andrea had moved the twin beds up here.

CHAPTER EIGHT

Andrea listened as John moved hesitantly around the room, getting ready for bed. He hadn't awakened her when he came upstairs; she had turned out her reading light only moments before. Sleep would be elusive tonight. She had known that when she'd climbed the stairs to the garret room, which she would now be sharing with somebody else. Her body was tired, but her mind was whirling, flashing conflicting messages of hope and grief.

Beside her bed, on the floor, were two piles of books: one, a stack of paperback romance novels, the other, various volumes of poetry. She loved the romance novels because they always had a happy ending. She loved the poems about unfulfilled longing because they were true.

> Downstairs I laugh, I sport and jest with all;
> But in my solitary room above
> I turn my face in silence to the wall;
> My heart is breaking for a little love.

The poem by Christina Rossetti somehow seemed appropriate reading for tonight. Andrea had underlined those words in shades of blue ink years ago. She didn't even need to read them now, she knew the lines so well. Had memorized them without trying. Had lived them for years.

She'd known John Sheldon almost all her life, their families' cottages being only half a dozen doors apart. When they were children, the three boys—Owen, John, and Jared—palled around together while she watched from a distance. Watched and waited. Later she poured her adolescent longings into her diary as she went on waiting. Eventually she was allowed to hang on to the fringes of their trio, joining them for a few hours while they swam or fished. They took her along to the amusement park, where she trailed behind them. They took her to the movies, where she sometimes sat a few rows ahead, sometimes a few rows behind. Only in hindsight did Andrea realize that Owen had probably been pressured by their parents to include her.

But at last the day came when John noticed her, as though she had suddenly slipped into a coat of flesh and become visible. She was eighteen and fresh out of high school. He was nineteen and one year into his studies at a community college in Rochester. Though Andrea never considered herself beautiful, she decided she must have finally blossomed enough to attract the person she'd been watching all her life.

That lovely summer of 1988 was one of shy infatuation. For the first time, Andrea realized that life could be kind and maybe even filled with promise. When John Sheldon showed up at the cottage, he didn't always come looking for Owen. Sometimes—in fact, most often then—he came looking for her. He took her for walks along the lake or to movies at the theater in town. Sometimes at night they sat on the dock and talked for hours while the stars winked down at them from an open sky. When he told her he loved her, she believed him, and her future seemed certain and bright. Owen kidded her about her beau. Her parents approved.

And then that fall John invited her to the Harvest Dance at the community college he attended. They went, not knowing that everything was about to go wrong. Before the dance was over they exchanged the party for the backseat of John's car, and when Andrea arrived home late that night, she was carrying in her belly the seed that would grow into Billy.

She still believed John loved her once. She held that belief in her heart like a piece of fine china, all wrapped up in layers of tissue paper. Sometimes she took it out and gazed at it longingly, then wrapped it up securely again and tucked it away.

That was what she was doing when she heard John creeping up the stairs. She quickly put away the memory of his love, as though he might catch her gazing at it. Shutting her eyes, she pretended to be asleep.

Even without seeing his face, she sensed his momentary confusion at the twin beds. She had done it for him, of course, to make it less awkward. He could come to her, or he could choose not to.

She wasn't surprised when he chose not to. That was how it'd been for a long time before the accident. Somewhere along the way she and John had stopped being lovers, had stopped being friends as well. They were just two people rolling along on parallel tracks through the same lonely territory.

Though his territory had been a little less lonely. At least he'd had way stations of companionship, she thought bitterly. He'd been unfaithful. He thought she didn't know, but how could she not? A wife could sense those things. What amazed her was that he had never left her, had never gotten off the train for good at one of those stations and left her to go on without him.

But then, she hadn't left him either, though she certainly had grounds. She'd entertained the thought at times and had been nudged in that direction by her brother and sister-in-law. Owen and Selene had spent the last few years trying to convince her to find someone else. She deserved someone better, they said. Why would she stay with a man like John?

She could hear Selene's voice even now. *"Listen, honey, if you're afraid you won't find anyone else, don't be."*

They were at the beauty salon one day at closing time. Selene was at the front desk scribbling notes in her appointment book while Andrea swept up locks of hair with a wide-headed mop. *"It isn't that, Selene,"* she had said.

Her sister-in-law looked up from her book, one strand of frosted hair falling over her brow. She unwrapped the foil from another piece of

Wrigley's Juicy Fruit and popped the gum into her mouth. *"Then what is it exactly?"* she asked.

What was it exactly? Andrea's mind echoed. She was too embarrassed to say, so she resorted to clichés. *"I'm staying with him for the kids."*

Selene rolled her eyes, snapped her gum. *"Yeah, right,"* she said. *"Like he gets the father of the year award or something."*

"Well, he is their father, you know. I can't change that."

"So maybe you can give them a stepfather who's not in prison."

The words had stung, but Andrea let the comment slide. She couldn't afford to argue with Selene or get on her bad side. She had to work with her sister-in-law at the beauty salon until John got home.

Now John was home, and Andrea had to wonder whether Owen and Selene hadn't been right after all. She might have at least looked around, allowed herself to test the waters—just to see if there could be someone else for her out there.

What she couldn't admit to Selene, though, was that she didn't want someone else. She wanted John. In spite of all the ways he'd hurt her, she couldn't seem to fully untangle him from her heart. She wished she could. She'd rejoice if she could. But he was like a tree whose branches had grown into and around a chain-link fence. She'd have to take an ax to the root to cut the stubborn thing out.

If he left her, she would accept it. But she would not leave him.

She wondered about this coming-to-Jesus thing that he claimed had changed him.

"It's hard to explain, Andrea," he'd told her, *"but I'm different now. I'm a different person."*

She had told him that was a fine thing. She was glad he'd found religion. She hoped it would make him happy. And he'd looked disappointed, as if she'd said all the wrong things, though she didn't know what else to say.

"I know it's hard to understand . . ." he'd said.

And that was the end of the conversation there in the visiting room in the prison two years ago. As though there was no use going on because she would never understand.

Well, if he really was different, he didn't have to explain, as far as she was concerned. She'd be satisfied simply to see it.

In the other bed John was asleep now, breathing slowly, snoring lightly. Andrea was almost afraid to breathe herself, afraid to wake him. How strange it was to have him here. How strange all of it was: his coming home, his lying there beside her in the dark.

How strange their marriage.

If one could call it that.

CHAPTER NINE

Billy and Phoebe sat side by side on the glider, as they often did in the cool of the morning. He pushed lightly against the porch's painted boards with the soles of his flat bare feet, rocking the two of them gently. Phoebe rested her head on his shoulder while he quietly sang a song he'd learned in Sunday school, something about God making all the birds in the sky and the fish in the sea. He couldn't remember all the words, but when he got stuck, he filled in the blanks by humming. He often sang to Phoebe, because she asked him to and because he liked to sing. His one rule about singing, though, was that he would only sing happy songs, never sad songs.

When he finished, Phoebe looked up at him with her blue eyes wide and whispered, "Billy, do you like that man?"

Billy had to think a minute. Finally he asked, "What man?"

"You know, the man that came here yesterday."

"You mean Dad?" He laughed lightly. He couldn't help it.

She stared at him, then nodded.

"Phoebe," he said, "that's our dad. He's . . . he's—of course I like him. I love him. Don't you?"

She shook her head. "I'm scared of him."

"Oh, Phoebe, you're scared of everything."

"No I'm not."

"Yes you are."

"I'm not scared of you."

"That doesn't count."

Phoebe didn't respond. For a moment the two of them sat quietly together, saying nothing. From the kitchen came the sounds of pots clanging; Mom was making oatmeal and sausage links for breakfast. Dad was at the sink in the bathroom, shaving. Beka, Billy figured, was probably still asleep.

"Phoebe?"

"Yeah, Billy?"

"Give Dad a chance."

She didn't say anything.

"You'll like him," he went on, "when you know him."

"I don't think so, Billy."

"You didn't . . . you don't remember him from before, do you, Phoeb?"

She shook her head. "Do you?"

"Sure I do." He nodded proudly. "He was a good dad."

"Really?"

"Really."

"Then how come he went to jail, where all the bad people go?"

"It was an accident. Dad's not a bad person. He had an accident."

"Mom said he was in a car wreck."

"That's right."

"You can go to jail for having a car wreck?"

"Yeah. If someone dies, you might go to jail."

Phoebe was quiet a long time. Then she said, "I don't ever want to drive. I don't want to go to jail."

"Well, I want to drive. Mom thinks I can't. I drive the boat with her there, but I'll never drive the car."

"Maybe you're lucky, then."

"No, it's not lucky. I want to do things by myself, not have people always driving me around like I'm a kid. I want . . ." He stopped, knowing if he kept on, he'd just make himself upset. He blinked a few times to chase away the bad thoughts, then smiled down at his little sister. "But anyway, Phoeb, you can't always be scared of things. You'll never be happy that way."

She shrugged her shoulders. "I can't help it."

"Maybe you can."

"Aren't you scared of anything, Billy?"

Billy squinted as he considered that. Finally he said, "Yeah, I am. Scared I'm going to miss breakfast because I'm out here talking to you."

Phoebe giggled at that. He liked it when he could make her laugh.

"Really, Billy. I guess you're not scared of anything."

"No, that's not true. I am sometimes. But then I just sing that song to myself."

"What song?"

"You know, the one that says 'angels watchin' over me.'"

"Oh yeah. I like that one."

She rested her head back against his shoulder. "Billy?"

"Yeah?"

"How long is he going to stay?"

"Dad?"

"Uh-huh."

Billy sniffed at that and shook his head. "He's home, Phoebe. He's home for good."

She looked away. "Oh," she said. It was a small sound, like the squeal of a mouse.

"Aren't you glad? You don't want a dad?"

She shrugged her small shoulders. "I don't know."

"You don't know? Every kid wants a dad, Phoeb."

"But what do I need a dad for, Billy, as long as I've got you?"

He found he didn't have an answer to that. He smiled when he heard Phoebe give off a small, contented sigh.

"Billy, sing me that song."

"Which song?"

"The one about angels watching over me."

"Okay." He moistened his lips with his tongue. Then he lifted his chin and sang, "'All night, all day, angels watching over me, my Lord. All night, all day, angels watching over me. . . .'"

CHAPTER TEN

John patted his face dry with a towel and slapped some aftershave on his reddened cheeks. Andrea had thought of everything: new pack of disposable razors, a can of shaving cream, a bottle of the brand of aftershave he'd always used. He hadn't even had to ask, hadn't even thought ahead to what he might need when he got home. But she had.

He looked at his reflection in the mirror, the same mirror that had been throwing his image back at him since he was a kid perched on a step stool at the sink. In the interim he'd made a mess of things. He wanted to do things right this time.

"God help me," he said aloud, repeating his simple prayer of the night before. It was the overarching prayer of a desperate man, and he knew it.

He slipped on a T-shirt and stepped into a pair of shorts. Both were brand-new. He'd found them, neatly folded, in a drawer of the dresser upstairs. *"I picked you up some new clothes—not much, just some casual wear for the summer,"* Andrea had told him. He zipped up the shorts and reached into the right-hand pocket. Sure enough. Same old Andrea. She'd tucked a handkerchief into the pocket, ironed and neatly folded. All the years of their marriage, whenever he'd complained that he didn't like handkerchiefs and she shouldn't bother, she came back saying, *"Yes, well, you never know when you're going to need one."*

With a wry smile, he stuffed the handkerchief back into the pocket and then stepped hesitantly forward into his first full day at home. As he moved from the bathroom into the hallway that served as Billy's bedroom, something shiny in the window caught his eye. He noticed now what he hadn't noticed coming through—the row of Special Olympics medals Billy had laid out along the windowsill. John had forgotten all about that, had forgotten about watching his son's triumphs in the water year after year. *"A real fish, that one,"* the coach had proclaimed of Billy Sheldon. *"One of the best swimmers I've seen at the Specials."* And everyone had been proud of Billy, including Billy.

Now here he was in the summer before his junior year of high school, working a job and earning money, attempting to take care of the cottage and to be the man of the house in his father's absence. At one time John would never have believed it.

Certainly he wouldn't have foreseen it on the day the boy was born. Some hours after the birth the doctor came back to the room, looking solemn. *"I'm sorry to say your son has Down syndrome,"* he had told the new parents apologetically, as though the condition had somehow been his fault instead of a genetic mishap. Either way, the announcement put a damper on John's hope that, with his son's birth, something good had come of his mistake.

John's first thought, and his first suggestion, was to put the child in an institution. That might be best for all of them, he said. But Andrea would have none of it. As she looked up from the face of her newborn son, John saw something in Andrea's eyes that he'd never seen before, something fierce and tender at the same time.

"I'm not giving my baby away," she said firmly.

John felt helpless. *"I just don't think I can deal with all this, Andrea."*

"You don't have to," she shot back. *"He's mine and I'll raise him."*

And so she had. Raised him right into manhood. He'd be turning eighteen in another few weeks, and that made him an adult.

John looked past the front room and out the window to where Billy sat on the glider with Phoebe. He felt a shiver run through him, a shiver that he recognized as fledgling pride for the son who had once so disappointed him. He walked to the porch door, and through the screen he greeted his children cheerfully. "Good morning, you two."

"Good morning, Dad!" Billy's eyes shone at the sight of his father.

Phoebe, though, only leaned closer to her brother and kept her eyes downcast.

"Did you sleep good, Dad?" Billy asked.

John thought it interesting that he hadn't noticed yesterday what was so obvious today, what had nettled him for years. Billy always dropped the ends of his words so that his sentence came out sounding like, "Di you slee goo, Da?" John had once cringed constantly at how the boy's tongue seemed to get in the way of everything. Though it wasn't his tongue that was too big, but his mouth that was too small. Common in kids with Down syndrome. Billy's mouth just couldn't seem to fit around an entire word. He always had to bite off the end to get the bulk of the letters out.

It doesn't matter now, John told himself. *I'm proud of my son.* Aloud, he said, "I slept just fine, Billy. How about you?"

"I slept good. I always do. I like to sleep." *I slep goo. I alway do. I li to slee.*

John nodded and smiled at Billy. Then he moved his gaze from his son to the little girl. "Hello, Phoebe."

She squirmed. She raised her eyes momentarily without lifting her head from Billy's shoulder. Her mouth moved, and she might have said hello, but no sound came out.

John waited but was met with a continuing silence. Finally he said, "Well, it smells like your mother is fixing breakfast."

"Yeah, and I'm hungry," Billy said. "Tell her to call me when it's ready."

John followed the aroma of frying sausages to the kitchen, where he found Andrea at the stove. She glanced up at him briefly. "Good morning. Sleep okay?"

"Fine, thanks."

"Hungry?"

He nodded. "Starving."

"Breakfast is almost ready. There's coffee in the pot. Help yourself if you want some."

At that moment the door to the adjoining bedroom flew open, and Rebekah appeared on the threshold wearing a summer robe, her hair disheveled, her makeup smeared. She looked at her father as though he were a tree fallen across the very road she needed to travel. He was in the way.

"You out of the bathroom?" she asked.

"Yes. It's free now."

"Finally." As she stomped through the kitchen she announced loudly, "We're never going to survive with five of us in this horrible little shack."

"Oh, Beka," Andrea sighed. "Breakfast is almost ready," she called after the girl.

"I'm not hungry!" In another moment the pipes beneath the cottage groaned as Rebekah drew herself a bath.

"This having one bathroom is going to be a problem," John muttered.

71

Andrea let go a small laugh. "Going to be? It's been a problem since we got here. Especially since the toilet has a nasty habit of getting backed up. We're living like sardines in a cottage that's slowly falling apart, John."

And another fish just squeezed into the tin, he thought. "I'm sorry, Andrea. I know it's not ideal. . . ."

She dismissed his comment with a shrug. "You do what you have to do. At least there's two things we can be thankful for—the place has been winterized, and better yet, we don't have a mortgage."

"Yeah." He nodded solemnly. "At least there's that. Do we have anything left from the sale of the Virginia Beach house?"

"Oh yes. Less every month, of course."

John fidgeted, thinking about what it would take to fix this place up a bit. He couldn't afford to tear down and rebuild as so many around the lake had done in recent years. Some places weren't cottages at all anymore but regular houses, with two stories, garages, and landscaping that rivaled the best backyards in Rochester. No, he couldn't do that, but he was going to have to do something. Which made him think about bringing home a paycheck. "What time does Owen want me and Billy at the restaurant today?" he asked.

"Eleven. That's when the lunch rush starts."

"And you say Billy knows how to take the bus?"

She nodded. "You can catch it right up across from the Steiners' place. You know, six doors down."

"Yes, I remember."

"Not a whole lot of buses come along here, and the ones that do aren't always reliable, but it's better than nothing. It gets you there eventually."

"Okay, I just didn't realize . . ." He stopped, momentarily lost in thought.

"Realize what, John?" she prodded.

He looked up. "It's going to be real inconvenient not having a driver's license."

"You'll get one eventually."

"Yeah, a year from now. Not soon enough." He shook his head, remembering how it felt yesterday to open the front door of the cottage and step outside. The wonder of such a simple act! But he knew now it wasn't enough. Freedom wasn't feeling the grass beneath your feet. It was having wheels under you, being able to go where you wanted to go. He wasn't free yet.

"Listen, you told Selene, right?" he asked. "You told her you won't be working for her anymore?"

"She's known all along I wouldn't be working once you got out of—" She stopped suddenly. John knew she didn't want to say the word. She tried to smile. "You know," she suggested, "I can drive you and Billy into town today if you want. I don't mind."

"You can't leave Phoebe here alone."

"She won't be alone. Rebekah's here till four, when she has to leave for work."

John looked out the window at the two old cars parked behind the cottage. "Where'd Rebekah get that beat-up old Jetta?"

"Owen. Used to be Selene's till they got her a better one."

"Uh-huh. You really think anyone should be driving that thing?"

"It's a clunker, but it runs."

"All right." John sighed. He looked around the kitchen, cleared his throat, watched as Andrea turned the sausages one last time. His eyes settled on her face in profile. She looked pale, tired. A dark crescent moon hung beneath that one eye, and etched about the corner of her mouth was a certain sadness. He knew it was because of him, and he felt a pang of guilt and of regret. But he was going to make things right now that he was home. He was going to make it all up to her. Somehow.

He stepped to the coffeemaker and poured some coffee into a waiting mug. He settled the carafe back onto the burner and stared into the lilting surface of the small black pool in the cup.

He'd been sipping a cup of coffee just two evenings ago when Pastor Pete came to say good-bye. The two men chatted awhile before John suddenly confessed, *"You know, Pete, I'm not sure I have the strength to go back to them, to be a husband and a father to my family."*

"John," Pete had said, holding John's gaze, *"you won't have to be strong. You will have to be tender."*

Remembering that, John turned to Andrea. He took a deep breath. "The kids," he started, "they look good. They . . ."

She didn't seem to be listening. She was preoccupied with getting the sausage links onto a serving plate.

"I mean . . . thanks, Andrea, for keeping the family together while I was . . . away."

She froze momentarily, and he watched a streak of color rise up her neck and fan out across her cheeks. She lifted her eyes to him slowly.

"You're welcome, John," she said quietly. She smiled briefly before dropping her eyes again. She settled the empty skillet on the stove and lifted her shoulders in a small shrug. "But what else could I do?"

"Well, I—" He was flustered, searching for words. "I know it hasn't been easy, but you've managed really well. I mean, look at Billy. He's become a responsible young man. You've done a great job with him."

She seemed pleased even while she tried to wave off the compliment. "Billy has done well for himself. He's always been extremely capable."

"But I don't think he'd have come so far if you hadn't worked with him all these years. I mean, you've done so much for him—more than most people would have, I think."

She shrugged again. "I don't know, John. I've only done what any mother would do. Any decent mother anyway."

He wanted to say more, but he was interrupted when Billy hollered from the porch, "Is breakfast ready yet, Mom? I'm starving to death."

"Come and get it," Andrea hollered back. "I can't have anyone dying on me around here."

She gave John another brief smile and then carried the plate of sausages to the porch.

CHAPTER ELEVEN

John knew the story only too well, how Donovan's Diner had became Laughter's Luncheonette back in 1995 when Owen Laughter bought the restaurant in downtown Conesus from Stan Donovan. The name of the place was the biggest draw, Owen said, even though everybody pronounced it wrong, including Owen himself. The family name was *Lau'-ter,* but who thought of *Lau'-ter* when the sign said Laughter? No one! Wasn't it great? Because, as Owen pointed out, who didn't want to laugh? Of course, Harold Laughter, Owen and Andrea's father, was initially reluctant to accept the butchering of the family name, but he eventually came around. Whenever he and Sylvia were vacationing at the lake, they ate almost every meal at Owen's place. Seated at the table closest to the cash register, they could see for themselves that Owen was on to something. The equation of burgers, fries, and laughter totaled up to a tidy sum.

Now, as John looked up at the neon sign above the restaurant's door, the last thing he wanted to do was laugh. He felt something icy in the pit of his stomach, and he wished he could turn around and get right back into the car and go home. But Andrea had already pulled away from the curb, and Billy was tugging on his arm and urging him toward the door.

"Come on, Dad," Billy said. "Don't wait. Come inside."

Telling himself he wouldn't be a busboy forever, John followed Billy into the restaurant. He hoped it was only his imagination that every eye in the place landed on him when he stepped inside. Surely there wasn't something about his presence that warned, *Ex-con approaching.*

"Once you've been in," Roach had told him, *"you're never out again, even when you're out. You always got the smell of the big house on you, and people smell it a mile away."*

He had never liked Roach when he was in prison, and he sure didn't like him now.

A woman approached wearing an apron stuffed

with drinking straws, pens, and order pads. Her dark hair was cropped short, and her colorless face was narrow and pinched, and John couldn't help noticing that in spite of the name of the place, she wasn't so much as smiling. He tried to smile at her anyway, but his cheeks quivered like horseflesh bothered by a fly. He offered her a taut nod instead.

"Maggie," Billy called out, "Maggie, here's my dad. He's working with us!"

"Yeah." Maggie looked from Billy to John and back again. "I know. Aren't we lucky?"

Billy beamed proudly. "Yeah, we're lucky!"

"Well," Maggie went on, "I'll show him around. Billy, you can go ahead and clock in. We have a little bit of paperwork for your dad to take care of, and then he'll join you out front."

"You want me to show him how to do the job?"

"Naw, don't bother. I can tell him what's expected of the busboys."

John flinched at that last word. At least in prison he'd been a clerk in the infirmary, typing reports, filing charts, handing out sick passes. It was a clean job and, within the penal system, about as respectable as you could get. Now he'd be gathering dirty dishes, crumpled napkins, and who knew what else.

On the drive in Billy had told him about the occasional surprises he'd come across—the muddy sock, a hearing aid, a full set of dentures, eight artificial fingernails painted hot pink. *"It's like a treasure hunt, Dad!"*

John shivered.

"And, Maggie, show Dad the clean dishrags and the rubber gloves, and—"

"Don't worry, Billy," John interrupted. "I'm sure Maggie will tell me everything I need to know."

Billy smiled and went to the kitchen to clock in.

John followed Maggie to an office where his brother-in-law sat behind a desk, bent over a pile of papers. Owen Laughter glanced up without raising his head. "Hello, John." He waved a pen. "Have a seat."

John sat. He waited for Owen to stop scribbling, a pause that stretched on for a good thirty seconds. Finally Owen put down the pen and slid the pile of papers across the desk. "We just have a few things for you to sign—tax forms, things like that."

"All right."

While he was looking over the forms, he heard Owen say, "You get settled in all right yesterday?"

John nodded. "Sure." He thought of the one plastic bag he'd carried home on the bus. "Not much unpacking to do."

But Owen already knew that. He was, after all, the one who'd met John at the bus station in Rochester, met him with the new change of clothes, a candy bar, and a can of Coca-Cola Classic. John had changed into the clothes in the bus station's men's room, stuffing the prison issue he'd been wearing in the trash can. He ate the candy bar and drank the soda on the long drive home. He and Owen had forty-five minutes to talk on their way to Conesus, and they'd hardly said a word. Finally, and maybe just to break the silence, Owen pointed to the plastic bag at John's feet and asked what was in it. John said it held a few personal items, like legal papers, a couple of sweaters, several pairs of socks, and the family's letters to him from the past five years. He failed to mention the Bible at the bottom of the bag, figuring Owen's reaction to that would not be favorable.

When John finished signing the papers, he looked up and said, "Thanks for what you're doing for me, Owen."

His brother-in-law's face remained passive. "I'm not doing it for you, John. I'm doing it for Andrea and the kids."

Owen had liked him once, way back when. They'd been friends long before John and Andrea were married. Owen, John, and Jared were drinking buddies all through those high school summers at the lake. They'd had some wild times together—talk about laughter! The three of them plus John Barleycorn—a sure combination to bust a gut.

But Owen had grown up, gotten responsible, put the adolescent drinking behind him while John and Jared went on indulging. Owen hadn't been happy with John for getting his kid sister pregnant, but he'd accepted it. It wasn't the shotgun wedding that did the friendship in. Ironically, the glue that held the friendship together in the first place was what finally broke it up. The liquor took John to prison, and Owen Laughter wasn't about to forget a thing like that. Even Jared had kept his distance ever since that particular ax fell. Drink had a way of killing off relationships, especially with those people a man used to drink with.

Owen thought his sister deserved better than a drunk and a convict. John couldn't disagree.

"I understand, Owen," John said as he pushed the papers back across the desk.

Owen nodded toward the woman leaning against the doorframe. "Maggie can show you what to do."

John rose. He wondered whether he should extend his hand across the desk but decided against it. Once again he followed Maggie, this time to the kitchen, where she pointed to a layout of the restaurant tacked up on the wall.

"This will be your station right here," she said, tapping the laminated sheet. "Keep your eyes open. Soon as a party leaves a table, you go clear it. Be sure to spray it down. I'll show you where the bottles of cleaning solution are in a minute. You'll carry one around with you, and I'll show you how to refill it. When the table's clean, you carry the tub back here to the window. Follow me."

They walked through the kitchen, where a trio of line cooks worked feverishly. One man chopped vegetables with an oversized knife, another stirred something in a pot on the stove, still another stood with a spatula over a grill that sizzled with a variety of hamburgers and thinly sliced steaks. Maggie didn't bother to introduce John but walked on through to the window where a young man was rinsing off dirty dishes with an industrial-sized sprayer hose.

"Okay," Maggie said, "you'll bring your tub to this window. First thing you've got to do is separate out the trash and throw it in the garbage can. You don't pass anything through this window except dishes and flatware. And make sure you don't throw away any of the flatware; sometimes it gets lost in the napkins and whatnot. If the trash can is full, it's your job to tie up the bag and put in a clean one. Now, a lot of people forget and leave things on the table—cell phones, sunglasses, that kind of thing. Those you take to Lost and Found in the office."

When Maggie paused, John ventured a question. "What about dentures?" he asked. "What do I do with those?"

Maggie didn't crack a smile. "Dentures?"

"Yeah, Billy said . . ." He thought a moment, then decided to drop it. This lady wasn't budging an inch.

"Okay, so you can pass the whole tub off to the dishwasher," Maggie went on, "and pick up another one here." She pointed to a stack of tubs. "Got any questions?"

John shook his head. "I don't guess so."

"Think you can handle it?"

John didn't bother to reply.

The trick, he thought, would be never to make eye contact. He'd move through the sea of patrons without stopping, zeroing in only on the empty table, the dirty dishes, the task at hand. If he kept his head down, he could be a nonperson doing a nonjob, not worth noticing. Anyway, since he himself had never lived in Conesus year-round, he didn't expect to know or be recognized by many people, which he considered a good thing.

Maggie showed him where to find the bibbed aprons, the rubber gloves, the spray bottles and dishrags. Then she thrust a tub in his hands and told him to get to work.

John stepped hesitantly into the dining room. The place was already in the midst of the lunch-hour rush; almost all the tables were full, and the hostess was seating yet another group of patrons at a booth Billy had just cleaned. John moved to his assigned area, a cluster of tables and booths in the far corner of the room. A heavyset man and a bottle-blond woman were at that moment rising from a booth, the man tossing a couple of dollars onto the table for the waitress. He belched loudly as he hiked up his pants, and then he and the woman headed toward the cash register. John looked down at the remains of their meal. He suddenly longed for his desk in the infirmary, even with its view of the prison grounds through a window reinforced with wire mesh.

He picked gingerly at the soiled napkins, tossing them into the tub. He gathered up the plates, the glasses, the flatware, trying to arrange them in such a way that the drinking glasses wouldn't break. His cheeks and his forehead burned, and a small wave of nausea rippled through his stomach. He remembered the way the *w* key always stuck on the portable typewriter in the infirmary, how mad that used to make him. He sure wouldn't be mad about it now. No, he sure wouldn't.

When the table was cleared, he lifted the spray bottle of cleaner from where it hung by the nozzle on his apron string. He sprayed the table down, rubbed it clean with a dishrag.

There, one table done. He wondered how many tables he would bus before he could quit this place and move on.

The lunch hour passed and the early afternoon

crawled by with John and Billy repeatedly passing each other as they moved from the tables to the dish window and back again. Billy was all smiles—for his dad, for his uncle Owen, for Maggie, for the customers. Billy smiled even when there was no one to smile at save his own self. John wondered at the boy's satisfaction and found it enviable.

When he had a spare moment, he watched his son at work, watched how he tackled each table in the same way. First Billy gathered up the trash, then the flatware, the plates, the bowls, the glasses, the coffee cups. The order never varied. When the table was clear, he sprayed the bleach solution in a left-to-right pattern, starting with the upper left corner of the table and working his way to the lower right. He sprayed five streaks of cleaner over each booth, four over each table, since the tables were slightly smaller. Then, starting again in the upper left corner, he rubbed circles over the table with a dishrag in the same left-to-right pattern until the whole thing was clean.

That was Billy for you, John thought. Orderly and determined, like most kids with Down syndrome. He didn't like to change his routines, and he didn't like to give up. The trait could be aggravating for him and for everyone around him, but then again, he eventually got the job done, and that was what mattered.

Around four o'clock John was clearing yet another table when Billy showed up at his elbow.

"I'm working up a big hunger, Dad. You too?"

John realized then that he hadn't had lunch and his stomach was starting to rebel. Billy was allowed to break for his shift meal at five o'clock, John at five-thirty. One free meal every shift, which was just about the only fringe benefit of the job.

"Yeah, I could eat," John said.

"Try the Philly cheesesteak, Dad. It's the best."

"Oh yeah?"

"Yeah. With hot peppers." Billy patted his stomach.

"Okay, sounds good."

Just as Billy moved on to his own station, a pretty, dark-haired girl about Rebekah's age waved at John from a nearby booth. He looked at her, turned, and glanced over his shoulder, then looked back at her.

"Hey," she hollered, "you Billy and Rebekah's dad?"

Caught already, on the first day. He didn't want to admit that he was Rebekah's dad, more for her sake than his own. But he knew he couldn't lie and expect to get away with it. He moved over to the table where the girl sat across from a young man with a bowl haircut and a face sporting the first bloom of downy whiskers.

"You know my daughter?" John asked, which,

as soon as he said it, he knew was stupid. Of course the girl knew his daughter.

"Yeah." The girl was all smiles. "We go to school together. So you're back?"

John nodded hesitantly. "Yes, I'm back."

"Way cool!" the girl exclaimed. "So what was it like?"

John felt himself stiffen, felt his throat constrict. He didn't want to talk about prison with a child he didn't know. "Well—"

"I always wanted to go to Peru!" the girl said.

John frowned then. His head moved slowly from side to side. "Peru?"

The girl slapped the table excitedly with the palms of both hands. "Rebekah's dad has been on an archeological dig in Peru," she said to the boy.

John's eyes moved slowly across the cluttered table to the boy. The shaggy teen was already staring up at him with admiration in his brown eyes. "Whoa, dude! Like, whatja find?" he asked.

"Well, I—"

"Didja come across any human bones?"

"Well, I—"

Long after he left the restaurant that day, John considered it a gift of fate that Billy, at that very moment, had dropped a too full bin, scattering dishes, flatware, and shards of glass all over the linoleum floor. John rushed to clean it up while Billy, distraught at his own clumsiness, was whisked away by Maggie to Owen's office, where he spent twenty minutes calming down. John hated to see his son so upset with himself for what was simply an accident, but at the same time he silently thanked the boy for creating a distraction when he needed one.

John could understand Rebekah not wanting to tell other kids her father was in prison, but—Peru? John wasn't sure he could so much as point to the place on a map.

CHAPTER TWELVE

Every time she woke up with the throbbing headache, Rebekah tried to convince herself it was worth it. She couldn't remember even half of what had happened the night before, but she was sure she'd had a good time. Besides, by now she knew how to handle the pain. Pop a couple of ibuprofen, keep your eyes shut, and wait for time to do its trick.

"Beka?"

She reluctantly opened one eye and squinted against a shaft of blinding light. "Yeah?"

"You feeling all right?"

"Yeah." She shut her eye and hoped her father would go away.

After a moment she realized he was still there.

"Are you sure?" he asked.

"Of course I'm sure."

"You've been lying here on the glider for the past hour."

"And your point is?"

"I just wanted to make sure you're all right."

"I'm just resting. Is that against the law?"

"Well, no."

Idiot, she thought. *He doesn't even know a hangover when he sees one. And he, the king of hangovers himself.*

She shifted her position and set the glider in motion, an unfortunate mistake that sent waves of nausea lapping across her stomach. She clenched her jaw against the juices creeping up her throat. That was all she needed right now, to toss the remnants of last night's partying all over her father's shoes.

A few deep breaths helped settle the queasiness, but still, thousands of tiny tipsy feet beat out a chorus line across her brain. If only she could remember the fun. If only payback wasn't expected for something she could hardly remember.

"Beka?"

"What?" She stifled a moan.

"Can I ask you something?"

"No."

She sensed his surprise at her answer. Her one word was an attack he hadn't expected. She liked that.

He sighed. "Well, I'm going to ask anyway."

Just shut up and go away. She fought the temptation to cover her ears with her hands. She tried to think about being in David's arms, leaning against him as he in turn leaned against a gravestone in the small cemetery behind the church. That was their favorite place to meet late at night—she and David, Lena and Jim. Sometimes a few others, whoever wanted to sit among the stones and down a few bottles. They laughed at the thought of the A.A. meetings held every Wednesday night in the church basement, and made a point of lining up their empty bottles— vodka, rum, beer, whatever—all along the threshold of the back door. *In your face,* the bottles said to all those anonymous drunks trying to stay dry.

Lena had introduced Rebekah to alcohol a couple of years ago, when they were both fourteen. Lena was a good friend. Rebekah knew she was indebted to her. It was the alcohol that melted her shyness so that she could simply be with people. The love of it gave her the courage to climb out her window at night and walk along the dark road to meet David and Lena and Jim for their midnight gatherings.

Her father was still standing over her; she could hear him breathing. He had said something and was waiting for an answer. In an attempt to clear her head, she rubbed a temple. "What?" she asked.

"I said, did you tell your friends I've been on an archeological dig in Peru?"

She almost laughed—might have, if the thought of moving that much didn't send her head spinning. "What was I supposed to tell them? That dear old dad was in the slammer?"

She waited for his anger, but it didn't come.

"I understand why you did it, Beka," he responded quietly.

She clenched her jaw again. *Don't think it's going to win you any points being nice to me. I'm not buying it.*

"But"—he sniffed and cleared his throat— "don't you think your friends are going to wonder why an archeologist is working as a busboy?"

She didn't know what to say. Finally she muttered, "Who cares?"

"Well, I care, and I think you care too. Somehow, word's going to get out what really happened, and then your friends are going to wonder why you told them I was in Peru."

Not even David knew where her dad had really been. In the three months they'd been seeing each other, they hadn't talked about her dad very much. She'd given him the dig-in-Peru story, but he hadn't seemed very impressed. What seemed to matter most to David was the fact that Rebekah didn't have a father around to interfere in their lives.

But now her father *was* here, and he was right—

David and everyone else would eventually know he'd been serving time. Word got around in a small town like Conesus.

She wondered how David would take it and what it would mean for them. She didn't want to lose him because of her father. She would have to do something to make sure she didn't lose him.

"Listen, Beka," her dad was saying, "I'm sorry."

"That's not going to change what happened, though, is it?"

"No, nothing's going to change what happened, but—"

"Then save your apologies for someone who cares."

There, that should do it. That should make him go ballistic. She would enjoy listening to him yell, even if it crushed her brain like a vise. She was tired of being the only angry person around here.

But when he spoke, his voice was tender. "Beka," he said, "I never meant to hurt you."

To her surprise she felt an aching in her chest, as if something heavy had suddenly crash-landed there.

Her dad went on, "You were always the special one. You were always special to me."

Good thing her eyes were shut; her lids could catch the tears. It was the headache, the hangover. Feeling sick always made her weepy.

"I never meant to hurt you," he said again.

"Well," she replied, "for not meaning to, you did a pretty good job of it."

Silence. And then footsteps. And then the squeaking of the screen door as it opened and shut.

Now she could go back to getting rid of the pain. God knew she wished she could get rid of the pain. In her head. In her heart. Everywhere.

CHAPTER THIRTEEN

The long-suffering fan by the open window in the kitchen was no match for the humid heat of summer. Here it was the eighth of June, and it was already—as Billy would put it—"hotter than blazes." One of the chores made more miserable by the hot weather was washing the dishes, all of which had to be done by hand. Andrea wore rubber gloves to buffer her skin from the steaming water in the sink, but her hands felt sticky inside the gloves, and beads of perspiration gathered on her forehead and trickled down her temples. The hair so recently colored and styled was a stringy mess, held out of her face by two large barrettes.

She chided herself now for spending the money to have her hair done. Selene had given her a discount—but never mind that. The point was, her effort had gone right past John. She had hardly expected to dazzle him, but she had hoped he might say something, whatever it is men say when they're trying to compliment their wives. *Hey, your hair looks pretty,* or even, *You do something different to your hair?* Anything to tell her he'd noticed.

She patted her face with a damp dish towel, then went back to washing the bowls and plates that had accumulated throughout the day. She didn't know which bothered her more, the heat of summer or the cold of winter, which here on a lake in upstate New York was a brutal and relentless cold. But when she was in the midst of one, she always longed for the other.

She remembered the rhyme her mother had so often recited:

> As a rule, man's a fool,
> When it's hot, he wants it cool,
> When it's cool, he wants it hot,
> He's always wanting what is not.

That fit her, she figured. Always wanting what was not.

"Can I dry those dishes for you?"

Andrea looked up with a start. She was surprised to see John standing in the doorway, even more surprised by his offer. Her momentary joy, though, was swallowed up by her own self-consciousness. She was all too aware of the apron, the rubber gloves, her tired body wilted and damp in the moist heat.

"You don't have to," she said shyly, "but if you'd like . . ." She pulled a dry dish towel out of a drawer and handed it to him.

He picked up a plate from the drying rack and rubbed circles on its surface. "I'm sorry this old cottage doesn't have a dishwasher."

She shrugged. "When Beka's home, she and Billy are my dishwasher. She washes, he dries. They don't say much to each other, but they get the job done."

"That's good." He nodded. "I'm glad they help out around here."

"Of course they do. They're good kids, John."

"I know they are. You're lucky to have them."

They're both of ours, she thought. *We're both lucky to have them.* But she didn't say the words aloud.

"Well," he went on, "things at work went a little better today than yesterday. At least Billy didn't drop a bin full of dishes."

"That's good. You know how hard he is on himself when he makes mistakes or even thinks he's done something wrong."

"I remember."

John paused, and Andrea realized he didn't know where to put the plate. "In the cupboard above you," she said.

He opened the cupboard. "Thanks."

They went on working quietly. Finally Andrea said, "I know it's not easy for you, John, working at the restaurant. Not exactly what you've always dreamed of, is it?"

He exhaled heavily. "It's only temporary, until I can find something better in Rochester and get us settled back up there."

Andrea kept her eyes on the soapy water in the sink. "I've been meaning to talk with you about that."

"Yeah? How so?"

"Well, the kids—Billy and Rebekah, anyway—they want to stay here till they graduate. I can't say I blame them, John. I hate to uproot them, and . . . well, maybe you can understand how they feel."

He didn't respond right away. Then, "There's not many job opportunities around here, Andrea."

"Something better is bound to come along."

"Doing what?"

"I don't know. But . . . something." She wished she had an answer, but John was right. Not many opportunities in Conesus. "It's just two years, and then they'll both be graduating."

"You expect me to bus tables for two years?"

"No." She shook her head. She didn't want their conversation to dissolve into an argument. "No, I don't. But I don't like the idea of uprooting the kids either," she repeated. "They've got friends here."

"They had friends in Rochester."

"Years ago. That was another life. Anyway, Rebekah's seeing someone."

"She is? Who?"

"A boy named David Morgan."

"How'd she meet him?"

"School."

"Is he a nice kid?"

"From what I know of him, he seems like a nice boy."

"I bet."

"What's that?"

She glanced over at her husband. He seemed agitated. "I can't say I like the idea of Beka and some boy going out together."

"Well, I wouldn't exactly say they're going out. They mostly just see each other at the amusement park because they're both working there for the summer. He's taken her to a movie once or twice. So don't worry. It's nothing serious. And anyway, they're both good kids."

She heard him sigh. He was worried. So was she. But she was more worried about Rebekah's relationship with her father than her relationship with the boy.

"Anyway," Andrea went on, "I think it'd be a mistake to disrupt the kids' routine at this point."

John polished a fork, held it up, and raised his brows at Andrea.

"In the drawer just to your right there," she said.

He opened the drawer and dropped in the fork. He grabbed a handful of flatware and wrapped it in the towel. "Maybe I can find something in Rochester and commute back and forth."

"How do you plan to do that when you can't drive?"

She heard him mutter quietly. Then he said, "I almost forget about that sometimes."

So maybe, she thought, *maybe you could just go on up to Rochester and live there. Find a job and a small apartment on the bus line and send us some money every once in a while.*

It wasn't the first time the thought had gone through her mind. After just two full days with John around, she knew it would have been better for Rebekah if her father had been gone two more years. By then Rebekah would be off to college or working full time. Either way, she'd most likely be living somewhere else. She wouldn't have to deal with a father coming home from prison.

The thought rose, flashed across her mind, then swam off like a goldfish descending into murky water. John was home, and Andrea wanted him here—in spite of what it meant for Rebekah. Rebekah had the whole of her future ahead of her; the one thing Andrea had was this second chance and the irrational but persistent hope that she could make a marriage with the one man she had always loved.

John finished drying and sorting the flatware and shut the drawer. "Well," he said, "not to change the subject, but I'll be starting A.A. meetings next Wednesday night. The closest meetings are up at Grace Chapel, where Billy goes to church." Then he added, "I can just walk there."

"Yes," she agreed, "that'd be best."

"Maybe through the people I meet in A.A., I can start networking—find out what opportunities there are as far as work around here."

"Sure, maybe." Though she hoped he wouldn't strike up any partnerships with someone who was also a former drunk. Working with Jared, his brother and drinking buddy, had been one of the worst decisions he'd ever made. "And then you have to report to a probation officer? Let him know you're going?"

"No." He shook his head. "I'm on unsupervised, remember?"

She lifted her head in thought. "Oh yes. They're just going to trust you to go to A.A."

"They can trust me."

"And you're on probation for a year?"

"That's right."

Andrea pulled the plug in the sink and let the dirty water go down the drain. She dried her hands on her apron, then took it off and hung it on a hook by the refrigerator. She turned and looked at her husband. "You have an interesting year ahead."

He caught her gaze. "I'm not going to mess up, Andrea."

"If you drink—"

"I'm not going to drink. I'm staying clean."

She nodded. She wished she felt as sure as he sounded.

CHAPTER FOURTEEN

John sat in the bluish glow of the television set watching the eleven-o'clock news. Andrea had put Phoebe to bed as soon as they'd finished washing the dishes and then had gone upstairs to read and unwind before falling asleep. Billy too had retreated to his room early with a set of head-phones tucked into his ears. He said he was lis-tening to music Rebekah had earlier helped him download from the computer into what he called an iPod. John hadn't seen one before, and Billy tried to tell him about it, but the whole thing made John nervous and uncomfortable. Half a decade locked away with no computer and little television had left him in something of a time freeze. He'd had to stand still while the world spun rapidly forward into strange new technolo-gies and unfamiliar forms of entertainment and communication. Kids downloaded music into hand-held contraptions, and people talked with each other via cameras embedded like the eye of Cyclops into the hardware of their computers.

John had emerged into a world eerily like the world of science fiction he had known in his youth. He didn't know how he was going to keep pace with the culture again, or whether he even could.

At least he still knew how to use the remote control for the television, since it was the same one they'd had in the cottage before he went to prison. His thumb rested on the volume button, which he'd turned down low. The front room was dark except for the flickering shadows coming from the TV screen. With no way to shut off the front room from Billy's hallway, John didn't want to disturb his son while he slept. He listened to Billy snoring softly and was pleasantly surprised at the sense of satisfaction running through him. Everyone in his care was asleep and safe. Except for Rebekah, who wasn't yet home from work.

John moved his thumb to the power button, thinking he might just as well turn off the news and go to bed. But before he could follow through, he heard the sound he'd been waiting for: the tires of the Volkswagen Jetta rolling over the graveled drive. He heard the car door open and close, heard footsteps up the slanted walkway to the porch. Then a key in the kitchen door.

"Beka?"

Silence. Then more footsteps, hesitant now, across the linoleum floor. Rebekah stopped in the doorway, her unsmiling face half hidden in shadow as the kitchen light shone behind her.

"You know," she said, "you don't have to wait up for me."

"I'm not. I'm just—" He sounded apologetic, or embarrassed, or maybe just plain weak; he wasn't sure which. What he did know was that he didn't sound like a father. But then, technology wasn't the only thing that had changed while he was away. His daughter had moved from pliant child to unpleasant teen, and he'd fallen out of step with her. He had no idea how to jump in at this point and be the parent she needed. Fidgeting, he tried to smile. "I guess I'm just a night owl."

Her whole body seemed to slump at that. "Well, that's just great," she murmured.

And then she was gone.

John switched off the television, stood and stretched, then walked quietly across the room. He treaded softly in his stocking feet up the steep stairs to the garret room. Waiting for Rebekah to come home was one reason he'd stayed up late watching the news. He knew he'd never fall asleep until everyone was in and accounted for. But that wasn't the only reason he stayed up. For the third night now, he wanted to make sure Andrea had had enough time to fall asleep before he climbed up to his own bed.

He paused at the top of the stairs, listening for Andrea's rhythmic breathing. Yes, she was asleep. She didn't stir as he slipped quietly around her bed to his own. He figured, though, that if he ever did wake her when he came to bed, she wouldn't let on. She'd pretend to be asleep so they wouldn't have to acknowledge each other's presence. Since that was how she wanted it, best to play along. He was lucky to have a place to come home to. Beyond that, he didn't want to stir the waters.

He squeezed between the foot of his bed and the overstuffed chair beside the window. He eased himself down on the edge of the mattress, not wanting the box springs to squeak too loudly. He sat there for a while, feeling the cool breeze that drifted into the room from the two open windows. The temperature had finally dropped a few degrees. A waning moon gave off just enough light so that when he turned toward his wife, he could see the contours of her face. She looked almost pretty lying there, her hair spread out against the pillow, one bare arm thrown up over her head. Sleep had drained her face of tension, and she looked peaceful and yet somehow expectant, as though she were waiting for something good to happen.

Andrea. John mouthed her name silently. He had so much to tell her, and he didn't know where to begin. He felt the burden of it inside, five years' worth of words, and he knew that among them was an apology, but it was an apology that was so fractured and for so many different mistakes, he didn't know how to piece it all together and make it presentable.

He had tried to express his remorse to her when she first started showing up for her twice yearly visits to the prison. The setting was less than ideal, as they were never alone in the visiting room. Once a year she brought the two older kids with her. But even those times when she came alone, the room was busy with other prisoners and their families milling about, talking, sharing snacks, listening to everybody else's conversations—or so it seemed to John.

Finally one day, in exasperation, he had blurted, *"Listen, Andrea, you deserve better than this. I think you should go ahead and divorce me. I won't contest it. I promise. Take the kids and start a new life. When I can, I'll start sending you child support."*

She didn't speak or even move for what seemed a long time. She looked stunned, as though someone had slapped her hard across the cheek. At last she asked, *"Is that how you want it?"*

He shook his head. *"What kind of life is this for you? Coming down here twice a year to visit your husband in prison. Taking care of three kids by yourself—"*

"But I don't want a divorce, John."

They looked intently at each other, the way an art student studies a sculpture from every angle, hoping to unveil the message chiseled in stone.

"But why, Andrea?" John asked quietly. *"Why stay with me?"*

She sat up straighter. One muscle in her jaw twitched as her mouth grew firm. *"Because I love you, John,"* she said. The words were strong— fortified, he sensed, by something like anger. But the firmness subsided to pain as she added, *"But you wouldn't know about that, would you?"*

He cringed at her words now, just as he had then. What did he know about love? Apparently, for most of his life, very little. What he knew most about love was that it never satisfied. Maybe for a while, but then the hunger returned, and the loneliness, and the void that was somehow larger than any tangible thing.

John remembered with regret the series of brief affairs he had had. There'd been a number of them over the years—he couldn't recall how many. They weren't so much affairs as simply flings. A burst of infatuation that quickly dwindled. Roman candle relationships, Jared called them. John thought of them more as duds, hardly worth the stress of cheating on his wife. The initial flash of excitement wasn't what he was looking for anyway. Not really. That flash and burnout seemed to be the pattern for his life, though—had even been the case with Andrea back when they were dating. With her, though, Billy had been conceived before the candle had burned itself out, so by the time the dust settled,

John found himself married to someone he didn't know how to love.

He lay down on top of the bedspread without bothering to change out of his clothes. He was tired, but he wasn't sure he could sleep. He tucked his hands under his head and stared up at the ceiling.

He'd had wandering eyes, and he knew it. A pretty face could still turn his head, though he'd seen few enough of those in the past five years. But he liked to think that what he had been looking for in his wanderings was more than skin deep, was something that would somehow satisfy not desire but longing. The endless drum-beat of wanting to know and be known.

That longing had colored his every decision and influenced his every action before he went to prison. Oddly, and unexpectedly, that same longing had been fulfilled behind the walls and barbed wire of the state penitentiary. He was a different man now, and he hoped to live a different kind of life. That was what he needed to tell Andrea, but he realized abruptly that something had been nagging at him for a long time. Fear. He was afraid to tell Andrea what had happened to him in prison. That one time when she was visiting he'd gotten as far as saying he'd prayed the sinner's prayer with the chaplain, but the look she gave him told him she was skeptical. *"Well, I'm glad you found religion,"* she'd said. And he wanted to tell her that it wasn't like that at all, but something prevented him from speaking.

Maybe it was what he'd seen happen too many times. Some of the men who came to Christ in prison went around telling everyone, as if they'd suddenly been reborn into holy-roller street-corner preachers compelled to share the Gospel with all the hell-bound passersby. That always made John feel a little sick. The only thing those men got in return was ridicule. Even when some of the believers shared their faith in quieter ways, their words were still mocked, sworn at, laughed over. He supposed you couldn't expect much from a bunch of criminals, but still, John remembered that the world viewed Christians in much the same way the convicts did—as a bunch of intolerant, narrow-minded, self-righteous hypocrites.

John sniffed lightly. Yeah, he knew. He'd been of the same opinion once. That was before he looked far enough beyond the Christians to gaze directly on the face of Christ. Once he did that, he understood. Once he did that, he had something for the first time in his life that meant more to him than life itself.

There was another believer behind bars, a dark-skinned fellow named Sid. Two hundred and fifty pounds of muscle, fists like basketballs, legs like telephone poles, and eyes like a child's. John had never met a more tender soul anywhere.

They'd commiserated once over the mockery of their faith.

"You know," Sid said, *"you tell some people about Jesus, it's just like casting your pearls before swine. Hard to see something so precious treated like garbage."*

John understood completely what Sid meant. Not that people like Andrea were swine, but still, it was hard to open your arms and pour out your treasure to people who might respond by labeling you a fool.

Rebekah, apparently repeating what she'd heard Andrea say, had called what happened to him a jailhouse conversion, one that would only last till he got out.

He would have to prove them wrong. But because he was afraid of casting out his pearls, he would, for the time being, have to do it quietly, without saying a word.

CHAPTER FIFTEEN

Billy watched as Phoebe broke through the surface of the lake, arms flapping, water splashing everywhere. As soon as she caught her breath, she laughed loudly.

"Watch me again, Billy!" she yelled.

She dog-paddled to the ladder and climbed up onto the sun-warmed dock. Then, legs pumping, feet stomping out wet footprints on the wooden planks, she ran to the end of the dock and cannonballed into the lake.

Billy applauded when her head once again popped out of the water like a cork. "You made a really big splash that time," he said. "You got me wet!" He was sunning in an inner tube several feet from the dock, using his hands as paddles to keep himself from drifting out too far.

Sundays were the best day of the week for Billy. His uncle always gave him Sundays off, even though the restaurant was open. That way Billy could go to church and afterward spend the rest of the day with the family. Mostly he palled around with Phoebe because Beka had to work, but that was all right. He and Phoebe had plenty to do—swimming, playing games, lying in the sun, fishing from the dock, taking the motorboat out with Mom. Billy was always happy to be with his little sister.

She swam to him and rested her arms on the inner tube. "What do you want me to do now, Billy?"

"I don't know." He shrugged. "You got goose bumps. Want to sit on the dock? Warm up some?"

"Okay."

Billy rolled and belly flopped out of the inner tube. The two of them put their hands on the tube and kicked their way back to shore. There, Billy dragged the tube up toward the bank while

Phoebe, shivering, ran off to wrap herself up in a beach towel.

In another moment Billy joined her at the end of the dock, where she sat with her legs dangling over the water. She had thrown the towel up over her head so that only her eyes peered out at Billy.

"You look like Mary in the Christmas pageant with the towel like that."

"I don't want him to see me," she answered quietly.

"Who?"

She motioned with her eyes toward the porch. Billy looked over his shoulder and saw their dad in one of the wicker chairs reading the Sunday paper.

He turned back to Phoebe. "You mean Dad?"

She nodded.

"That's silly, Phoeb. You don't have to hide from Dad."

"He's always watching me."

"No he isn't."

"Yeah he is."

"No he isn't."

"Yes he *is,* Billy."

"Well, okay. Maybe he is. Because he wants to know you."

Phoebe didn't answer.

"You'll like him someday," Billy said. "Wait and see."

She looked as if she didn't believe him, but she let the towel drop to the dock and leaned her head against Billy's arm. "Sing me a song, Billy."

"Which one?"

"I don't care. Any one."

"All right." He thought a moment, coughed, and cleared his throat. Then he started to sing.

"Jesus is love.
He shows us the way.
He's always watching over us,
Both night and day . . ."

Billy was kind of proud of this one; he'd written it himself. The tune was a bit different every time he sang it, and sometimes he even changed the words around, but it didn't matter to him, and it didn't seem to matter to Phoebe either.

"Jesus is peace.
He takes away my fear.
When I am afraid,
I know He is near."

His little sister linked her arm through his and shut her eyes. That, and the sun, made Billy feel warm all over.

"Jesus is life.
So when my days are done,
I know He'll come for me,
And take me home."

As he sang, he didn't notice the dock quivering beneath the weight of his father's footfalls. He looked up in surprise when he heard his father ask, "What are you singing, Billy?"

"Oh, hi, Dad." Billy smiled. "It's just a song I made up."

"Mind if I join you?"

"Have a seat."

Billy patted the dock beside him. He couldn't help noticing that when his father sat down, his feet actually reached the water. Billy watched the long, narrow toes sink beneath the surface, watched as hungry minnows gathered around and then, disappointed, flickered off again.

"Have a nice swim?" his dad asked.

"Yeah, Dad, the water's great. You want to come in?"

"Not right now. Some other time, though."

"Maybe we can go fishing sometime too. Take the motorboat out somewhere."

"Yeah, sure. You got rods?"

"Three of them. One for me, one for you, and one for whoever else wants to come."

"That works."

"You want to come with us, Phoeb?" Billy asked. "We'll let you hook the worms."

Phoebe made a face and shook her head. Billy laughed. "She doesn't like to touch the worms."

"Well, I don't blame her. They're kind of slimy, aren't they?"

Phoebe glanced at her dad, at Billy, at the water. The three sat silently a moment. Then Billy chuckled.

"What's funny, son?" his dad asked.

"Nothing, Dad. I'm just happy. I mean, you, me, and Phoebe all sitting right here together on the dock. I can't think of anything better than that."

"I'm glad you feel that way, Billy."

"Can you, Dad? Can you think of anything better?"

"No, I guess I can't." He leaned forward and tried to catch Phoebe's gaze. "What do you think, Phoebe?"

Billy felt the child shrug, felt her cling more tightly to his arm. He answered for her, "She thinks she likes it too." He felt a small pinch on the inside of his arm, but he ignored it. "I'm teaching Phoebe how to swim, Dad," he said proudly.

"Yeah? Well, I'm glad you are, Billy. I saw your medals on the windowsill. I'd forgotten how good you are in the water."

"I like to swim. Coach said I'm like a fish."

"I know you are. You going to do any more racing at the Special Olympics?"

"I don't know. Maybe."

"You should if you have the chance."

"I don't know, Dad. It was fun when I was a kid, but I got grown-up things to worry about now."

"You do? Like what?"

"Uncle Owen's going to teach me everything I need to know about owning a restaurant."

"He is? You going to buy the restaurant from him?"

"Maybe someday. I like the work."

"I know you do, Billy."

"And I got to make a living somehow."

"Yeah. We'll talk about that. We'll get it all figured out."

"I can do it, Dad."

Silence. Then, "I don't doubt that, son." Dad leaned forward again, looking past Billy to Phoebe. "Phoebe, I think you need a nap."

Phoebe shook her head. "No I don't."

"You look like you're falling asleep."

"No I'm not."

"You know, you might sleep better at night if you didn't sleep on the floor in Billy's room."

"I like the floor."

"I'm just suggesting you might be more comfortable in your own bed."

She narrowed her eyes, pulled her mouth into a taut line.

Billy said, "She doesn't like it in with Beka."

"So I've been told. What's the matter, Phoebe?"

When she didn't answer, Billy said, "It's all right, Phoeb. You can tell us."

She was quiet another moment before saying, "Beka has scary things."

"What kind of scary things?" Dad asked.

Phoebe looked at Billy. He nodded at her to go on. "She has candles and things."

"Candles? Oh, are you afraid she'll set the room on fire?"

Phoebe shook her head.

Dad prodded, "What is it, then?"

When Phoebe didn't answer, Billy patted her hand. "You can tell us, Phoeb," he said. "We're here to take care of you."

Finally she said, "She has books with scary pictures in them."

"What kind of scary pictures?" Dad asked.

Phoebe shrugged. "I don't know."

A motorboat sped by close to the end of the dock, cutting a wake in the water. Billy watched as the series of small waves rolled to shore.

His father leaned forward again to look at Phoebe. "Do you know what the books are?"

"No," Phoebe whispered. To Billy's surprise, she added, "She uses them when she casts her spells."

Billy had to think about that for a minute. Suddenly, he laughed. "You mean, like Beka is a witch or something?"

Phoebe narrowed her eyes at him, and Billy stopped laughing.

"What makes you think she's casting spells, Phoebe?" Dad asked.

"Well, once she got mad at me and said she was

115

going to put a spell on me if I didn't go away and leave her alone."

"She did?" Dad looked at Billy. "Is that what kids are into these days, Billy?"

"Not me, Dad." Billy shook his head. "I don't know anything about it. Maybe she thinks she's Harry Potter or something. She and her friends were crazy about all those movies."

"Oh yeah," Dad said. He nodded and then smiled at Phoebe. "Listen, honey, it's just pretend. Beka can't really put a spell on you. All that stuff in the movies—that's just pretend too. You know that, don't you?"

Phoebe looked out over the lake. She didn't answer.

CHAPTER SIXTEEN

The moon wasn't anywhere near full, and today wasn't the right day of the week for this kind of thing, but Rebekah decided to go ahead and do it anyway. It couldn't hurt. She could do it now and do it again later. After all, as Lena had explained, that was what was so wonderful about all of this; you were free to do whatever you wanted, however you wanted to do it. Rebekah had the power within herself to make things happen; she had only to find the right way to unleash that power. At least that's what Lena said.

Glad that Phoebe had already made her nightly

trek to Billy's room, Rebekah pulled back the double doors of her closet to reveal her sacred space. That was where she kept the wooden crate she used as an altar, her candles and incense, her herbs and oils—all the tools of the Craft that she'd been collecting over the past months. The crate lay on its side with the open end facing out so that she could use the crate itself as a sort of cubby for her belongings. She also had a small collection of magic books given to her by Lena and Lena's aunt Jo, who knew just about everything there was to know about the Craft. Rebekah's most important book, of course, was her Book of Shadows, a spiral notebook in which she recorded her thoughts, her feelings, and her own made-up spells.

She glanced at the luminous face of the clock on the nightstand beside the bed. Just past midnight. At least it was a good time, she thought, to call on the elements to make her more beautiful. She had to be beautiful for David because she didn't want to lose him. The thought of being without him terrified her, but she tried to push it away. She didn't want to be pulling down any negative thoughts when she should be envisioning only good things. If she did this right, she could bend even the universe to her will. She wanted badly to believe that. She needed badly to believe it. She reminded herself that some months ago she had cast a spell, asking the universe to send her love, and right after that David had shown up. That had to be more than coincidence.

Rebekah lit two candles on the altar—both red, the color of love. Around the base of the candles she sprinkled cinnamon, ginger, marjoram, and thyme, all of which were an aid in love, and all of which she had conveniently found in her mother's spice rack.

For just a moment she hesitated. Maybe she should wait for the full moon after all. But no, that was two, maybe three, weeks off, and she couldn't wait that long. She had to do something now. David was sure to find out the truth about her father, and that might change his mind about her. On top of that, she had seen him tonight talking with Jessica Faulkner while he collected tickets at the Ferris wheel. They had talked a little too long and had laughed a little too much, as far as Rebekah was concerned.

When Rebekah and David met at closing time, she asked him what he and Jessica had been talking about. David had shrugged and said, *"I don't know. Nothing much. Why?"*

"No reason. Just looked like you were having fun."

"Not jealous, are you?"

"No." Yes. She was jealous and afraid, but she wouldn't let on.

"Want to meet tonight?"

"I've got to lie low for a while."

"How come?"

"My dad's back, remember? It's harder now to sneak out and back in without getting caught."

"Yeah. Okay." He'd obviously been irritated.

"Soon, though, David. We'll meet soon. I promise." Because if she couldn't spend time with him, he'd find someone who could.

On the floor in front of her she dumped the contents of a plastic bag. These were the items she would need for the ritual: her makeup, soap, shampoo, lotions, several pieces of jewelry, a hand mirror, and a mister filled with holy water consecrated beneath a full moon. Carefully she placed each of the items on the crate that served as her altar.

She stood then to cast her circle. *"You can never forget to cast your circle,"* Lena had warned, *"or you leave yourself open to negative energy."*

Moving clockwise, Rebekah defined her circle by placing stones on the floor to create a perimeter. Next she placed her elemental representations on the points depicting north, south, east, and west: a jar of dirt for earth, a feather for air, a tiger's eye gemstone for fire, and a shell for water. As she did so, she pushed back a stray doubt about what she was doing, knowing that the doubt itself would work against her, interfering with what she wanted to accomplish. Once the elements were laid, she used a small broom to brush away any doubts and all negative thoughts; the circle was a sacred place and needed to be pure. To fill the space with positive energy, she opened a jar of salt water coated with rosemary and, dipping her fingers in the mixture, flicked the water around the circle's edge.

When she finished, she paused a moment, unsure what to do next. She didn't want to mess up. Sitting cross-legged on the floor, she shut her eyes and pictured Lena. In her mind she heard again what her friend had told her so many times. *"You can't do anything wrong, you know. That's the beauty of it. Anything you do is right. Just do what works for you."*

She picked up the mister and sprayed each item on the altar with holy water. Each time she sprayed, as the mist tumbled down upon each object, Rebekah whispered, "The power of beauty in me, around me, on me. The power of love in me, around me, on me."

She paused and took a deep breath. It was time to center herself. Before she could go on with the ritual, she would have to purify her mind and draw up positive energy from the earth, letting the power sink into every part of her body.

"You will learn," Aunt Jo had told her, *"that you yourself are divine. You are a part of the goddess and the god, the lady and the lord, the universal one. You can do anything."*

Rebekah stood and raised her arms. She shut her eyes and tried to release the nagging doubts, tried to dwell on the divinity within her. She hoped that Lena's aunt was right and that she could do anything, because losing David would mean losing the best thing in her life.

CHAPTER SEVENTEEN

The cramped church basement smelled of mold and old coffee and somebody's too-sweet perfume. Eleven people sat in a circle on metal folding chairs, some chatting quietly, a few sitting silently as they waited for the meeting to begin.

John looked down at his hands, clasped loosely at his knees like two people caught in a conversation they didn't want to be in. Nothing about his body felt right at the moment because he really didn't want to be here, exposing himself as something he still didn't like to accept.

He'd grown used to the A.A. meetings in prison, but it had taken a couple of years, mostly because in prison he was struggling to see himself not only as an alcoholic—which he had long denied—but worse, as a criminal. Granted, he was a lousy husband, a second-rate father, and an unreliable provider, but still—how do you go from that to a convicted criminal seemingly overnight? One day you're holding a low-wage but honest job and the next you're in the slammer without so much as a clear memory of the events that got you there.

For a long time he refused to put himself on a par with the other prisoners. They were the real criminals, the conscious wrongdoers. They had robbed convenience stores at gunpoint, sold crack cocaine on street corners, committed fraud, abused children, killed their wives. John Sheldon hadn't done anything like that. He'd had no desire to kill a man and no intention of killing the man he did kill.

Only after thirty-three months and probably a hundred talks with Pastor Pete did John realize there was something about the human heart that could make a man do even things he didn't want to do. Only after all those months of being locked up did he come to understand that there was something to the idea of good and evil, and if you didn't choose the one, you'd be chosen by the other.

That was when he surrendered, seeing himself for what he was and knowing he'd go on spiraling downward if goodness didn't intervene. God broke in then—safety net, savior, life itself.

Still, John didn't want to be here at this A.A. meeting, admitting to strangers he was something he didn't want to be. He wouldn't have come if it hadn't been a requirement of his probation. He certainly didn't need A.A. to stay dry. Killing someone, he'd discovered, had a way of putting a person off alcohol for good.

John looked up with a start when a man across the circle began to speak. "Good evening, ladies and gentlemen," he said as he rose to his feet. "This is the regular meeting of the Conesus Lake group of Alcoholics Anonymous. My name is Larry, and I'm an alcoholic and your secretary."

He was a tall, gaunt man, about sixty-five years old. He had a narrow, fleshless face and thinning gray hair, and he wore a pair of baggy trousers that appeared to be held up not so much by his belt as by his protruding hip bones. He might have appeared more dead than alive except for the uncanny warmth in his eyes and a voice so rich in compassion it seemed to settle like a down comforter over the entire group.

"Let's open our meeting tonight with a moment of silence and the Serenity Prayer." He shut his eyes and bowed his head. Everyone in the circle followed suit.

In the next moment John heard the murmurs of the Serenity Prayer rise up around him. He heard himself join in, heard the words tumble from his own reluctant lips, heard above everything else Larry's strong voice leading the group like a shepherd gently herding his flock.

John liked Larry instantly, knew there was something good and solid about him, and would have gone on listening to the man with intrigue if, upon looking up at the close of the prayer, he hadn't found himself gazing directly across the circle at a woman who hadn't been there a moment before. She must have slipped in quietly when everyone had their eyes shut. She had settled in the vacant chair right next to Larry, and though she'd come in late, she looked as unrushed and serene as if she'd been there the entire time.

Larry looked down at her and chuckled. "I hardly heard you come in, Pamela. Glad you could make it."

"Sorry I'm late, Larry. Car trouble."

"That's all right. Car running okay now?"

"Yeah. I called Triple A and got it jumped. That was all it needed."

"Good, good. Well, let's get on with the meeting, then, shall we?"

Larry talked on, but John didn't listen. He was too busy trying to steal glances at the woman named Pamela. He'd never seen anything like *that* at the A.A. meetings in prison, had never seen anything like that in prison at all, save in his own imagination. She was no doubt the kind of creature that invaded the dreams of every man behind bars, their waking dreams, their sleeping dreams, those gut-wrenching dreams that leave a man tossing feverishly in the dead of night.

She was lovely and classy and soft, without that hardened look of so many women who'd spent years cradling a bottle. She was young, but not so young that she hadn't lived. She had an open, serious face and full red lips and hair the color of mahogany and doelike eyes that held a look John knew well. He was acquainted with that look from his years inside, had seen it often in the eyes of the prisoners, an expression that spoke of a loneliness so deep it seemed to be bottomless. How could a woman like this know such loneliness?

". . . one new face," Larry was saying. "Would you care to introduce yourself to the group?"

John realized with a jolt that Larry had spoken to him and was now waiting for him to respond. He shifted in his seat, cleared his throat. "Um . . . hi, I'm John. I . . . I'm not new to A.A. I've been in A.A. for about five years down in Virginia. I just moved back here again. I'm from here, or Rochester really, but we live here now."

He pressed his lips together so as to stop stumbling over his words. He looked at Pamela. She looked at him. She smiled.

"Welcome, John," Larry said. "We're glad to have you here. Now I'd like to ask Rick to read a section from chapter five of the Big Book, and after that I'll introduce the discussion topic for the evening."

An hour and a half later, when John was walking home through the dusk, he remembered little of what was said at the meeting. He did, though, recall feeling annoyed at a man who repeatedly and loudly blew his nose into a soiled handkerchief. He remembered cringing in shared embarrassment at a woman who stuttered painfully, trying in vain to announce seven years of sobriety. He also knew he had reached into his wallet and pulled out a five to drop into the basket when it was passed around.

But beyond that, all he could remember were those eyes. Those deep, brown, lonely, lovely eyes.

The circle had joined hands at the end and recited the Lord's Prayer. When they came to the plea about "lead us not into temptation," he had squeezed his eyes tight, trying to rid his mind of unwanted thoughts.

O Lord, he prayed silently now, *deliver me from evil.*

But as he went on walking home through the fading light, he was all the while thinking of Pamela.

CHAPTER EIGHTEEN

Every time Billy stepped through the entrance gate of the Conesus Lake Amusement Park, he felt happy and excited. He loved the crowds, the rides, the midway games, the ice cream and cotton candy and fried foods on a stick.

The park was also the place that sucked Billy's

pockets dry of any spare change he had after he put most of his paycheck in the bank.

"Come on, Phoebe," he said, tugging at his sister's hand. "Let's get to the arcade and win some tickets." Once he'd played enough games and earned enough tickets, he could claim the prize he'd had his eye on for a couple of weeks now.

"You said you'd ride the merry-go-round with me," Phoebe reminded him.

Billy nodded. "I will later. I want to go to the arcade first."

"Is Beka working there today?"

"I don't know. We'll see."

As they wound their way through the crowd on the midway, Billy was aware of the stares, especially from other kids—little kids, teenagers—but he tried to ignore them. Hadn't they ever seen a person with Down syndrome before? There were plenty of them around, so Billy didn't know what the big deal was. Anyway, he wasn't nearly so freaky as the kids with dreadlocks, piercings, and tattoos, or the kids with a load of fake gold chains around their necks, their pants hanging down so low you could see the brand of underpants they wore. Now *they* were worth staring at. Billy pulled Phoebe along, cutting a determined path through the crowd, focused on reaching the arcade.

"Hey, Billy!"

Billy stopped short, and Phoebe stumbled into him. "Sorry, Phoeb," he said. "I thought I heard my name."

"Hey, Billy!"

Phoebe lifted one skinny arm and pointed toward the Toss-a-Ball game just ahead of them. "Look. It's Beka's boyfriend."

David Morgan beckoned to them with a baseball in his hand. "Billy! Come on over and win your little sister a stuffed animal!"

Billy rocked on the balls of his feet, unsure of what to do. He wasn't any good at the Toss-a-Ball game. He'd tried it a couple times before and didn't like it. It looked as if it'd be easy to win that game, to smash that pyramid of cans all over the place, but the ball wasn't a real baseball, and it was too light to do any real damage. One, maybe two cans fell, but never all six.

He felt Phoebe squeeze his hand. "Billy," she said. "Look at those pandas! Maybe you could win me a panda."

He shook his head. "I don't know."

"Come on, Billy. Just try, all right?"

He knew it couldn't go well either way. If he played, he wouldn't win. If he didn't play, she'd be disappointed in him for not trying.

He allowed Phoebe to pull him over to the booth. David Morgan gave them a wide smile. But Billy wasn't smiling. "No one wins this game," he said.

David laughed. "Are you kidding? People win all the time. I just restocked the prizes an hour ago." He turned to Phoebe. "You want Billy to win you a stuffed animal, don't you?"

Billy followed David's gaze to Phoebe's eager face. Her eyes were wide as she nodded happily. He felt his teeth clench as he looked at the cans stacked on the board. "Okay. Give me one ball."

"Listen, Billy," David said, "it's a better deal to go three for five. Five dollars gets you three tries, and there's no way you can't empty the shelf on three tries, is there?"

Billy had never liked David very much. He didn't know why, but every time he saw the guy, he felt something turn over in his stomach. It may have been the fact that David Morgan was good-looking and he knew it. He had the kind of face that showed up on the cover of those Hollywood gossip magazines. Nice features, thick dark hair, perfect white teeth—the whole works. A face like that did something to a person, turned him into someone you couldn't trust. Especially when he was dating your sister.

"I don't know, David—"

"Here you go, Billy-boy. Three balls. Don't disappoint the little kid there, all right?"

Reluctantly Billy reached into his pocket and pulled out a five. He laid it on the counter and picked up the first of the balls. He was surprised again at how light it was. He thought he might as well be tossing a marshmallow at bowling pins. He could have used the five dollars at the arcade, winning tickets for the prize he wanted.

He drew back his arm and hoped his anger would smash the pyramid. But he let go a ball that dropped short of the target by several inches, swerving off to the left and ending up in the tarp beneath the board.

"Tough luck, Billy," David said. "But hey, you've got two more balls. Put a little more muscle into it and aim it just off center."

Billy tried not to look at Phoebe, who was clapping her hands and hopping up and down. He took a deep breath, drew back, and tossed the ball. This one hit the target, and he felt a shiver of hope as the ball shaved off the peak of the pyramid.

"You got one!" David announced. "Okay, last ball. You can do it, bud."

For a split second Billy thought maybe he could. If he aimed just right, if he threw hard enough, he could win that panda for Phoebe. In his mind he saw all five remaining cans explode outward, sailing off the shelf in different directions. Pulling his arm back like a pitcher on the mound, he collected all his strength and threw out his arm, sending the ball sailing. It soared in a trembling arc toward the target, but like the first ball, it fell short, missing the mark by a wide margin and landing with a thud on the tarp.

"Aw, too bad, Billy-boy." David grinned, then winked at Phoebe. "Maybe next time, huh?"

Billy clenched his teeth. He didn't take his eyes off the cans that had outdone him. He wanted to tell David there wasn't going to be a next time. He wasn't going to fall for this one again and waste his money. He wanted to yell at David, tell him the game wasn't fair, because someone who'd thrown the balls as hard as he'd thrown them should have knocked down all the cans. Something wasn't right here if a person tried so hard and couldn't win.

He felt Phoebe squeeze his elbow. "It's all right, Billy," she said. "Never mind. Let's just go to the arcade."

He ignored her for a moment but finally gave in as she tugged him away from the booth. Holding hands, they stumbled on down the midway, their tennis shoes pressing against steamy blacktop, through sticky puddles of melted ice cream and discarded cotton candy, over generator wires stretched out like black snakes in the sun. Billy thought Phoebe might have said something, but he couldn't hear her over the carnival barkers and the music coming from the rides. He didn't bother to ask her what it was. He looked straight ahead, seething until they reached the arcade.

Rebekah stood behind the counter, collecting tickets and handing out prizes. Billy marched to the glass case holding the toys and trinkets, searching for the one item he wanted.

He let out a sigh of relief. It was still there.

"That's the last one, Billy," Rebekah said, tossing a handful of tickets into a bucket.

Billy looked up anxiously. "Are you sure? There's no more?"

"Nope, they're gone. We only had a few, but apparently there were people out there who wanted the silly things."

"It's not silly." Billy looked back down at the nightlight that was nestled in one corner of the glass case. On the white plastic covering was the picture of a tiny lamb sleeping on a patch of grass.

"They're for babies," Rebekah said.

"No they're not." Billy shook his head. "They're for anyone, and I like it."

Rebekah shrugged. "Whatever."

Billy was sure the lamb was the one his Sunday school teacher had read about from the Bible, the one that lay down in green pastures and walked with the shepherd beside still waters. He liked that, and he wanted to have the lamb in his room, where he could see it every day.

"How many tickets do you have, Billy?" Phoebe asked.

Billy rubbed his forehead as he thought. "I remember. I have seventy-nine."

"Are you sure?"

"Yeah. Dad counted with me. We counted three times."

"So how many more tickets do you need?"

Billy pulled a slip of paper out of his pocket and looked at it. "Two hundred and twenty-one."

"Wow. That's a lot."

"Yeah. I better get busy."

"Can I help? I usually win some tickets playing that bowling game."

"Okay, sure. Here's a dollar, Phoeb. You get four tokens."

"Don't worry, Billy. We'll win the nightlight."

"I hope so." Billy looked up at his sister behind the counter. "Can you hold it for me, Beka? Don't let anyone else buy it?"

She shrugged again. "Sorry, Billy. I have to sell it if somebody wants it, you know? I could lose my job if I didn't."

Billy looked at the nightlight again. He had to have it.

He went to the token machine and started feeding it dollar bills.

Chapter Nineteen

Andrea pulled the bedsheet up to Phoebe's chin, then bent down to kiss her cheek, her forehead, her nose. That always made Phoebe smile. "Good night, sweetheart," Andrea said.

"Good night, Mommy."

"Do you think you can stay in your own bed all night tonight?"

"I don't know." The child pursed her lips, looked up at her mother with big round eyes. "I'll try," she promised. "But I wish I had my own room."

"Someday you will. Your own room with all your own things."

"Okay, Mommy."

"Good night, Phoebe." Andrea moved to the door and switched off the light.

"Mommy?"

"Yes?"

"We forgot to say my prayers."

"Oh yeah. Okay, I'm listening."

"Now I lay me down to sleep, I pray the Lord my soul to keep. May angels watch me through the night and wake me with the morning light. Amen."

"Okay, go to sleep now, Phoebe."

"Mommy?"

"Hmm?"

"Billy says angels watch over us night and day. Do you think they're watching me right now?"

"Well, yes. I'm sure they are. So you don't need to worry. Now go to sleep."

Andrea pulled the door shut with a sigh. She knew Rebekah would wake Phoebe up when she came home from work, and Phoebe would end up on the floor by Billy's bed again. She hoped Phoebe would soon outgrow her fears.

She poured herself a cup of iced tea from the fridge and carried it to the overstuffed chair in the front room. She sat down heavily and put her feet up on the tattered hassock. She was tired, bone tired, but not quite ready to go upstairs to bed.

She would drink her tea and revel in a few moments of quiet first. She loved the evening quiet, filled as it was with the night songs of crickets and cicadas and the occasional gentle lapping of waves on the shore. Here, by the open window, she could even feel a bit of cool breeze rising up from the lake.

She drank deeply, put her head back, listened. From somewhere out there in the dark came the sound of Billy's voice and John's response. They weren't on the glider outside the window; Andrea thought they must be sitting together on the porch steps.

"So you want to come, Dad?" Billy asked.

"Sure, Billy. Sure I do," John answered.

"You'll like Pastor Gunther. He's real nice."

"What time does the service start tomorrow morning?"

"Ten o'clock. I get there early so I can get a seat right down in front."

"Right down in front, huh?"

"Yeah. That's okay, isn't it, Dad?"

"Sure. That's okay. And then after church you go to your Sunday school class?"

"They don't have Sunday school in the summer. Just church."

Andrea thought maybe she should go on upstairs; she felt like she was eavesdropping. But she changed her mind when she heard John say, "So your mother and sisters don't go to church with you, Billy?"

"Naw. I've asked them, but they don't want to go."

True. Billy had asked her numerous times, and she always said no. Rebekah would fight the whole way there, and both Rebekah and Phoebe would fidget throughout the service, making the hour miserable for all of them. It just wouldn't be worth it.

"Let me ask you something, Billy," John said.

"Sure, Dad."

"How long have you been going to church?"

Billy was quiet a moment. Then he said, "I don't know. Maybe about two years."

"And you just started going by yourself?"

"Yeah."

"Weren't you scared?"

"Scared of what?"

"I don't know. Just going out and being with a bunch of strangers, I guess."

"Naw, I wasn't scared."

"Well, that's good, then. But I'm wondering why you started going."

"To learn about God."

"But, we never—I mean, before I had to go away, we never went to church, never talked about God. Who told you?"

"What do you mean, Dad?"

"Who told you God was there?"

"He did."

"He?"

"God. God told me just the same as He tells everyone."

"He did?"

"Sure. Didn't he tell you, Dad?"

"Well, I had a lot of long talks with a man we called Pastor Pete. He was the one who kind of . . . helped me to understand it all."

In the ensuing silence Andrea could imagine Billy frowning, trying to make sense of what his father had said.

Finally Billy asked, "What didn't you understand, Dad?"

"Well, everything. I didn't even really know for sure that God existed."

"But, Dad," Billy protested, "that's easy. We wouldn't be here if He weren't there. Everyone knows that."

"Not everyone, Billy. For some people, it isn't easy at all. For some people, there's just too much to figure out—so much that they can never stop wondering and just settle on believing."

A long pause followed. Then Billy said, "You know what I think, Dad?"

"What, Billy?"

"I think they're making it too hard."

"You may be right about that, son."

Another pause, then, "Dad?"

"Yeah?"

"Think we should ask Mom again, see if she wants to go with us now that you're here?"

"No, I don't think so."

Andrea's heart sank, though she wasn't surprised by John's answer.

"Why not, Dad?"

"Well, it'd be nice if we all went together as a family, and maybe someday we can. But for now, let's not push it."

Andrea sat up a little straighter. If John wanted her to go to church, she would go. They could take Phoebe and leave Rebekah at home. She'd be fine alone for an hour.

Andrea decided not to interrupt John and Billy tonight. She'd just plan on being dressed and ready in the morning when the two of them announced they were going to church. She couldn't wait to see the look on Billy's face. She only hoped John would be as pleased.

CHAPTER TWENTY

By 9:52 A.M. on Sunday morning, John, Billy, Andrea, and Phoebe Sheldon were seated in the front pew, pulpit side, of Grace Chapel. John tugged at his collar and resisted the urge to fan himself with the church bulletin the way Andrea was doing down the row on the far side of Billy and Phoebe. The sanctuary was already warm in spite of the trio of ceiling fans whirling overhead, and John dreaded the thought of being stuck for an hour at the feet of a rambling preacher. For a moment he envied Rebekah, who had declined his invitation to join them by moaning and rolling over in bed.

Beside him Billy sneezed loudly three times. John reached into his pocket, pulled out his handkerchief, and offered it to Billy.

Billy raised a hand. "I got my own, Dad." He sank down in the pew so he could more easily dig into his pocket.

John watched as his son pulled out his own neatly folded handkerchief, snapped it open, and blew his nose. Then the boy crumpled it up in a ball and pushed it back into his pocket.

From down the row Andrea smiled mildly at John, as though to say, *See, you never know when you might need a handkerchief.*

John offered a small smile in return and then

dropped his eyes to the bulletin dated Sunday, June 17. Father's Day. At his place at the breakfast table that morning he'd found a card from Billy and Phoebe, homemade. Colored paper, ribbons, glitter, and the words "Hoppy Fatter's Day." He hadn't even been able to speak for a full thirty seconds or he would have broken down in tears. He'd never seen anything quite so beautiful.

He opened the bulletin and was glancing at the service notes when he felt Billy nudge him in the ribs. "Hey, Dad. Pastor Gunther's going to talk about David and Goliath."

John nodded absently. "Yeah?" he murmured. He fidgeted, looked over his shoulder, scanned the dozen or so pews between himself and the church doors. He didn't recognize a single face and didn't find the one he was looking for.

Turning forward again, he dropped his eyes to the black shine of his bargain-basement Oxfords. *God, help me,* he prayed silently. He knew it wasn't much, only a fragment of the plea he should be offering to God, and he chastened himself for limping along on these three small words since coming home from prison.

"I like the story of David and Goliath, don't you, Dad?" Billy went on.

"Sure, I guess so."

"I like it 'cause the little guy wins. All he's got is that slingshot, but he goes out there against the

140

giant and, wham-o, hits that monster right in the middle of the forehead. Goliath bites the dust without hardly knowing what hit him."

John chuckled quietly. "Yeah, I guess that's about right."

Before they could say more, the quiet of the sanctuary was shattered by a sudden blast of organ music. In his peripheral vision he saw Phoebe and Andrea jump, startled awake after nearly succumbing to the drowsy warmth of the place. Andrea, he realized, had turned to look at him. He glanced at her, tried to return her smile, failed miserably. His gaze went back to the Oxfords, to a smudge on the otherwise polished right toe.

He was annoyed with himself, annoyed with the thoughts that plagued him, annoyed at the interference that made a difficult task even harder. How did he expect to make a workable family unit out of five unlikely people when his mind was crowded with thoughts of Pamela?

Hoppy Fatter's Day. Billy had beamed, gathered him up in a huge bear hug, whispered, "You're the best, Dad." Even Phoebe had managed a shy, reluctant hug and couldn't help smiling when he complimented her on her fine artwork. Andrea had stood by watching, taking it in, looking satisfied for once. The sight of her standing there in her apron made him think of the mother in *Leave It to Beaver* or *Father Knows*

Best. How many women still wore aprons and puttered around the kitchen in early twenty-first-century America? Maybe he was lucky to have a wife who cooked and cleaned and cared for the kids and folded his handkerchiefs, all without complaint.

Even as he thought of Andrea, he glanced over his shoulder again. When he realized what he was doing, he made fists of his hands, swore silently at himself, forced himself to look up at the pulpit and pay attention to here and now.

"Fool," he muttered.

Billy leaned toward him. "What, Dad?"

John shook his head. "Nothing, Billy. I just—" He stopped abruptly when a man wearing pastoral garb climbed into the pulpit. The pastor looked directly at John, nodded a greeting, and announced to the congregation, "Please open your hymnals to page two twenty-four."

As Billy flipped through a hymnal, John asked, "Who's that?"

Billy glanced up, then back at John. "That's him, Dad. That's Pastor Gunther."

"That's Pastor Gunther?"

Billy nodded. "Why, Dad? What's wrong?"

"Nothing."

Nothing, except that Pastor Gunther was Larry, alcoholic and secretary of the Conesus Lake chapter of Alcoholics Anonymous.

As though reading his thoughts, Pastor Larry

Gunther looked down at John again, nodded and smiled, then broke into the first verse of "Jesus! What a Friend for Sinners."

John almost laughed—might have if he weren't quite so baffled. Did the congregation know they played the flock of a besotted shepherd? Or rather, he corrected himself, a one-time imbiber, even if he'd been clean now for—how many years did he say? Twelve without a drink? But just two fingers of gin and the guy could be gone again, right back to drinking himself into the ground. He was that close to ruin, and what kind of pastor was that? Still, the congregation must know that about the man. How could they not?

John had seldom been to church, save for the chapel services in the prison, but he followed the service by taking his cues from the bulletin. He stood when they were supposed to stand, sang when they were supposed to sing, followed along as a lay reader read the day's Scripture from the Bible, sat when the congregation was supposed to sit. The one task he didn't do well was listen to the sermon. He was too busy alternately puzzling over the pastor and pushing thoughts of Pamela from his mind.

When the hour was over and the congregants filed out, John stalled for time by asking Billy his impression of the service and feigning interest in the boy's answer. He waited until the sanctuary was nearly empty, save for the last few stragglers shaking the pastor's hand and thanking him for a wonderful sermon. Finally John trailed his wife and kids down the aisle. He listened while an excited Billy introduced them all to the pastor, heard Andrea say, "Very glad to meet you," heard Billy say, "This is my dad, Pastor Gunther. Remember, I told you he was coming home?"

John knew then that Larry Gunther knew he'd come from prison, but in light of Larry's own history, John didn't feel quite as bad as he might have otherwise. Why should he cringe when the face he was staring into had the telltale web of broken vessels, the ruddy sunken cheeks of a one-time heavy drinker? He extended his hand and felt it received with a warm grasp.

"Hello again, John." Larry smiled placidly, but his eyes laughed merrily, as though he were amused.

"Hello, Pastor Gunther."

The man shrugged, waved a hand. "It's still Larry up here, the same as down in the basement."

"Oh? All right, Larry."

"I'm glad you could be here this morning."

"Thank you. I'm . . ."

"Surprised to see me in the pulpit?"

"Well, yes. To be honest."

"Tell me, John, have you ever read Graham Greene's novel *The Power and the Glory*?"

"I don't remember. I'm not much of a reader."

"So you're not familiar with the whiskey priest?"

"No, I don't guess so."

"Well, you see, as Greene put it, 'He was aware of his own desperate inadequacy,' " Larry quoted. "Page eighty-two."

"Oh?"

"That's what made him strong."

John frowned but at the same time offered an almost imperceptible nod of his head. "All right," he said quietly.

"See you Wednesday night?"

"I'll be there."

"Good. Till then, one day at a time, right?"

"Sure thing, Larry. You too." John wondered whether that was the proper thing to say to a pastor, but it was already said, and Larry was already walking away, unzipping his robe.

As they exited the church and moved down the wooden steps, John was aware of Andrea's gaze. "What in the world was that all about, John?"

He shrugged and loosened the knot in his tie. "Tell you the truth, Andrea," he said, "I'm not completely sure myself. Though I suppose at some point I'm bound to find out."

CHAPTER TWENTY-ONE

Working the ticket booth was the worst job in the park, way off the charts on the boredom factor, as far as Rebekah was concerned. Take the money, count out the tickets, slide them under the glass along with the change. She'd rather work the arcade or one of the concession stands, though even those assignments were already getting old. Really, compared to what she could be doing with her time, this whole working thing was becoming one huge pain in the neck.

The crowds were down today, as was usual for a Tuesday, or what was known in the trade as the midweek slump. Between the boredom and the heat, Rebekah was certain that if she shut her eyes for even a second, she'd be asleep. The small fan on the floor of the booth was turned up high, but it didn't shoot out enough air to either keep her cool or keep her awake.

Rebekah rubbed her temples and moaned in frustration, then reached for the can of Coke one of the carnival hands had just dropped off at the booth. Gary, she knew, had a thing for her, though he was a dozen years older and, in the opinion of everyone at the park, uglier than sin. His mountainous nose sprung up sharply from the valley of his lipless face, and dark horn-rimmed glasses distorted his small blinking eyes like mirrors in a fun house. The girls who worked at the park laughed and called him Gargoyle when they thought he couldn't hear them, though sometimes he did.

But that didn't discourage Gary from dropping off cans of soda for Rebekah from time to time. He carried his offerings in a hand slick with grease so that Rebekah had to wipe the can with whatever paper napkin or rag she could find before opening it. She accepted the sodas because they were free, and because she knew that he knew she wouldn't be caught dead with some-body like him. Besides, she was David Morgan's girl. Everyone at the park knew that.

She took a long, refreshing sip of the drink and then held the can to her forehead to let the cool of the aluminum seep into her skin. She thought of Gary's greasy hand, but she was too hot to care. When she settled the Coke back on the ledge, she realized with a start that someone was standing at the booth.

"Twenty tickets," the girl said, sliding a twenty-dollar bill under the glass.

Rebekah silently counted out the tickets, then shoved them under the glass without lifting her eyes or saying a word. She knew very well what Jessica Faulkner looked like without having to look. She hated the sight of her. Hated the star-tling beauty that made the girl stand out like a Hollywood icon right here in Backwater Heights.

Jessica accepted the tickets with an equally silent disdain and wandered off, followed by three girls Rebekah thought of as the parasites.

As she watched them blend in with the crowd, another familiar face appeared beyond the glass. This face was less attractive, with close-set eyes and a too-large mouth, framed by flyaway hair the color of winter wheat. Lena Barrett sometimes threatened to grow dreadlocks. Rebekah thought it would suit her.

"Hey, girl," Lena said.

"Hi, Lena. I was just thinking about you."

"Yeah, I know."

Rebekah sniffed. "Okay, whatever." Lena was her best friend, but sometimes she was so strange it was annoying. "Listen, I just sold some tickets to Jessica Faulkner and her minions."

"Yeah, I know that too. That's why I'm here."

"What do you mean?"

"I followed her over here from the arcade. She's been there for the past hour, playing pinball."

"So?"

"So you know that's where David's working today. At least he was working when he wasn't too distracted by other things."

Rebekah felt something cold crawl just beneath her skin. "So what are you saying, Lena?"

"I'm saying, I think we need to be proactive here. Know what I mean?"

"Not really, no."

"Beka, listen. You want to keep David, don't you?"

"You think he likes Jessica?"

"Does he like Jessica? Think about it, Beka. I mean, what guy *doesn't* like Jessica? The problem is, does *she* like *him*?"

Before Rebekah could answer, a man came up behind Lena and asked, "You buying tickets?"

Lena looked startled a moment, then shook her head. "Oh, sorry, mister. No. You go ahead."

"How many?" Rebekah asked.

"Give me forty, will you?"

Rebekah noticed her fingers trembling as she counted out the tickets. She slid them under the glass, along with the man's change.

"It's a rip-off, you know," the man said, "a dollar a ticket."

"I didn't set the price, sir."

"I got three kids. . . ." He waved a hand at the three heads bobbing around him at waist level. "I can drop a hundred bucks in two hours easy around here. Come on, kids, let's go."

Lena reclaimed her spot at the window. "So take the brats swimming," she said, glancing over her shoulder. "It doesn't cost a nickel, and maybe you'll get lucky and they'll drown."

"Good grief, Lena," Rebekah said. "You're full of good advice."

"In fact I am, Beka. And I'm telling you, you better do something about little Miss I-get-whoever-I-want before she goes in for the kill."

"You think she wants David?"

"I know she wants David."

"What have you been doing—spying on them the past hour?"

"You bet I have."

"What for?"

"What for? I thought we were friends. I'd expect you to do the same with Jim, if you thought he was cheating on me."

"I never said David was cheating on me."

"Not yet. But as your friend, I'm telling you to nip this thing in the bud."

"And what exactly do you expect me to do?"

"I know the perfect hands-off spell."

Rebekah sighed and bought some time by taking a long sip of Coke. "I did a beauty spell, Lena, but I'm not sure it did any good."

"You must have done it wrong."

"You said there was no right or wrong way to do it."

"There isn't really, but—listen, Beka, you have a lot to learn. You're just lucky Aunt Jo and I are willing to teach you. Meanwhile, I'll show you what we can do by getting rid of Jessica."

"Getting rid of her? What do you mean by that? I don't want to hurt anybody. And anyway, do no harm, remember?"

"We're not going to hurt anybody. We're just going to make her quietly go away."

Rebekah shook her head. "I don't know, Lena."

"You want to keep David, don't you?"

"Of course!"

"Then harness your power, girl."

Rebekah sighed again. "It just seems like I should be able to keep him without any hocus-pocus."

"Hocus-pocus? Beka! Listen, this isn't hocus-pocus, it's the real thing. It's using the power you were born with, the power you have a right to use."

"I'll think about it. But, listen, don't do anything without me."

"I won't."

"Shouldn't you be at work or something?"

"I'm off today." She shrugged. "But I'll tell you, it's still only June and I'm already tired of selling popcorn and Raisinets to a bunch of fat slobs at the movie theater."

"Yeah, well, it's right up there with selling tickets here."

"You know, Beka, it's too bad we're not like Jessica. She doesn't have to work summers, you know. Her parents are divorced, but still, her dad is some bigwig real-estate developer or something. The guy's like filthy rich. I've heard she has a trust fund and everything."

"Yeah? Well, good for her."

"I think she needs to be knocked down a notch or two."

Rebekah wanted to get off the subject of

Jessica. "Listen, Lena," she said, "I'm meeting David in half an hour at the pavilion for break. I'll ask him if he wants to meet out behind the church tonight. What do you think? You and Jim up for it?"

"Up for it? I'd say we're long overdue. And as fate would have it, Mom restocked just yesterday. You should see the place. We could start our own drive-through bar selling gin and tonics out the kitchen window. She'll never miss a couple of bottles."

"Okay. What do you say—midnight, then?"

"I'd say you're on."

CHAPTER TWENTY-TWO

John awakened with a start. He stared up at the ceiling in the darkened room, trying to clear his head of fragmented dreams. He wondered what had pulled him up out of a heavy sleep. Rolling on his side, he glanced at the glowing face of the clock. Almost three-thirty.

He shut his eyes again, then opened them quickly as a heavy thud sounded downstairs. He shot from the bed and rushed down the narrow staircase, his mind and heart racing. At the bottom he paused a moment, listening, wondering which way to go, which of his children needed him.

In another moment Andrea was there beside him. "Beka," she whispered.

They moved as one through the front room and into the kitchen, where John pushed open the bedroom door and switched on the light. The bed was empty, the covers thrown back to the footboard. Phoebe had already made her nightly trek, abandoning this room to her older sister, who was slumped against the frame of the open window, half in, half out.

"Beka!" Andrea cried. "What's the matter with you?"

Rebekah managed to swing the second foot inside. She steadied herself, took one tentative step toward the bed, swayed, and crumpled to the floor. John rushed to her side and, gently gathering her up in his arms, cradled her head in his lap. His stomach recoiled at the sick, sodden smell of alcohol. For an awful moment he couldn't breathe. In his daughter's ashen face, he saw at once his own past and Rebekah's future, a future he didn't like and couldn't bear to imagine. Somewhere in the pit of his stomach, he felt a deep loathing for himself, for the weakness of flesh that was his legacy.

Andrea knelt beside him and touched their daughter's face, as though searching for fever. "She's sick, John. We've got to get her to a doctor."

John shook his head. "She's not sick, Andrea. She's drunk."

"Drunk?" Andrea repeated the word dully, as though it were foreign to her.

John nodded. He scooped Rebekah up in his arms and lifted her onto the bed. Tenderly, as though she were a newborn, he straightened her legs, took off her shoes, and pulled the sheet up over her. "She'll have to sleep it off," he said.

Andrea's eyes were wide, her face pale. "Will she be all right?"

Do you mean, John wondered, *in the morning or in the years to come?* "She probably won't feel very good when she wakes up."

He watched his wife's gaze travel from their daughter's face to his. If she accused him, said this was his fault, he would readily agree. But when she spoke, her voice was quiet, almost sorrowful.

"She's never done anything like this before."

"Are you sure?"

"Of course I'm sure. Don't you think I'd know if she came home drunk?"

Would she? John's own parents hadn't known when he and Jared stumbled into the cottage, a couple of teens sneaking home after a night of boozing. Hadn't they climbed in through this very window?

John turned to the window, pulled down the screen that Rebekah had opened to climb through. "She's been sneaking out at night for a while now."

When he turned back, he wondered for a moment at the tears in his wife's eyes, how they

154

pooled there without spilling over. Her eyes, magnified, glimmering, were wandering stars in a dark sky. Andrea Sheldon looked hopelessly lost.

"John," she whispered, "what are we going to do?"

He tried to sound calm. "For now, we're going to go back to bed. We'll deal with this in the morning. Don't worry, Andrea. Everything's going to be all right."

They climbed back up to the garret room and stretched out on the parallel beds. "Try to get some sleep, Andrea," he said softly.

"But, John . . ."

"What?"

"She's only sixteen years old."

"I know."

"You think she's been drinking for a while?"

John took a deep breath, let it out slowly. "I don't know. Maybe. It's what kids do."

"How could I not have known?"

"You didn't have a clue?"

"None."

"You trusted her."

"Yes. I just never thought . . ."

The room fell quiet. Then John said, "Just because you were never a drinker, Andrea, doesn't mean your daughter won't drink." *She is, after all, my daughter too,* he thought.

"All of a sudden I feel like I don't know who

she is, like she's somebody else's child," Andrea went on.

"Kids like to push their limits. That's the way it is."

"Billy never did."

"Billy's different. I mean, he never faced the kind of peer pressure Beka must be facing."

"Well, we've got to put a stop to it."

"Of course."

"I don't want to lose her, John."

"We're not going to lose her, Andrea. Now get some sleep. We'll deal with it in the morning."

In a little while he heard her breathing take on the slow and gentle rhythm of sleep. He tucked his hands under his head and, listening for some kind of assurance that never came, finally let go just enough to sink into troubled dreams.

CHAPTER TWENTY-THREE

Rebekah told herself everything was all right now that she was out of the cottage and seated on a park bench beside the mini-donut concession stand. Yes, she was in deep trouble with her parents, but she'd had a good reason for what she'd done, and he was seated there beside her, his arm draped casually around her shoulder. David. This, right here, was the center of her universe. As long as she was with David, everything was all right.

She laid her still throbbing head on his shoulder and smiled wanly as she felt his hold on her tighten. The pain was more of a dull ache now, instead of the pounding sledgehammer that had awakened her this morning.

The minute she'd opened her eyes, she knew she'd been caught. She was lying on her side, facing the window. The screen was lowered. She'd never been able to lower the screen. When she was sober, yes, but not when she stumbled in drunk. She'd always awaken the next morning and find the window wide open with nothing between her and the flies buzzing over the trash cans outside. But now the screen was closed, and there was only one explanation: someone else had closed it.

She was almost afraid to move, wondering what was waiting for her beyond the bedroom door. She heard movement out in the kitchen, the voices of her mother and father. She thought briefly of escape, of climbing back out the window and leaving for good. She might have done it if the hammering in her brain wasn't keeping her nailed to the bed.

She didn't remember anything about getting home. She didn't remember much about the night at all. Her mind carried pieces and fragments but nothing that fit together to make a whole. She remembered a bottle in her hand, the first warmth of alcohol flowing through her veins. She recalled the flickering of flashlights, whispered voices, music coming from somewhere. She had an image of Jim falling over a gravestone, falling flat on his face, and Lena laughing. And too, there was David beside her, the hard ground beneath her, a whole slew of stars overhead.

A few other kids were there too, she remembered, kids Lena knew from the movie theater where she worked. Rebekah thought she might have seen them rolling joints, but she wasn't sure now. The rest was a blank screen with no reception, not even snow, and as she gazed at it she sensed a certain fear gnawing at her stomach. She didn't know what she had done in the lost hours.

By the time her mother had come into the room and stood by the bed, Rebekah had already resolved to stop drinking so much. The last thing she needed was the look on her mother's face, her eyes so grieved Rebekah might have been lying in her coffin, stiff with embalming fluid instead of simply sick with 80 proof. Then her dad had appeared and stood beside her mother. As he looked down at her, she sensed she was seeing his face through the end of Phoebe's kaleidoscope, at an ever-changing scene of grief, anger, hurt, puzzlement. Couldn't he settle on just one negative emotion and leave it at that? She couldn't deal with so much at once.

Her father said, *"You probably don't feel very good right now."*

"Yeah, you would know, wouldn't you?" she

said. At least she thought she spoke. She wasn't sure the words actually came out. She was so dry she could hardly peel her tongue off the roof of her mouth.

An hour later she was sitting across from her parents at the kitchen table, sipping hot tea. When Billy happened in looking for something to eat, he was told he'd have to wait for lunch and that for now he should go outside and take Phoebe with him.

Billy, wide-eyed, asked, *"Is Beka in trouble?"* Without waiting for an answer, he looked at her in alarm. *"Beka, what'd you do?"*

Nothing you'll ever do, she thought. *Perfect child. Mama's golden boy.*

After Billy left, Rebekah sat quietly nursing her tea while her mother threw out anguished questions and her father lectured her on the evils of alcohol. He made sure he was holding her attention when he warned, *"Beka, keep it up and you're going to ruin your life."*

And Rebekah had stared him right back in the eye and said, *"Not much chance of that. You've already ruined it for me."*

This time she got the words out, and if she and her dad had been dueling with swords, that would have been a slice right to the heart. She could see it in his eyes, on his whole frozen face.

She had felt triumphant then, but only a short time later the memory of that moment made her feel pained, as though somehow the sword had been turned back on her.

And now she was going to have to tell David. She drew in a deep breath to steel herself. "Hey, David?"

"Yeah?"

She lifted her head and looked at him. "Listen, my parents found out. They heard me come in last night."

He swore quietly, narrowed his eyes. "So what's the fallout?"

"I'm grounded. Two weeks."

"Yeah? And what's that mean?"

"No phone calls—"

"What? You were just on your cell phone with Lena."

"Yeah, I can have the phone when I'm at work—in case of emergencies, they say. But once I'm home I have to hand it over."

"Oh yeah? So what else?"

"No e-mail, no seeing friends, no seeing you."

He laughed. "Yeah, right." He kissed her, laughed again. "A little hard to keep us apart when we work at the same place. Idiots."

Rebekah stiffened, suddenly defensive. But she decided to brush off David's remark. Let him say what he wanted, as long as he didn't break up with her.

"Listen, I'll be more careful next time," she promised. "I won't get caught again."

He shrugged, looked disinterested. "Like it matters," he said.

She wanted to ask him what he meant, but she was afraid of the answer. When she was with him, she wanted everything to matter.

He asked, "Do they know you were with me last night?"

"No." She shook her head. "I wouldn't tell them who I was with, though they could guess about Lena. I didn't tell them they were right, though. I just said I was with a group of kids I'd met at the park."

"Okay, so they don't know I was there, but they still don't want me to see you."

"It's just part of the punishment. They don't have anything against you."

David seemed to think about that for a minute. Then he said, "So when do you think we can have a repeat of last night?"

Rebekah chewed the inside of her lip. "Soon."

"Man, it was great."

"Yeah." She wished she could remember.

"Listen," David said, "we'd better move it. The boss'll have my head if I'm late again."

"All right." She sighed.

"Meet me at the pavilion for lunch, okay?"

"Yeah."

He kissed her, smiled, wandered off. Everything at home was a mess, but at least she had David.

Rebekah took a deep breath. She couldn't afford to be weak, not unless she wanted someone like Jessica Faulkner to come between them. Rebekah's hold on David was threadlike, and she knew it. There were plenty of other pretty girls around to tempt him, plenty of reasons he might wander off for good without a backward glance. She needed to tighten her grip, and she would—even if it meant doing everything in her power to keep him.

CHAPTER TWENTY-FOUR

Andrea snapped open a fresh sheet and watched it settle gently over her bed. She smoothed the wrinkles and tucked in the corners. She had always loved the feel of cool clean linen beneath her hands, had always loved to crawl between crisp sheets at night, even if she was alone.

Which, she realized at once, was exactly what she was, in spite of the wedding band she wore.

She stood up straighter, shut her eyes. *Never mind,* she thought. She hated self-pity. She wouldn't indulge in it.

Still, it would be nice if someone knew who she was, what she wanted, what she needed.

"Listen, honey," Selene had told her, *"you don't want to go through your whole life without loving someone."*

But that wasn't the problem. Andrea did love

someone. What she wanted was to be loved *by* someone.

Wearily she tried to put the thought aside, to set her mind on the task at hand. It was good to stay busy, doing what needed to be done. Satisfied that the sheets were smooth and tight, she tucked her pillow into a clean case, plumped it, and laid it at the head of the bed, then draped the white summer spread over the sheets.

She turned to John's bed and paused when she heard Phoebe's timid voice downstairs. "I'm going to play on the porch."

The girl was talking to her father, who was no doubt lounging in the overstuffed chair and reading the newspaper from Rochester, the *Democrat and Chronicle.* "Okay, Phoeb," John said. "What have you got there? Chinese checkers? Want me to play with you?"

Andrea could well imagine the look of fear in the child's eyes. Two weeks with her father home and Phoebe still regarded him as an intruder. She'd given him a Father's Day card over the weekend only because Billy had insisted they make one together.

Andrea listened hard but couldn't quite hear Phoebe's response to John's question. She knew what it was, though, when she heard John say, "Well, it's a little hard to play Chinese checkers by yourself, isn't it?"

The screen door opened, slammed shut.

Andrea stepped to the window and looked out over the lake. She shouldn't be so surprised. She had known all along that she might be disappointed, that John's coming home might not be that second chance she wanted, that it might in fact spell only disaster.

Things fall apart, she remembered, *the centre cannot hold.* The snatch of poetry bubbled up from somewhere, from long-ago school days. She didn't know the name of the poem or who wrote it. She only knew the line, and that it was true.

She saw bits and pieces of her life breaking off, floating away. . . .

Rebekah, angry and alienated, and worse, flirting with alcohol just like her father. She might be lost completely, drifting off right under their noses if they weren't careful to reel her in.

Billy, her son, joy of her heart. He'd be eighteen on June thirtieth, less than two weeks away. Legally, he'd be an adult. And in spite of his disability, he was growing more and more independent. Andrea often wished she could have stopped time long ago, kept him a child, the vulnerable one who needed her.

Phoebe, the baby. How quickly she was growing up! She'd be starting first grade in the fall. Then all of Andrea's children would be in school. Some women looked forward to that. Not Andrea. She wanted to gather each of them to herself and keep them forever under her wing, where she could protect them. Which was, of course, the opposite of what a mother was meant to do.

And then there was John. What a strange and tenuous relationship they had. Somewhere along the way they had stopped pretending to be lovers and had settled into this routine of tolerable coexistence. It was hardly the stuff of a woman's dreams.

She wondered what would become of her. Well, no, she didn't have to wonder. She knew. Her children would grow up and move out—even Billy, who talked about having his own apartment someday. She would have to let them go. And then, she supposed, not even John would stay. Why should he? Unless something changed, it didn't seem likely that he would stay even until then. The most probable scenario was that she would end up alone, with only occasional visits from children and grandchildren. And that was all.

It didn't seem near enough, couldn't possibly be the sum of an entire lifetime, but no matter how she worked the equation, it all added up to the same impossibly small measure.

"Dear God," she whispered. Only after a moment did she realize the words were a prayer. What she had meant as a statement of disapproval, or at best a sigh of resignation, sounded for all the world like a plea. And she was surprised, because she was not one to pray, though she supposed there was a God out there somewhere.

She turned back to John's bed and stripped it of its rumpled sheets. Just as she reached for the clean linen, she heard Phoebe let off a wail on the porch. Andrea sighed, recognizing it as an angry cry. That child was always frustrated over something. The screen door banged again, and John's voice floated up from the porch.

"What's the matter, Phoeb?"

"My marble!"

"What happened?"

"Down there!"

"You mean it rolled through the slats?"

"Down that hole!"

How many times had Andrea told Phoebe not to take her Chinese checkers out to the porch? *"You'll lose the marbles if you do,"* she'd warned. The old floorboards had too many crevices that could swallow up a marble in seconds.

Andrea left the bed and headed for the stairs, reaching the bottom just as John stepped back into the front room.

"Hey, Andrea," he said, "do we have a flashlight around here somewhere?"

"In the kitchen. Why?"

"Phoebe lost one of the marbles."

"Under the porch, right?" She was talking to his

back. In a moment he returned with the flashlight. "You're going to crawl under there and try to find it?"

"Well, sure."

"You'll never find it," she said, but he was already moving down the porch steps. Andrea followed him outside, where she found Phoebe curled up in a wicker chair, crying. She started to say she had told Phoebe time and again not to take the Chinese checkers out to the porch, but the child's mournful wails stopped her. Instead, she said, "Don't worry, honey. Daddy's going to look for your marble."

She watched as John moved around the porch, scouting out a break in the latticework. He was at the far end near the bay window when he cried out, "Aha! I think I can squeeze through here."

Phoebe lifted her head and looked expectantly at her mother. Andrea gazed at the child's tearstained face and smiled reassuringly. They waited. Beneath their feet they heard a scraping, then a sputtering, like John was spitting out cobwebs. They saw a light flicker and flash between the floorboards. Then a bump.

"Ow!"

"You all right down there, John?" Andrea called.

More sputtering. "I'm all right. Just a mild concussion is all."

"Maybe you should come out."

"I just want to look around a minute."

Andrea looked at Phoebe again. The child had stopped crying, and her eyes were wide.

"What do you see down there, John?"

"We've definitely had recent visitors. The neighbors' cats, I think. And . . . ah, something dead."

"Don't tell me it's a mouse."

"All right, then. I won't tell you."

Phoebe ventured a grin.

"Hey, I think I found"—the child's brows flew up—"my father's old penknife. It's—oh, never mind. It's just a piece of metal off of something. I don't know what."

"What about the marble, John?"

"Just a minute. I'm looking."

The light flickered and flashed some more. Phoebe got down on the porch floor and put her eye to the hole where the marble had disappeared.

"I see you," she said, almost playfully.

"Oh, hey, Phoebe. That's a good idea. That lets me know where—ouch!"

"You okay, John?"

"I think I just crawled over a nail. It's—wait, let me see." The light swung wildly, stopped.

"You're going to get tetanus down there if you don't come out."

"Can't get tetanus. I had my shots. Anyway, it's not a nail. Just a sharp little stone that decided to dig its way into my kneecap."

"Well, if you're going to be down there, you should be wearing pants instead of shorts."

"I'm sorry, Andrea, but I didn't know I'd be crawling under the porch when I got dressed this morning."

Phoebe, her eye still to the hole, said, "Do you see the marble?"

"Not yet, Phoeb. I'm still looking. Let me— aha!"

"Did you find it?"

"I'm coming out now."

"But did you find it?"

John didn't answer. He emerged, streaked with dirt, crisscrossed with cobwebs, looking triumphant. He climbed up to the porch and extended his hand to Phoebe. "Is this your marble?"

Phoebe stood to see what was cradled in her father's palm. She clapped her hands while jumping up and down on her toes. "You found it!"

"Here you go, kiddo."

Phoebe took the marble and clutched it tightly, fist to chest. "Thank you, Daddy," she breathed out happily.

"You're welcome, Phoeb." John smiled and nodded. Then looking down at himself, he said, "Guess I'd better go clean up a bit."

After he stepped inside, Andrea said to Phoebe, "Why don't you take the checkers inside now too, so it doesn't happen again."

The child obeyed, and Andrea lingered on the porch a moment, marveling. She wondered whether John had noticed it too. This was the first time Phoebe had called her father Daddy.

The lake seemed to wink at her, and in the distance a tangle of gulls took flight over the water.

CHAPTER TWENTY-FIVE

John put down the newspaper and glanced at his watch. His lunch break was over; he had to get back out on the floor. He carried his dirty dishes through the kitchen to the dishwashing area, scraped the remains of his sandwich into a garbage bin, and settled the plate and glass onto the stainless steel counter.

"How's it going, José?" he asked the young man at the sink.

"Going good." José nodded and tugged on the sprayer as he rinsed a rack full of dishes.

"You wouldn't want to switch places, would you? I'll take over the dishwashing while you bus the tables?"

The young man laughed. "No, no. The boss wouldn't like. He hired me to wash the dishes, so I stay here, washing dishes." He let go of the sprayer and pointed at the dishes in the sink.

"You sure, José? You work out front, you can talk with all the pretty ladies that come in."

José laughed again while he waved both

hands. "No, no. No pretty ladies. I can't afford. I got to send money back home."

John nodded. "Well, okay. Just thought I'd ask."

"I'm here fair and square, you know," José added. "No sneaking over the border. I work hard."

John smiled and gave him a friendly slap on the shoulder. "I know, José. You're a good worker. Well, catch you later, huh?"

He grabbed an empty tub and headed for the restaurant floor. Scanning the room to do a table check, he zeroed in on the tables in his section that needed cleaning. He made a beeline for the first one, keeping his head down and trying to avoid eye contact. He had two reasons for that: one, the remains of his weighty but battered pride, and two, the tug of his persistent weakness.

As he went about the task of collecting dirty dishes, he wanted to remain as unobtrusive as possible. He didn't like to be seen doing this kind of work. On break and at meal times he read the employment section of the Rochester *Democrat and Chronicle*, dreaming of the future. Eventually he'd move the family back up there and make a fresh start. A genuine fresh start. Not this halfway house of small-town probation with the added indignity of punching his brother-in-law's time clock. But for now, he had two years of this ahead of him, till Rebekah and Billy graduated high school. Unless he could find other work here in Conesus, which wasn't likely.

Another reason he kept his head down was he didn't want to see those same pretty ladies he'd used as bait for José. After five years in an arid place, temptation was suddenly blooming everywhere. He didn't want to be distracted—not when he was trying to put his family back together.

He smiled as he thought about Phoebe and the marble he'd rescued that morning. One huge step forward with the youngest daughter—she'd called him Daddy. Thank God for that.

He barely had time to rejoice, though, when thoughts of Rebekah crowded in. He cringed at the memory of her passed out cold on the floor. He could only assume it was one more consequence of his own drunk driving. Rebekah might never have picked up a bottle if he'd been home to stop her. But he hadn't been there, and she'd been without a father, and he knew only too well the pull of alcohol when a person feels in need of anything: a boost for the ego, an anesthetic for the mind, a salve for the heart. Or even just a lubricant for the jaw, so that social settings were something less than terrifying. He knew how easy it was to view alcohol as the consummate panacea for what ails you. As far as his older daughter went, he'd been losing ground for a long time.

John set the tub down on the table and briefly studied the remains of the meal. Two salad plates and a couple of iced teas, heavy lipstick on the rim of the drinking glasses. No doubt a couple of dissatisfied ladies meeting for lunch, chatting up their marriage woes, dreaming of escape from husband and kids. *And I said to Roger, I said, Listen, either you bring home more money or I'm outta here. And Roger said—*

It was a game John played to pass the time, to divert his mind from the task at hand. In John's imagination, no one in Conesus had a happy marriage. He wasn't sure it was possible. Though God knew, he wanted it to be.

After piling the dishes into the tub, he lifted the bottle of bleach solution from where it hung on his apron strings and sprayed the table.

"Hey there, Dad."

John looked over his shoulder and saw Billy passing by. "Hey, son. How's it going?" he called after him.

"Great, Dad."

"That's good." John rubbed circles on the tabletop with a dishrag.

"Oh, you were too quick. I—"

Aware that he was being spoken to again, and that this time the speaker was a woman, John straightened up, then stiffened.

"I had to get change to leave a tip," the woman finished.

John's mind tossed about, trying to come up with a story, some reason for his being here bussing this table. But nothing he might say could make any difference, and he knew it. He held out a hand, tentatively. "I'll see that your waitress gets it."

She laid the three dollar bills across his palm. The corners of her mouth turned up. She had already applied a new layer of lipstick. "You're . . . John. Right?"

"Yes, that's right."

"I'm Pamela."

He dropped his eyes while tucking the bills in the pocket of his apron. "I remember."

"You work here?"

"Just temporarily." He glanced up, then down again. He was acutely aware of the color of her lips and the scent of her perfume. "The owner's my brother-in-law. I'm helping him out for a while, as a favor."

"I see."

Undoubtedly she did. Part of the picture anyway. A boozer and a loser, resorting to bussing tables.

But, then again, she must have a story too.

"You going tonight?" she asked.

"To the meeting?"

She nodded.

"Yeah, I'll be there." He wasn't about to mention that he had to be there as part of his probation.

174

"Listen, John, do me a favor, will you?"

He cleared his throat. All the thoughts he had more or less successfully stifled since the previous Wednesday rose to the surface again. "Sure."

"Tell Larry I can't be there tonight, all right? I've got to run out of town for a day or two with my sister."

"Sure," he said again. "I'll tell him."

"Thanks."

He thought they were finished and that she would leave now, but she didn't. An awkward silence settled between them. He didn't like the way it needled him, making him feel nervous and inadequate.

He lifted the tub full of dishes and backed up from the table. "Well, see you around, then," he said.

She looked as though she wanted to say something. He didn't wait to find out what it was.

CHAPTER TWENTY-SIX

Billy, in the passenger seat of his mother's Volvo, tapped his fingers on his knees excitedly as the car headed down Lake Road toward Conesus Lake Amusement Park.

"Why are you so nervous, Billy?" Mom asked.

"I'm not nervous. I'm happy."

"Oh?"

"I've almost got enough tickets to buy that prize I wanted."

From the backseat, Phoebe explained, "He wants to buy a nightlight. It has a picture of a little lamb on it."

Billy's drumming picked up speed. "Yeah," he agreed.

"You don't need a nightlight, Billy," his mother said. "Is it for Phoebe?"

"No." He shook his head. "It's for me."

"Well, okay. If it's something you want."

"I might get enough tickets to get it today. If someone hasn't already got it."

"Don't worry, Billy," Phoebe assured him, "Beka won't let anyone take it."

"What's today, Mom?"

"Thursday. Why?"

"I want to get the nightlight before my birthday party on Saturday."

"Then you have today and tomorrow to get enough tickets. Speaking of your birthday," Mom said, "what kind of cake do you want?"

Billy laughed loudly. "You know what I want, Mom!"

His mother smiled. "Vanilla, right?"

More laughter. "No, Mom!"

"Spice cake?"

"No!"

"Liverwurst?"

"Mom!"

Shrieks of laughter from both the front and back seats.

"Oh, I think I remember."

"What?"

"Chocolate cake with chocolate icing."

"That's it!"

"But that's what you have every year. Don't you want something special this year?"

"But chocolate cake *is* special."

"All right, then. It'll be chocolate."

As they neared the entrance to the amusement park, Billy heard his mother sigh heavily.

"What's the matter, Mom?" he asked. "You don't want chocolate?"

She laughed quietly. "Yes, I want chocolate. But I just can't believe my baby will be eighteen years old. All grown up."

"Aw, Mom, I haven't been a baby in a long time."

"I know, son. But still . . ."

She smiled at him, but it didn't look like a happy smile to Billy.

"Don't worry, Mom," he said. "I'll always be around to take care of you."

His mother reached over and squeezed his hand. Billy squeezed back. He liked this feeling of being a man and taking care of people.

The car rolled to a stop, and his mother shifted into park. "Okay, you two," she said, "I'll pick you up right here at the entrance at eight o'clock.

Billy, you've got the watch. You keep track of the time, all right?"

"Sure, Mom."

"I don't want to have to come in there looking for you after dark."

"Don't worry, Mom. We'll be here. I promise." He leaned over and gave his mother a kiss. He was always surprised at how soft her cheek was.

Once they were out of the car, he grabbed Phoebe's hand and together they headed for the arcade.

"If Beka's boyfriend tries to get you to play that game, don't stop," Phoebe said.

"Don't worry, I won't."

"You're going to buy me some cotton candy, aren't you?"

"Yeah. But not right now."

"Can we go on some rides?"

"Yeah. Later. Did Mom give you any money?"

"No. She said she spent it all on your birthday present."

"She did?" Billy stopped walking and smiled widely. He looked at Phoebe. "Did she tell you what it was?"

Phoebe shook her head. "No, she wouldn't say. She said I couldn't keep it a secret if I knew."

"Yeah, Mom was right. Guess I'll find out Saturday."

They started up again, moving quickly past the few people milling about the midway. Billy didn't even notice the games, the carnival barkers, the concession stands. He just wanted to get to the arcade and make sure the nightlight was still there.

Rebekah was behind the counter counting tickets for a couple with a little girl. She glanced up when Billy and Phoebe entered the arcade. She acted as if she didn't recognize her own brother and sister.

Billy moved right to the spot where the nightlight had been displayed.

"Where is it, Billy?" Phoebe asked, squeezing his hand.

He didn't answer. A shiver of anxiety slid through him. He let go of his sister's hand and moved back and forth in front of the glass display case, looking for the nightlight among the items on display.

And then he saw it.

The little girl was clutching the light in her hands, rubbing one dimpled index finger over the lamb.

Billy drew in one sharp breath and looked up at Rebekah. He waited until the girl and her parents moved away from the counter. He didn't have to say anything. Rebekah knew what he was thinking.

"I'm sorry, Billy," she said. "They wanted it, and I had to give it to them."

Billy's lips trembled. "The last one?" he whispered.

Rebekah nodded.

"Beka," Phoebe scolded, "you should have hid it so no one else could buy it."

"I couldn't do that, Phoeb. You want me to lose my job over a silly nightlight?"

Billy didn't want to cry in front of his sisters. He didn't want to cry in front of the other kids playing games in the arcade. He was almost a man now, eighteen in two days, and he didn't want to cry.

"Listen, Phoeb," Rebekah said, "why don't you guys go ride some rides or something." To Billy, his sister's voice sounded gentle but far away. He was vaguely aware of her digging around in her jeans pocket. "Here's a few extra bucks. Go on, hit the midway. No use standing around here gawking. It's not going to bring the nightlight back."

Billy felt Phoebe tug at his hand. His feet were as heavy as cinderblocks, but he willed them to move. *Grown men don't cry,* he told himself. He wiped his eyes with the back of one hand as his little sister led him out of the arcade.

CHAPTER TWENTY-SEVEN

A sign was taped to the door of Laughter's Luncheonette: "Closed for family celebration. Open again at 4:00. Come on back for supper!"

Inside, several tables had been pushed together

to accommodate the birthday crowd. Billy sat at the head of the gathering, king of the day, crowned with a festive party hat, the elastic strap digging a trench into his fleshy neck. He didn't seem to mind. Billy was all smiles.

Andrea, sitting to his right, gazed at her son. How she loved him. So much so that the love was a physical ache in her chest, a good ache.

She felt a hand on her shoulder, a squeeze. She turned to Owen, who said quietly, "You've done good."

"He's a good boy," she responded.

"He's a lucky kid, with you as his mother."

She raised her hand to his, patted it. "Thanks."

Owen smiled, his rugged face taking on a tenderness that Andrea always found comforting.

"And thanks for closing the restaurant so we could have the party here," she added.

"Hey, anything for Billy." He squeezed her shoulder again, then looked around the table and hollered, "So who wants more spaghetti?"

As gatherings go, it was a small group. Just the five Sheldons and the four Laughters—Owen, Selene, and their two teenaged sons, Russ and Stuart. And one of Billy's friends from school, Arthur, and his mother. Arthur, also a child with Down syndrome, was a year younger than Billy and several years farther down the scale in mental age. He didn't say much, but he grinned constantly and laughed a lot, and Billy liked him.

Sitting directly across the table from Andrea, his face was one huge grin now beneath his party hat. His eyes grew large at the mention of more spaghetti.

Billy raised his fork in the air. "More spaghetti for everyone, Uncle Owen! And more meatballs!"

"Coming right up!" Owen lifted a small bell from beside his plate and rang it. In a moment a waitress wearing a party hat showed up with a pitcher of water in one hand, iced tea in the other.

"Hi, Elaine!" Billy hollered at her.

"Hi, Billy. How's the birthday boy?" She moved around the table, refreshing drinks.

"Still hungry. We all want more spaghetti."

"I'm on it! Be right back."

She went to the kitchen and came back with Sally, a young woman who seemed reluctant to make eye contact. She was obviously self-conscious and annoyed by the party hat that sat askew on her head. Each waitress pushed a cart with a large steel pot on it, one with pasta, the other with tomato sauce. Elaine dished up the noodles while Sally followed behind, dipping out large ladles of sauce and meatballs. When finished, they pushed the clanging carts back to the kitchen and disappeared behind the swinging door.

Andrea gazed at the small group of partiers. She felt a rare satisfaction as she watched everyone eating, talking, laughing. John sat at the far end of the long table, opposite Billy. He was having an animated conversation with his nephews Russ and Stuart. Andrea couldn't hear what they were talking about, though John was obviously enjoying the boys, who had grown into gangly young men while he was away.

Rebekah sat next to her cousin Russ, but she didn't pay much attention to him. Andrea was surprised to see Rebekah talking quietly with Phoebe instead. She was still grounded, but she'd apparently decided to leave her anger and sullenness at home for once. She almost looked like the Rebekah of several years ago, the pleasant little girl at the tail end of childhood, still innocent and happy. She even occasionally laughed with Phoebe while wiping spaghetti sauce off the child's face.

Phoebe was the only other person at the table wearing a party hat. The hats had been Phoebe's idea, along with the noisemakers that had—thankfully—been laid aside when the food was served. Phoebe had blown on her noisemaker so hard the paper had become limp with moisture. She loved a party, and a birthday party for Billy was almost as good as a birthday party for herself. That's what she'd told Andrea earlier when she was putting on her favorite pink dress. *"Because Billy's the best brother in the world,"* she'd said.

Andrea was deep enough in thought that Owen

startled her when he hollered, "Enough of the spaghetti and meatballs, huh? It's time to open your presents, Billy!"

"Bring 'em on!" Billy yelled, waving his fork. "I'm ready!"

Elaine and Sally were summoned back to clear the dirty dishes and make room for the gifts. As the waitresses worked, Billy called down the length of the table, "Hey, Dad, get this! We're at the restaurant, and we don't have to bus the table!"

Andrea heard John laugh, but it sounded unnatural. It was a laugh that, for Andrea, forced a crack in the wall of the party and allowed the stress of their daily lives back in. She looked at John and felt the full weight of their strained relationship, as stilted and contrived as John's laughter.

But she wouldn't think about that right now. Plenty of time for that later. Right now she wanted to drink in Billy's joy, his delight at the gifts set before him, a small but irresistible pile of colorful wrapping and ribbons. His face shone with this same excited glow every year, no matter his age.

"What are you waiting for, Billy?" Owen prodded. "A golden engraved invitation?"

Billy looked at his uncle wide-eyed. "It's just so pretty, Uncle Owen. I hate to mess it up."

John, from the far end of the table, called out,

"Well, if I'd known you just wanted to look at the wrapping paper, I'd have wrapped an empty box and saved myself a ton of dough." This time his laughter was genuine.

"Open them, you silly goose!" This was from Phoebe, who found a working noisemaker and blew it in Billy's direction.

Billy held up a hand. "All right! All right! Which one should I open first?"

"Mine!" Phoebe said.

"Open mine last, Billy."

All eyes turned to Rebekah as Billy asked, "How come, Beka?"

She shrugged. "I don't know. I just want you to."

"All right. Which one is yours, Phoebe?"

The next few moments were a tangle of ripping paper and shouts of glee as Billy tore through his gifts. From Phoebe, a hand-drawn picture of Billy and Phoebe together. "Looks just like us, Phoeb!" From Arthur, a box of assorted chocolates. "Hey, Artie, you know what I like!" From Aunt Selene and the cousins, an electric razor and a bottle of English Leather cologne. "Now I'll smell good for the ladies!" From Uncle Owen, a framed Certificate of Honorary Ownership of Laughter's Luncheonette. "Wow, Uncle Owen, you mean it? I'm honorary owner? Now I'm a businessman! I'm a real businessman!"

Andrea felt a small thrill run through her as

Billy's hand touched the gift from her and John. The item was small, no larger than his hand, but she suspected it would leave him feeling like he owned the world. She watched his face as he tore through paper, ribbon, and tape to expose the thing inside.

When he saw what it was, Billy jumped, knocking the table with his knees. "It's a cell phone!" he cried. "It's a cell phone. Look, I have a cell phone just like Rebekah's. I can call people! I can take pictures!" He held the phone up and waved it in a circle around the table for everyone to see. Then he stopped, as though something had suddenly occurred to him. He looked at Andrea. "Does it work?"

"Of course it works," Andrea said. "Give it a try."

"Who should I call?"

"Anyone you want."

Billy smiled, flipped open the phone, punched some numbers. Seconds later Owen's pocket rang.

Owen smiled, shifted, dug out the phone. He feigned a serious expression. "Owen Laughter here. State your business."

"It's me, Uncle Owen! I'm calling you!"

"So you are! Happy birthday, Billy!"

Andrea joined in the laughter. The phone was an extra expense that they could little afford, but her son was as happy as she had hoped, and that made it worthwhile.

"Thanks, Mom! Thanks, Dad!" Billy hollered.

Andrea, still gazing at Billy, heard John say, "You're welcome, son. Every grown man needs a cell phone, huh?"

"Yeah! And I'm a grown man now."

"That you are, son."

Billy held out a hand to her, and Andrea gripped it tightly. She wanted never to let go. Here was her strength, right here, the joy of her life.

"You're the best, Mom."

"Happy birthday, Billy. I love you."

"I love you too."

They shared a smile before Billy pulled away. "Hey, Beka," he said, "can you show me how to take pictures with this thing?"

"Yeah." She nodded. "It's easy."

"Speaking of Beka," John said, "don't you have one more present, Billy?"

Billy looked up from the phone, smiled again. "Oh yeah! I didn't open Beka's gift yet."

Rebekah's face remained passive, Andrea noticed, as Billy put the phone aside and sifted through the piles of scattered wrapping paper to find her gift. It too was a small package, neatly wrapped in the same paper Andrea had used. Andrea scarcely had time to wonder what it was before it was there, unwrapped and cradled in Billy's hands, but still, she couldn't quite make it out. She knew only that it rendered Billy as motion-less as stone, his brow furrowed, his eyes misty.

Slowly he looked up at his sister. "You said that little girl got the last one."

Rebekah gave one small nod. "She did. But I had already bought this one for you and put it aside."

Billy cupped it to his heart, shut his eyes. "It's the best gift ever, Beka," he whispered.

"I'm glad you like it, Billy."

Andrea held out her hand, and Billy laid the gift in her palm. It was the nightlight Billy had told her about, the one with the picture of a little lamb painted on the front.

CHAPTER TWENTY-EIGHT

She was studying him; John knew that. He could feel her gaze crawling over his skin, warm and inviting.

John shifted his position restlessly in the folding chair in the basement of Grace Chapel. He glanced up at the face of Larry Gunther, Whiskey Priest. Larry was talking about something. John didn't know what.

He was aware only of Pamela, that she was there, looking lovely, gazing intently, tormenting him.

John glanced at his watch, then realized that his right foot was tapping the concrete floor nervously. Smiling apologetically at the guy next to him, he slid his foot under the chair, willed it to stop.

He tried to tune in to the evening program. "So we're here by popular demand tonight," he heard Larry say, "even though it's the Fourth of July. Thanks for your commitment and for wanting to meet. We'll be sure to wrap this up on time so you can get home and enjoy the fireworks with your families."

With that, John left again, turning inward to take stock of his family. He realized there would be no one at the cottage when he got home. Andrea, Billy, and Phoebe had gone over to Owen's for a barbecue dinner with his family and a bunch of their friends. Rebekah, no longer grounded, was working at the amusement park and afterward was going to spend the night with her friend Lena Barrett.

"Let's begin," Larry said, "with the Serenity Prayer."

John looked at his hands, already clenched together in his lap. The air was warm and close in the windowless room, and he found it difficult to breathe. He mouthed the words while thinking of Andrea. She'd invited him to join them at Owen's after the meeting. *"You can get there in plenty of time for the fireworks show,"* she'd said. He'd hedged, saying he might just go on home and turn in early. The truth was, he didn't want to go. He didn't like being with Owen at the restaurant, and he sure didn't want to be with him outside of the restaurant if he could help it. Owen never said much to him—but then, maybe that was the problem. His brother-in-law's aloofness let John know he was not an appreciated member of the family.

When the prayer was finished, John told himself to go on praying. He had done little enough of that since leaving prison. He had brought his Bible home in the bottom of that plastic bag and left it in the drawer of his bedside table, unopened. It had been his very lifeline in prison, and now he never reached for it.

He remembered what Rebekah had said at dinner his first night home: *"He got that jailhouse religion. . . . Of course, it only lasts till they get out."*

He didn't want her to be right. Wouldn't let her be right. *God,* he thought, *help me. Help all of us. Show me how I can bring my family back together. Show me how to be a husband and a father. And . . . Lord, I . . .*

John looked up. A man whose name he didn't know was reading from the Big Book, and Pamela seemed to be listening. Her face was passive, though, her expression one of disinterest. John wanted to return to his prayer, but when the image of first Andrea and then Rebekah rose in his mind, he had no idea what to say. Words were too small to touch the helplessness he felt at the thought of his wife and daughter.

He tried to pull his gaze away from Pamela,

but slowly, before he could succeed, she turned her head, saw him staring. She smiled. No one else would have known it was a smile, but he knew.

Dear God, he thought. But the words were weightless, an aborted prayer, vanishing almost before the words were formed in that region of the mind where prayers are birthed.

He got through the meeting by latching on to the speaker, feigning interest, hanging on every word without comprehending a single one. He was there and not there all at once, hopelessly divided, pulled in two directions.

Afterward, as he walked home through the twilight, he breathed deeply of the warm, moist air. Only now—now that he had escaped the church basement—did his heart begin to settle, his thoughts to quiet. He wanted the woman he had left behind, but he didn't want to want her. He'd slipped out during Larry's closing comments to avoid her. She could only complicate things—everything he had dreamed of and lived for while in prison. He had made careful plans, had made promises to himself, had wanted somehow to make a life with the family that was waiting for him back home.

He strode forward, keeping close to the edge of the road to avoid the occasional traffic. He didn't have far to go when a car slowed down, easing itself parallel to him, its wheels barely turning. It was a Mustang convertible, and she was behind the wheel.

"Can I give you a lift, John?" she called.

He stopped. The car stopped. She was waiting for his response.

"Uh, thanks," he said, "but I live just down the road from here." He pointed with a thumb. "Not far. It's real close. I can walk."

Pamela seemed not to notice his bumbling response but instead leaned over and opened the passenger-side door. For a fraction of a second he thought of the stranger he had picked up the night of the accident.

"Where you going?"

"Anywhere."

"I can take you partway."

"Hop in, John," she said. "I'll take you."

He put his hand on the door. "I—"

She patted the seat, waved him in.

He felt as though he were stepping back and watching from a distance, even as he saw himself get into the car and pull the door shut. "I'm in the white cottage, number one-twenty-two."

She shifted into drive, and the car moved forward. The tires spat out gravel from the side of the road and picked up speed. John watched curiously as they passed his cottage and sailed forward over the asphalt.

He almost laughed. He marveled at how easy it was to let go of all resolve. The warring was over, and he was at peace. "Where are you taking me?" he asked.

She didn't answer right away. She seemed intent on the road. Finally she said, "Apparently I'm taking you to my place for a drink." Her mouth drew back in a small amused smile. She turned her head, locking eyes with him. "You don't mind, do you?"

He settled back into the seat and let her drive.

CHAPTER TWENTY-NINE

Rebekah lay on her bed staring up at the ceiling. She wiped at the corner of each eye with an open palm, not wanting her friend to see her cry. But it was too late.

"Listen, Beka," Lena said, "tears are for babies and weaklings, which we are not, okay? Besides, lying there crying isn't going to do you any good."

"But I'm going to lose him, aren't I?"

"Not if you listen to me and do as I say. Now get down here and give me a hand."

Rebekah sat up and looked over the side of the bed. Lena sat cross-legged on the floor by the open closet. She wore shorts and a tank top, and her feet were bare. Her skin, browned by the sun, glowed in the flickering light of the candles lined up on the crate Rebekah used as an altar. The room was otherwise dim, as Lena had pulled down the shade and closed the curtains against the afternoon sun. Lena had also bolted the bedroom door, even though the girls were alone in the cottage. Rebekah's father and brother were at work, and her mom had taken Phoebe to a dentist appointment in the next town over.

"What exactly are you doing?" Rebekah asked.

"Getting ready."

"But, I mean, what's going to happen?"

"Nothing bad. We're just going to throw down a little wall between David and Jessica, just to make sure she stays away from him."

"Can you make her ugly?"

Lena laughed, stopped suddenly, and narrowed her eyes. "I was going to say there's a limit to what we can do, but I'm not so sure there is. Now get down here and help me."

Rebekah slid off the bed and sank to the floor beside Lena. Her friend was sifting through the box of herbs and spices Rebekah had collected over the past months, bottles and bags of them.

"You got any nutmeg in here?" Lena asked.

"I don't know. Why?"

"Good for fidelity. Ah, here it is."

Rebekah watched as Lena added the bottle to a small pile on the floor. She looked at the pile skeptically and almost wished she hadn't asked Lena to come over. She'd just wanted to talk, to spill her feelings to someone. She'd been crying since yesterday when she saw David with Jessica again. Jessica had been leaning casually against the wall of the pavilion. David was standing over her, one hand against the wall above her head. *"We're just friends,"* David had sworn to Rebekah later. But friends don't stand that close, don't look at each other like that.

"Snap out of it, Beka," Lena said. "You're staring into space again."

Rebekah shook her head. "Forget it, Lena. It's no use."

Lena stopped her busywork and frowned at Rebekah. "You still don't get it, do you?"

"Get what?"

"The power you have. The power we all have."

"I haven't seen it work."

"Well, I have."

"Yeah?"

"Yeah. Listen, haven't I told you about Carl, the last guy my mom was dating?"

"I don't think so."

"I didn't like him. He wasn't any good for her."

"You just don't like your mom dating anyone."

"She can date someone, if I approve."

"Why is it up to you?"

"Because if she marries him, I have to live with him."

"Okay. So what happened to Carl?"

"Well, I'm not really sure, but the point is, I got rid of him."

"How?"

"I cast a spell, *this* spell. One night Mom and Carl were downstairs mixing up drinks and having themselves a little private party, and I was upstairs making sure it was for the last time."

"And it was?"

"Yeah."

"And you don't know what happened to him?"

Lena shrugged. "He just never came back."

"Well, you know, your mom might have really liked him."

"She did. But I did it for her own good. Everything I do is for somebody's good, Beka."

Rebekah looked at her friend. As the seconds ticked by, she understood what she had only vaguely sensed before: She didn't believe her.

And yet she wanted to.

"Listen, Beka," Lena said slowly, emphasizing each word. "You love David, don't you?"

Rebekah nodded.

"And you want to keep him, right?"

"Yeah."

"Then let's get started."

Rebekah nodded again. She took a deep breath. She'd do whatever she had to do to keep David.

CHAPTER THIRTY

John sat on the top step of the porch, a sweating glass of iced tea in his hand. He had occupied the same spot often as a boy, had sat there looking out over the water, daydreaming. He'd had so many dreams once. Nothing grandiose, nothing even very far beyond his reach. Just simple dreams of doing something with his life. Maybe owning a business, maybe designing buildings or bridges, maybe—and this was the grandest one— becoming an airline pilot and flying planes all over the world. Why not? John could do anything he put his mind to; that's what his father had said.

He remembered once as a kid pointing toward the strange fortress across the lake and saying, *"See the Castle over there, Pop?"*

His father, sitting on the steps beside him, nodded as he squinted against the sun. *"Sure do, son."*

"Someday I'm going to fix it up and make it nice again," John had boasted. *"That'll be mine. But I'll make a room for you and Mom, and you can live there too. Would you like that, Pop?"*

His father was drinking something like iced tea or lemonade or maybe iced coffee—something cold to ward off the summer heat. He lifted the glass to his lips and took a long drink. Then he said, *"Sounds like an agreeable plan to me."*

Good thing Pop wasn't here to see him now. John had grieved at his father's funeral, thought his death untimely, but now he knew what the old man had been spared. John hadn't built any castles. Hadn't even renovated any. Far from it.

John stiffened at the familiar squeak of the screen door behind him. He didn't turn to see who was there. He kept his face toward the lake while taking a long swallow of the tea.

From somewhere above him, just beyond his left shoulder, Andrea's voice rained down. "I thought you could use a little more to drink."

John marveled that words so gentle could cut so deep. She couldn't know, of course; she meant only to be kind.

He lifted his eyes no higher than her waist, saw the pitcher of iced tea in her hands. He held up his glass, watched the tea cascade from the lip of the pitcher.

"Thanks, Andrea."

"Get you anything else?"

"No thanks. I think I'm set."

For three days John had scarcely looked his wife in the eye. He didn't look at her now. He heard her footsteps on the porch, heard the screen door squeak open, slam shut.

The woman's name was Pamela Jarvis, and she lived with her daughter in a small cottage on the north end of the lake. She was divorced, had been divorced more than once, he gathered, but he wasn't quite sure. It didn't matter. She was alone, available.

"Your daughter—she . . ." He'd waved a hand while glancing around the unfamiliar room.

"She's at my sister's house. She spends a lot of time there. She has a couple of friends with her tonight, and they're watching the fireworks together."

He didn't learn the daughter's name. That didn't matter either, so long as the girl wasn't home.

"Drink?" Pamela asked, opening up a surprisingly well-stocked cabinet. Then she laughed. *"So how long?"*

"How long what?" he responded.

"You know. How long without a drink?"

"More than five years."

"Good for you."

He couldn't tell whether the words were laced with sincerity or sarcasm. He watched as she poured herself two fingers of bourbon. Small beads of sweat began to sting his brow. She was Thirteenth Stepping, as it was known in A.A. She didn't attend meetings looking for sobriety through the Twelve Steps. She was looking for something else, something beyond all that.

She held up the glass. *"You sure?"* she asked.

He shook his head. He had, at least, the strength to do that much, knowing that alcohol could send him right back to prison. But a woman. Now that was something else altogether. A woman could take him places he hadn't been in a long time.

"Daddy!"

Startled, John caught his breath. He hurriedly tucked his thoughts away, then smiled grimly to himself when he realized they were already hidden. He looked over his shoulder and saw Phoebe standing just inside the screen door.

"What are you doing, Daddy?"

John waved the girl outside. "I'm just sitting here drinking some iced tea. Want to join me?"

Phoebe stepped out onto the porch. "I will in a minute, but wait right here, okay?"

"I'm not going anywhere."

The child ran past him down the steps. She disappeared beyond the steep bank by the lake and then reappeared with something in her hand.

"What have you got there, Phoeb?"

"Smell, Daddy."

She opened her small hand, revealing a few crushed leaves. John inhaled deeply and relaxed into a genuine grin. She had gathered some wild mint for his tea.

"You want it, Daddy?"

"I sure do. Drop it right in there." He held out his glass for the mint, and she let it fall from her palm. "Thank you, sweetheart."

"You're welcome."

John patted the step beside him. "Have a seat."

The little girl sat, hugging her knees with both

arms. "Billy's coming out in a minute. He's been in the shower."

"Uh-huh."

"The toilet was all plugged up this morning when I got up—"

"Again?"

"But Billy got the plunger out and fixed it."

"Okay. That's good."

"Not without making a mess, though. That's why he's taking extra long in the shower."

"Oh yeah?"

"Beka says this place is falling down around our ears."

John sighed. "I suspect she's more than half right."

"But I don't care. I like it here."

"Well, I'm glad you do, Phoebe. I'm glad someone does."

"When Billy gets out of the shower, he said he'd play with me awhile before you guys have to go to work."

"That's good. What are you going to do?"

"I don't know." She shrugged. "Play Chinese checkers, maybe. Do you like the mint, Daddy?"

"I sure do. I used to pick mint for your granddaddy's iced tea. Did you know that?"

Phoebe shook her head.

"I wish you could have met your granddaddy. He died too young, before you were born. You'd have liked him, though. He was a good man."

"Like you, Daddy?"

"Well—"

"Billy says you're a good man."

"Well, I—"

John didn't have time to go on before Billy pushed past the screen door to the porch and, straddling several floorboards like a cowboy taking aim with a pistol, pointed his cell phone at them in a two-handed grip. "Hey, Dad, Phoebe, say cheese!" he said.

He was neatly dressed in a button-up shirt and slacks, his wet hair plastered to his head, the scent of English Leather cologne trailing him like a pungent afterthought. "Look, I took your picture!" he exclaimed. "Beka showed me how to do it!"

He proudly displayed the picture, holding the phone in front of their faces.

"That's great, Billy," John said. "You'll have to show me how to do that."

"It's easy, Dad," Billy responded confidently. "I can show you in no time."

John nodded. "You got some nice gifts for your birthday, huh, son?"

"Yeah, Dad, the best."

"How's that nightlight working out for you?"

"Whoa, Dad—it's so cool."

"It glows real pretty in the night, Daddy," Phoebe added.

"I bet it does," John remarked. "Nice of Beka to get it for you, Billy."

"Yeah." Billy laughed. "She sure surprised me."

Phoebe said, "Billy put my picture up on the wall. Did you see it, Daddy?"

"I sure did. It's beautiful, Phoeb."

"I told her it looks just like us. Don't you think so, Dad?" Billy asked.

"As good as any photograph, I'd say."

Phoebe smiled happily. Then she said, "Hey, Billy, can you show *me* how to take a picture on your phone?"

"Sure, Phoeb. Come sit here and I'll show you. It's real easy."

Billy and Phoebe moved to the glider while John moved up to the padded wicker chair. In just a little while he'd have to go inside, take a shower, get ready to go to work. He wanted to put it off for as long as he could. The thought of going to work was making him nervous.

Pamela had shown up at the restaurant yesterday, sat there drinking lemonade by herself. She had the paper spread out on the table as though she were reading it, but he never saw her turn the page. Their eyes met once, maybe twice. They didn't speak. They didn't have to. There was some sort of electric current running between them that said it all without a single word. It had brought that whole Fourth of July night rushing back like a tidal wave crashing onto the present moment. How was it that no one else in the restaurant felt it, a thing that big, that over-whelming?

Dear God, he thought now as he looked out over the lake. *What have I done? My children, my—*

He remembered the scent of her, the smooth softness of her skin. He clenched his jaw as he glanced over at Billy and Phoebe. He had lied to them and to Andrea. He had said he'd come straight home from the meeting, that he'd had a headache so he'd gone to bed early.

Dear God, he thought again. *What have I done?*

He sniffed then at the irony, at the absurdity of the question. He knew exactly what he'd done.

More than that he knew, given half a chance, he'd do it again.

CHAPTER THIRTY-ONE

Andrea glanced at the clock in the kitchen and then walked across the front room to the porch door. "John," she called out through the screen, "it's ten o'clock. Don't you think you should be getting ready?"

John flinched. He blinked slowly, as though coming back from far away. "Okay, thanks, Andrea," he said, his voice listless. "I lost track of the time."

"I just don't want you and Billy to be late for work."

"No, I'll get moving. Beka in the shower?"

"She's barely out of bed yet. The shower's all yours."

"Hey, Mom!" Billy smiled up from the glider. "I'm showing Phoebe how to take pictures. Look at the picture I took of Dad and Phoebe."

Andrea stepped out onto the porch and took the phone. She angled it so she could see the photo. There was Phoebe, smiling broadly, John, looking sullen, surprised at best. "Wonderful, Billy," she said, handing him the phone. "Has Beka shown you how to send them to the computer?"

Billy shook his head. "Not yet. But she said she would."

John finally rose from the chair. The porch floor creaked beneath his weight. Andrea turned toward him, saw the empty glass in hand. "I'll take that for you," she offered.

He barely glanced at her. "Thanks. I'll be out of the shower in a few minutes, in case Beka wants it."

"No hurry."

"Hey, Mom, say cheese!"

Andrea turned back toward the glider to find Phoebe snapping a picture with the phone. The child laughed. "I got you, Mom! I took your picture!"

"You didn't even give me a chance to smile."

"Yeah, Mom," Billy said, studying the phone in

Phoebe's hand. "You're not smiling. You look a little funny. Want to see?"

"No, thank you. I'll pass. Now listen, Billy, you've got thirty minutes, and then you and Dad are out the door."

"I know. I'm all ready to go. I'm just waiting on Dad."

Andrea stepped toward the door, stopped a moment. "By the way, Billy," she said.

"Yeah, Mom?"

"You smell nice."

While Phoebe frowned and sniffed the air, Billy tore his attention away from the picture and looked up at his mother. Deep crows-feet formed around his eyes as his small face opened up into a wide, full-toothed smile. For Andrea, there was no other face in the world that could match that one for joy.

"Thanks, Mom!" Billy said.

Andrea carried the image of that face with her back to the kitchen, where it promptly dissolved, mistlike, at the sight of Rebekah sitting at the table. In profile she looked like a little lost waif, her clothes rumpled, her hair disheveled, her face weary beyond her years. She stared absently into a tall glass of orange juice.

"Good morning, Beka."

"Hi, Mom."

Andrea settled John's empty glass in the sink. "You want something to eat?"

"Not yet."

Andrea poured herself a cup of coffee she didn't really want and carried it to the table. "Mind if I join you?"

Rebekah shrugged. "Sure. Whatever."

The pipes in the bathroom groaned as John started his shower. Laughter from the porch drifted into the kitchen. Andrea sipped her coffee. "Billy and Phoebe are out there taking pictures."

Rebekah didn't look up. "Oh yeah?"

"I appreciate your showing Billy how to use the phone."

Another lift of the shoulders. "Since you and Dad don't know how to use a cell, I'm the one that has to do it."

"I wouldn't say we don't know how to use a cell phone."

"Yeah, maybe. But taking pictures. That happened when Dad was—you know."

In prison. Yes, a lot had changed in the world while John was in prison.

But Andrea didn't want to think about that. "Billy really likes the nightlight, you know."

"Yeah. Weird, huh?"

Andrea pursed her lips, willed herself to be patient. "I'm just saying, I appreciate what you've done for him. It means a lot."

Rebekah finally met Andrea's gaze. Her face softened. "It's okay, Mom. Billy—I mean, it's easy to make him happy, isn't it?"

Andrea smiled. "It doesn't take much. We should all be so lucky."

Rebekah sipped her orange juice, looked out the window.

Andrea tried to sound cheerful as she said, "I've been thinking, honey. We need to take a family day, go somewhere, do something fun. Would you like that?"

"I don't know, Mom. I guess so."

"Maybe we could take a little trip up to Niagara Falls. We haven't been there in years."

Rebekah didn't respond, didn't even glance away from the window.

"Beka?"

"Yeah?"

"Can you tell me what's bothering you?"

Silence. Then, "I don't know. Nothing."

"Well, it can't be nothing. Sometimes it helps to talk."

The girl shrugged.

Andrea sighed. "Beka, is there anything going on I should know about?"

"No."

"I mean, like drinking. You haven't been out drinking again, have you—"

"No."

"Because you know what alcohol can lead to, right? We've both seen what can happen."

Mother and daughter looked at each other. Then Rebekah said, "I'm not going to kill anyone like Dad did, if that's what you mean."

"Well, I . . ." Andrea paused, swallowed her anger. "I just want you to be careful, is all. It's so easy to make bad decisions."

Rebekah looked back toward the window.

Andrea curled both hands around the mug and studied the coffee inside. It was already growing cold. "Listen, honey, I want you to enjoy the summer a little bit. I don't know when we can get away for a vacation, but in the meantime why don't you invite some of your friends over here, just to go swimming or something?"

"I don't know, Mom."

"Well, why not? I haven't seen Lena in ages."

"She's working at the theater."

"She must have some days off."

Rebekah didn't respond.

"Or David," Andrea persisted. "You know, your dad hasn't even met him yet. Why don't you invite him to have supper with us sometime?"

"I don't think so." The words were a whisper. Rebekah's eyes moistened.

"Beka?"

No answer.

For a long moment no one said anything.

Finally Andrea said, "What's the matter, honey?"

To her surprise Rebekah said, "I think he might be interested in someone else."

Andrea watched as one tear rolled down her daughter's cheek. "Did he tell you that?"

A shake of the head.

"Have you broken up?"

"Not exactly." Rebekah lifted a hand, brushed away the tear.

"I'm so sorry, Beka. I know how it hurts."

Rebekah responded with one small nod of her head.

"It probably doesn't help for me to tell you that you're young, that you have plenty of time to find the right one for you."

"No, it doesn't help."

Andrea pushed the coffee mug aside, reached across the table, and laid a hand on her daughter's arm. "I want so much for you to be happy, Beka. I want to help you not to make the same mistakes I made—"

As though to finish Andrea's sentence, John appeared in the doorway, freshly shaved, showered, and dressed. Andrea's hand fell to the table as Rebekah pulled her arm away. Before John could so much as say good morning, Rebekah slipped into her room and shut the door.

CHAPTER THIRTY-TWO

Rebekah gazed at the wilting daisies in the plastic cup on the arcade's display counter. It was a pathetic bouquet, but it filled her with a sense of wonder at how everything in the world could turn around so quickly. Just that morning she'd been sitting at the kitchen table crying, embarrassing herself in front of her mother because she thought David was dumping her for Jessica Faulkner. Now here she was, not eight hours later, high on love again because David had met her at work with a handful of daisies he'd stolen from his neighbor's garden. His offering and the kiss that came with it left Jessica Faulkner looking like one puny rival while the rest of life suddenly looked bright again.

Maybe, Rebekah thought, just maybe Lena was right after all. Maybe they did have the power to do anything they wanted, as long as they did no harm, as long as what they did was good.

And no question this was good.

She had asked the universe to keep David in love with her, and in spite of all her doubts and fears, the universe seemed to want to help out. Rebekah was grateful to whatever god or goddess or power out there had nudged David into

bringing her flowers and letting her know everything was all right between them. Apparently
something was watching over her, something that
heard her pleas and answered, and it was safe for
her to hope for good things.

She had just reached out and lifted up the sag-
ging head of one of the daisies when a child's
voice interrupted her thoughts. "Hey, lady, what
can I get for forty-two tickets?"

Rebekah looked over the side of the display
case and into the face of a small boy. In one
chubby fist he clutched a wad of tickets.

She smiled at him. "Everything on the bottom
row is worth five tickets. You can get eight of
those, or you can get four things worth ten tickets
each. Those are up here."

The boy gazed wide-eyed at the trinkets, and
Rebekah leaned on the glass case to wait. He was
a cute little kid, towheaded, freckle-faced. Maybe
she'd throw in a few extra tickets for him, give
him an even fifty. The boss said she could do that
if she wanted. It made them look generous and
kept the patrons coming back.

"Hey, kid."

"Yeah?"

"Tell you what."

"Yeah?"

"I—" Rebekah was cut off by a can of Coke
coming down hard on top of the display case. She
sighed. "Oh hi, Gary."

"Hi, Beka." The carnival hand smiled, pushed his glasses up the bridge of his nose with a greasy index finger. "I thought maybe you could use something to drink."

"Thanks." She turned her attention back to the young boy and hoped Gary would go away.

He took a step closer instead. "Hey, what do you think about what happened last night?"

Rebekah sighed again while Gary watched her expectantly, his eyebrows raised high above the rim of his glasses. "What are you talking about?" she said.

"Weren't you working?"

"I was off yesterday."

"Man, you missed it."

"I guess I did."

"And you didn't read the paper today?"

Rebekah noticed then that he had a newspaper tucked up under one arm.

"No." She shook her head.

"So you don't know about the accident?"

"No. But you're probably going to tell me about it, aren't you?"

"Yeah, old Benson's being questioned right now because he was the last one to do a safety check on the Scrambler."

"Yeah?"

"It could have been me." He drew a hand along his brow as though wiping away imaginary sweat.

"All right, Gary. I give up. Just tell me what happened."

"Well, the ride was going but not all that fast because it was just starting up."

"Uh-huh."

"But still it was fast enough, you know what I mean?"

Rebekah stared blankly at the man. She was rapidly losing patience. "Just spill it, Gary."

"Well, so the safety bar comes unlatched on one of the cars, you know, and some girl flies out. I could hear the screams all the way on the other side of the park."

Rebekah waited.

"Yeah, next thing you know there were sirens all over the place. Ambulance came, police came. They're not running the Scrambler today. Didn't you notice?"

"What happened to the girl?" Rebekah asked.

"They hauled her off to the hospital."

"Is she all right?"

Gary shrugged. "Hurt pretty bad, I guess. There's a write-up in the Conesus paper." He pulled the paper out from under his arm and laid it flat on the countertop. He tapped at the headline on the front page.

Rebekah followed Gary's finger to the head-line: "Girl Hurt on Amusement Park Ride." Her father always read the local daily. Why hadn't he mentioned it? But then, she hadn't given him a chance, had she? Hadn't even said a word to him when he came into the kitchen where she sat talking with Mom.

Rebekah pulled the paper closer and started to read. By the time she reached the third paragraph, she was sure she was going to be sick. She lifted her eyes and looked not at Gary but into the face of the little boy who'd been deciding on his prize. He was staring up at her impatiently, pointing at a trinket behind the glass.

"Can I have the—"

She didn't let him finish. She moved from behind the counter and headed to the open air.

"Hey, Beka," Gary called, "where you going?"

She paused long enough to say, "Cover for me, will you, Gary? Give the kid whatever he wants."

"What? This ain't my job. I don't know any-thing about—"

"Just do it."

She ran to the patch of barren ground behind the arcade and squatted among the crisscross of elec-trical cables. Taking a few deep breaths, she tried to steady herself. *It has to be a coincidence,* she thought. She dug in the pocket of her shorts for her phone and flipped it open with trembling fin-gers.

Four rings, then "Yeah, hello?"

"Lena?"

"Beka?"

"Lena, did you hear?"

"Listen, I can hardly hear anything. I'm at work, and there's a line like you wouldn't believe for the six-o'clock show. I'm up to my ears in popcorn. Can I call you back?"

"No! I've got to talk to you now."

"Listen, I could get in trouble. I wouldn't have answered except I saw it was you. I—hey, just a minute, kid. Can't you see I'm on the phone? Listen, Beka, let me call you—"

"Lena, there's been an accident. Jessica Faulkner's in the hospital."

From the other end of the line came a tangle of voices, calls for popcorn, sodas, licorice whips, and discernible above the rest, a young man telling Lena to hang up and get to work. Lena responded by telling him to stuff it, this was important. To Rebekah, Lena said, "So what happened?"

"She was riding the Scrambler, and she got thrown off. Last night. It happened last night."

"Wow, no lie!" Lena sounded interested now. "And she's in the hospital?"

"Yeah. It's serious. I mean, she's got some broken bones and a head injury. She's not even conscious."

"No lie!" Lena said again. "Well, hey, she's out of the picture for a while, then."

Rebekah slumped cross-legged to the ground. She felt weak, hot, dizzy. "Don't you get it, Lena?"

"Listen, Bek, I really gotta go before the manager catches me. Tony, here, is just about to go ballistic—"

"Lena, don't you get it? It's our fault!"

"Shut up, Tony, I'm getting off right now—"

"We did it to her—"

"What are you talking about, Bek? We weren't even there."

"You know what I'm talking about! We cast the circle to keep her away from David. But I didn't mean for . . ." She was crying now, squeezing the phone so hard her hand ached.

"That's crazy, Beka. We had nothing to do with it. It was some freak accident."

"We wanted her to stay away—"

"Listen, I'll talk to you later, okay? I really gotta go. Meanwhile, forget it. We had nothing to do with it. We—all right, Tony. I said I'm hanging up. Beka, I'm hanging up now, but I'll talk to you later."

The line went dead. Rebekah let the phone slowly fall away from her ear. She didn't even bother to snap it shut. With the hot sun bearing down on her, she shivered.

CHAPTER THIRTY-THREE

John tilted his head back and looked fully at the open sky. How big it was! A wide expanse of blue arching over the lake and finally bending toward earth somewhere off in the distance. Once, not so long ago, he couldn't remember the immensity of the outdoors, of distance, of space. He hadn't thought about it much during the years he was confined to small places. Even outside in the prison yard he couldn't look up without seeing walls and barbed wire and guard towers. He had forgotten what it was to sit in a boat surrounded by water, air, the warmth of the sun.

"We should have done this weeks ago, Billy," he said.

Billy tugged at his fishing line, then looked up at his dad and smiled. "I told you, Dad. I told you we should go fishing."

"You were right, son."

He'd been home just over a month, and the summer was slipping by. Here it was July eighth already. Before he knew it, August would roll in, followed quickly by September. Not long after that, those who lived year-round by the lake would start battening down the hatches in anticipation of another long winter.

John hesitated to admit even to himself why he had put off fishing till now. For all his love of the lake, he didn't like being too far from shore. Swimming from the dock was one thing, going out in a boat where only a thin layer of wood separated you from the murky water below—well, that was something else altogether. An hour earlier, when they'd packed up the boat, John told Billy not to take them out too far, saying he wanted to steer clear of the other traffic—the larger motorboats, the jet skis, the water-skiers. After all, the lake was a busy place on Sunday afternoons, with vessels zigzagging all over the place. So Billy had pointed the boat due north and hugged the shoreline until he reached a spot where he thought the fish might be biting. Then he'd cut the motor, dropped anchor, and baited the poles with the worms he'd bought at the bait shop earlier that afternoon.

Phoebe reeled in her line now, saw the remnants of a worm dangling on an otherwise empty hook, and said, "Aw, I thought I had one." She reeled the line in almost up to the bobber and prepared to cast again.

"Careful, Phoeb," Billy said. "Don't hook me like you did last summer."

"I know how to do it," Phoebe insisted. She drew back, swung the rod, pushed the release button, and watched her bait drop into the water a few feet from the boat. "There. See?"

John smiled. This was better than he'd imagined all those times he'd dreamed about coming home and being with his kids. In those dreams Billy was still a boy and Phoebe didn't have a face—not one that was clear to him, anyway. He knew it would be good to be home, but in his dreams he couldn't feel the pride he now felt for his son, couldn't feel the love he now felt for his daughter, and he couldn't feel the overwhelming sense of freedom that came with looking up at an unimpeded view of the sky.

It was all better than he had hoped. Except for one thing. When he'd dreamed about coming home to his family, there'd been no shadow of infidelity darkening the picture, not even one hint of it anywhere in his mind. The way he had pictured it, things were going to be different this time. He was a different person, and he was supposed to live a better life, one that didn't include his past mistakes.

One month. One month home and he'd already drifted back to the old way of life.

As he thought about it, though, he had to admit one thing *was* different now. This time around he felt something he hadn't felt before. Shame. From the minute he woke up in the morning until the minute he fell asleep at night, the shame was there, waxing and waning but ever present. Mostly it was a heavy emotion, pulling the heart all out of shape.

John looked at Phoebe, sitting there in the center seat of the boat, watching the bobber intently while willing a fish to bite. Then at Billy, at the far end, one hand holding his fishing pole, the other on top of the motor as though to protect it. Billy must have sensed his gaze, because he turned and smiled.

"I'm glad you're here, Dad."

John nodded. "Me too, Billy."

He had to nip this thing with Pamela in the bud. So he'd messed up once—okay, that didn't mean he had to keep messing up. He'd draw the line right here, resolve to do the right thing from now on, for the sake of these kids, if nothing else.

The trick was, he was going to have to be stronger than his own desires.

Phoebe fidgeted, scratched one leg, tugged at the uppermost strap of her life jacket. "You know, Daddy," Phoebe said, "if you weren't here, me and Billy couldn't be out here fishing."

"Billy and I," John corrected. "And no, you couldn't be out here by yourselves."

"But we're not scared," she countered. Her small face looked determined beneath the baseball cap that shielded her eyes from the sun.

"I know you're not," John said. "Still, you need to have an adult with you when you come out on the water."

"But I'm an adult now, Dad." Billy's protest was pained, his voice almost a whine. "I'm eighteen now, and that makes me a grown-up."

John wasn't sure how to respond. Finally he said, "Give yourself some time, son. You'll get there."

"No." Billy shook his head. "I can drive the boat, but not alone. And Mom thinks I'll never drive a car. I tell her, some people with Downs drive a car, but she still says no. I'll never be independent the way Beka is."

What Billy said was true, John reflected. Though Billy was far more competent than many people with Down syndrome, he would still never be completely independent. But John decided to let the subject drop. He didn't want worries for the future infringing on the afternoon.

"Hey, Billy," he said, "hand me some water out of the cooler, will you?"

Billy dug into the small cooler with one hand and pulled out a bottle of water. He handed it to Phoebe, who handed it to John.

John wedged the bottle between his feet while he reeled in his line. "Well, the fish aren't biting, so I think I'll just enjoy the ride for a while."

"But we aren't going anywhere, Daddy," Phoebe said.

"Exactly." John unscrewed the bottle top and took a long cold swallow. "You kids need to be drinking some water too. It's hot out here."

"It's even hotter when you're wearing a life jacket," Billy noted, pulling at the padded orange canvas around his neck.

"Yeah, Dad. Can we take them off?" Phoebe asked.

"Not a chance," John said. "You keep them on."

"You know it's no use asking, Phoeb," Billy said. "You know what Mom always says. She says everyone has to have one on, no matter what."

"Smart lady," John said, nodding.

"But I'm a good swimmer," Billy went on. "Better than you even, Dad."

John thought of the Special Olympics medals lined up on the windowsill in Billy's room. "Can't argue with you there. Still, let's not take any chances."

Billy frowned. He appeared to be in thought. Finally he said with a shrug, "Okay. Mom says it's better to be safe than sorry."

"That's right, son. Anyway, it'll cool down as the sun begins to set. Shouldn't be long now."

Billy handed a bottle of water to Phoebe and got one out for himself. John watched the kids fish quietly for a while before a passing motorboat jogged his memory of Billy's struggle to get their own outboard motor started. "Hey, Billy?"

"Yeah, Dad?"

"You always have trouble starting the motor?"

"Not always. Sometimes she starts right up. Sometimes, like today, it takes a while. When Uncle Owen gave us the boat, he told us the engine was finicky."

"Yeah," John muttered, "no wonder Owen got rid of it."

"What's that, Dad?"

"Nothing. Listen, when we can afford it, we'll buy a new motor, all right? No, we'll buy a whole new boat."

"Really, Dad?"

"Really."

"All right!" Billy slapped his knee and laughed happily.

"Someday," John continued, "we'll have a whole new everything. New boat, new cars, new house."

"Yeah!" Billy agreed. "A house with more than one bathroom."

"Right."

"And where the toilet doesn't always get clogged up," Phoebe added.

"Yeah, that too."

And nothing, John added to himself, nothing they owned would be from Owen. Not one thing. John was home now and these were his kids, and he was going to take care of them without the help of his brother-in-law.

After a moment John said, "Hey, Billy? Phoebe?"

"Yeah, Dad?"

"What, Daddy?"

John pushed the words past the ache in his throat. "I love you guys."

"Love you too, Dad."

"Love you, Daddy."

John nodded. It was all sweeter than he had dared to dream.

Thirty minutes passed as they floated on the surface of the lake, the boat a cradle, the breeze a lullaby. They caught no fish and John was glad; it would have broken the serenity. If this was it, John thought, if this moment was the whole of his life, he would be satisfied.

It was starting to get dark, and clouds rolled in over the lake, casting shadows on the water, letting loose small drops of rain.

"Let's head back," John said. "We don't want to get caught out here in a storm."

Billy nodded and reeled in his line. "Mom says, first sign of rain to get out of the water. She says it can get bad pretty fast, and you sure don't want to be in an aluminum boat like this if there's lightning."

"That's right, Billy. I think your mom has taught you well."

John helped Phoebe lay the fishing rods on the floor of the boat while Billy pulled up anchor. He watched as Billy stood, opened the fuel valve on the motor, and pulled the starter cord. The motor roared to life on the first try.

"I did it!" Billy yelled excitedly, waving a fist in the air.

John gave him a nod and a thumbs-up.

Billy smiled broadly, then hollered over the roar of the motor, "Last one home's a rotten egg!"

He steered the boat around to the south and headed toward home.

CHAPTER THIRTY-FOUR

Rebekah slapped the steering wheel with both hands, then pulled the key out of the ignition and stormed back into the cottage. The place was deserted. In the few minutes she'd spent in the Jetta talking on her cell to David, everyone had disappeared. She'd been late already when he called. Now Lena and Aunt Jo were going to start wondering where she was.

"Dad!"

"Upstairs, Beka," he hollered.

Just as he answered, she spotted her mother standing on the dock, watching Billy and Phoebe swim. For a moment she forgot her anger, forgot everything as she watched her mother clap for Phoebe, who had just dived like a champion off the end of the dock. Rebekah remembered her mother cheering her on once, just like that. But that was a long time ago, when she was a child.

She let out a breath, then stomped up the stairs with an exaggerated heaviness, her sandals slapping against the bare wood. "I can't believe it," she muttered.

"What's the matter?" her father asked.

He was sitting in that tattered old chair by the window, the one with the antimacassar draped over the back. The granny chair, she called it. Her dad looked kind of silly in it, sunk down as he was in the cushioned seat, an open book in his lap. He must have thought so too, judging by the look in his eyes. You'd think he'd just been caught doing something he shouldn't be doing.

"Beka?" he prodded.

"My car won't start," she told him.

He nodded slightly, almost smiled. "You mean that old rattletrap from Uncle Owen?"

She frowned at his comment, shook her head. "Well, yeah, whatever. It won't start."

"What's it sound like?"

"What do you mean?"

"When you turn the key, what's it sound like?"

"It doesn't sound like anything. Nothing happens."

"Must be the battery, then."

"Oh great."

"Did you leave an overhead light on or something?"

"No. I don't know. I mean, I was sitting in the front seat with the door open for a few minutes, if that's a problem."

"All right, Beka, don't worry. We'll give you a jump. You going to work already?"

Rebekah shook her head. "I'm off today. I'm going over to a friend's house."

227

"Oh? Hey, you know, I've been home for weeks, and I haven't met any of your friends yet. Why don't you bring them over here?"

Rebekah thought she might explode. The last thing she wanted was to introduce her friends to her father. The only thing she wanted right now was to get out of here. "Listen, Dad," she said, "can you just give me a jump or whatever so I can get going? I'm already late."

He gazed at her a moment—a little sadly, she thought—then closed the book in his lap. She noticed for the first time what it was. And yet she asked anyway. "What are you reading?"

"Well—" He looked down at the book, as though he had to check for himself. "It's a Bible I was given while I—"

"Why are you reading that?" Her words sounded sharper than she had meant.

"Well, actually, Beka," he said quietly, "I've been thinking I should tell you about—you know, what happened to me in prison. I haven't been very good about sharing all these things with you and Billy and Phoebe. I haven't even been very good about reading the Bible since . . ."

He seemed to realize then that she wasn't really listening, because he stopped talking. Silence fell over the room. Rebekah was aware only of the giant weight of fear in the pit of her stomach.

"Dad?" she whispered.

"What is it, Beka?"

"Do you think there's evil in the world?"

He seemed to wince at that, as though it pained him to answer. "I know there's evil in the world."

"But there isn't supposed to be. There's . . ." She didn't know how to go on. Aunt Jo had explained it all, had told her and Lena how evil was only an illusion and not really there at all. Everything was one, and it was all good, but beyond that Rebekah couldn't remember how Aunt Jo had explained the part about evil.

Her father was waiting for her to go on. "What is it, Beka?" he asked again.

"Do you think—" She stopped. She could hardly believe she was going to ask her father this question, but she had to ask somebody. She had to know. "Do you think we can put a curse on people?"

"A curse? What do you mean?"

"I mean, like, if you cast a spell that might hurt someone, do you think it would work?"

Her father seemed to think about that. Finally he said, "Listen, honey, in prison I came up against everything you can imagine. One of the guys there was into voodoo. He was forever ripping up his bedsheets to make dolls out of them to put curses on people. Finally the guards made him sleep without sheets."

"So he'd stop putting curses on people?"

"No, so he'd stop ripping up the prison's sheets.

That kind of stuff costs, and the warden doesn't like it when the prisoners waste money."

Rebekah cocked her head and eyed her father sideways. "So did he ever put a curse on you?"

"Yeah, he did. He thought I cut in on him in line once, when I really didn't. But that's a big thing in prison, especially when you're in the chow line, which we were. I heard that night through the prison grapevine that he'd put a curse on me."

"So what happened?"

"Nothing."

"Nothing?"

"No. A few days later he was transferred out of the prison and taken somewhere else."

"Are you saying there's nothing to any of this stuff?"

He laid the Bible on the bed, kept his hand on top of it. "Well, I'm not sure I'm the best person to ask, but I really don't think so. Why do you want to know?"

She shook her head. "Nothing. I just—I saw a movie. Yeah, there was a movie about that sort of thing, and it got me thinking."

"Oh." He tilted his chin, seemed to study her. "I think you watch too much scary stuff. It gives you nightmares. I've heard you wake up screaming more than once."

"Um, yeah." She tried to laugh, but it fell flat. "Well, I've got to get going. Can you . . . ?" She nodded toward the stairway.

"Sure." He stood. "I think your mom has some jumper cables in the Volvo."

Ten minutes later the Jetta was purring. Rebekah, behind the wheel, watched as her father pushed the hood closed and then disconnected the cables from the battery of her mother's car.

Cables still in one hand, he leaned his other hand on the sill of the open driver's-side window. "How far you going?"

"A couple miles."

"Well, listen, take the long way. You need to run this thing for a good twenty minutes. I suppose this is the original battery?"

She shrugged. "I don't know."

"Well, we'll have to get you a new one. Along with everything else around here. When we can afford it."

She frowned. "Yeah, okay."

He took a step back, started rolling up the cable.

Rebekah reached for the shift and put the car in reverse. She kept her foot on the brake and squeezed the wheel with both hands.

"Dad?"

"Yeah?"

"Thanks for the jump."

"Sure thing, Beka."

She wanted to say something else, but she wasn't sure what it was. And then the moment passed.

"Well," her father said, "have a good time at your friend's."

"Yeah." Her hands relaxed; her foot let up on the brake. A certain longing hung at the back of her throat. "I will," she said quietly.

She backed the car down the graveled drive, looked for traffic, eased out onto the road. She traveled around the lake for twenty minutes, trying unsuccessfully to erase from her thoughts the image of her father standing there alone by the cottage, one hand raised in a small wave as she drove away.

CHAPTER THIRTY-FIVE

"It's about time you got here," Lena said as she swung open the front door.

Rebekah looked beyond her friend's shoulder as she spoke. "Sorry," she said. "I—my car wouldn't start."

"So how come you didn't call?"

"I was busy. I mean, my dad and I—we had to jump the car and all. The battery was dead."

"Yeah? Well, I called you. Didn't you hear the phone?"

Rebekah's jaw tightened. She had heard her cell phone go off, but she'd ignored it. "I told you I was sorry," she said. "I would have been on time if the battery hadn't died."

"Uh-huh. I thought maybe you were chickening out on me."

Rebekah drummed up the courage to look Lena in the eye. "Listen, Lena," she said, "I'm here, aren't I?"

Lena's mouth grew small, but at the same time her face seemed to soften. She stepped aside and nodded toward the hall. "Well, come on in."

Rebekah took a deep breath and stepped inside. Lena shut the door, then led the way down the hall to the kitchen.

Aunt Jo's cottage was one of the newer ones on the lake, large and airy. The first time Rebekah visited, more than a year before, she'd simply walked from room to room, taking in the open spaces and the sunshine streaming in through the many large windows. While the place was unfamiliar, she felt oddly at home, almost as though she belonged there. Something about the cottage, she told Aunt Jo, made her happy.

Aunt Jo had been pleased. She had worked hard, she explained, to arrange everything in the cottage so that the energy would flow freely through each room, bringing balance and harmony. Rebekah had no idea what Aunt Jo was talking about, but in the months ahead, she would learn.

Rebekah and Lena entered the kitchen, where Aunt Jo was wiping the center island with a dishcloth. "Well, there you are, Beka," the woman said warmly. She smiled, laid down the dishcloth, and pulled Rebekah into a hug. She was tall and willowy, so thin there was hardly anything there to hug, thought Rebekah.

"We were beginning to wonder," Aunt Jo went on. "Anyway, I've just put a loaf of bread in the oven, so why don't we sit at the kitchen table while it's baking. I have some fresh lemonade in the fridge. Does everybody want some?"

Aunt Jo was a pretty woman, though she preferred what Lena called "the natural look." She used little makeup—maybe a dab of powder and blush, but nothing at all to highlight her eyes or color her lips. She didn't bother either to wash the gray streaks out of her otherwise dark brown hair, which she generally pulled back into a simple clip at the base of her neck. She most often, as now, wore a solid color cotton blouse and a long billowy skirt, the hem of which reached almost down to her slender bare feet. Her one indulgence was jewelry, which she wore a lot of. She seemed especially fond of weighty earrings that pulled on her lobes and tickled the sides of her neck. She also wore a variety of necklaces, bracelets, and rings—several at once, as though she couldn't settle on one or two. She even wore ankle bracelets and toe rings.

Her features were fine and even, her skin amazingly smooth except for the deep laugh lines around her eyes. That was what Rebekah liked most about her—the ready smile, the quick and easy laugh. She seemed to be in love with the world and everyone in it. The only exception Rebekah knew of was Aunt Jo's former husband, who had left her alone and childless some years before. She supported herself as a buyer for a department store in the next town over, though she earned a little extra cash reading tarot cards for clients on the weekends.

As much as Rebekah liked Lena's aunt, her stomach churned now as she watched the woman pour lemonade into tall, narrow glasses. She wished she hadn't come. She wished she had just kept driving in circles around the lake. She didn't want to talk with Aunt Jo about what had happened. She was here only because for more than a week Lena kept bugging her until she agreed to come.

When the three of them settled at the kitchen table, Rebekah thought she might be able to steer the conversation toward small talk. But Aunt Jo plunged right in. "Well, Beka," she said, "I'm sorry to hear about your friend."

"She's not our friend," Lena interrupted.

No, Rebekah's mind echoed, *she's not our friend.* Rebekah didn't like Jessica Faulkner, had had thoughts of her—no, it was wrong even to remember. She pursed her lips and shut her eyes for a moment. She had to be careful what she thought. Thoughts had power. Thoughts could change things.

"Well . . ." Aunt Jo paused and took a sip of

lemonade. Then she looked at Rebekah. "Lena tells me you think it's your fault, that you somehow brought about the accident."

Rebekah shrugged. Her breath quickened, though she tried to sound nonchalant. "We wanted her to stay away from David."

"So you tried to cast a spell?"

Rebekah glanced at Lena and nodded. "Yeah, we did. And then not long after that . . ."

When Rebekah couldn't finish, Lena jumped in. "After that Jessica got hurled from the Scrambler, and now Beka's afraid to practice the Craft."

Aunt Jo reached across the table and took Rebekah's hand. "First of all, you had nothing to do with it. Second, you and Lena have a lot to learn. The universe doesn't necessarily work the way you think it does."

Then how does the universe work? Rebekah wondered. She had thought she was beginning to understand, but now she was more confused than ever.

"Now listen, girls, I want the two of you to stop casting spells for a while. You're obviously not ready."

"But, Aunt Jo!"

"Hear me out, Lena."

"Maybe Beka's not ready, but I am. I've been ready for a long time."

"Lena, you have so much to learn. Casting spells isn't the most important thing—"

"Then what is?"

Aunt Jo let go of Rebekah's hand and laid an open palm over Lena's forearm. Rebekah felt relieved to have her hand back. She dropped both hands to her lap as she listened to the answer.

"Learning is," Aunt Jo said, speaking quietly but firmly. "That's what's most important. That's why we're here. To grow spiritually, to learn to live in harmony with all things. But you don't want that—especially you, Lena. You're still more interested in having your own way. You wrestle with the universe rather than walking in tune with it. You'll never achieve anything until you cooperate with the goddess and the god."

Lena didn't respond, though her face was tight with annoyance. Aunt Jo gazed at Lena placidly for a long while. She seemed to be willing her to understand.

Finally Aunt Jo turned again to Rebekah. Rebekah dropped her eyes, chewed at the inside of her cheek.

"Beka, honey, listen. You have nothing to be afraid of. Everything about the Craft is good and beautiful. You know that, don't you?"

Rebekah shrugged. She couldn't look into Aunt Jo's face. "I guess so," she said.

"The only evil is the evil we ourselves create. If you live in harmony with nature, and with the goddess and the god, you are perfectly safe."

Rebekah nodded. She had heard all this before,

months ago, when Lena and her aunt had introduced her to the Craft.

Then she had welcomed it all. And even now, she still wanted to believe it. The Craft had grounded her when she'd felt herself floating, given her something to hold on to when everything in her life seemed out of control. She needed both the peace and the power that Aunt Jo had promised back at the beginning.

She lifted her chin slowly and met Aunt Jo's gaze. "So you don't think we did it to Jessica? I mean, you don't think we made the accident happen?"

Aunt Jo gave a small, reassuring laugh. "Of course not, Beka."

"But it's possible, isn't it, to put a curse on people?"

"Some people seem to be able to do that kind of thing, but they're not like us. We vow only to do good. Remember what I told you the foundation of the Craft is?"

Rebekah nodded.

"What is it?"

"Love."

"That's right. Love for all people, for animals, for nature, for all things."

"Sometimes," Rebekah said, "it's hard to love certain people."

Aunt Jo nodded, offered a small smile. "Even when it's hard, you must allow the divine in you to honor the divine in them. We are, after all, all part of each other, all part of the divine."

The room was quiet a moment. Rebekah sensed her fear beginning to lift. She drew in a deep breath.

"So, Beka, do you want to go on learning?"

Rebekah nodded. "Yeah," she said quietly. "I do."

Aunt Jo smiled at her, and then at Lena.

"Anyway, Beka," Lena said, "if it'll make you feel any better, I heard Jessica's going to be all right."

"She is?" Rebekah asked eagerly. "Where'd you hear that?"

"Some guy at the movie theater. I heard him talking about her while he was waiting in line for popcorn. So when he reached the counter, I asked him. He said her parents moved her to a hospital in Rochester for a while, but they expect her to be okay."

"See there?" Aunt Jo said happily. "All is well."

"So why didn't you tell me before?" Rebekah asked.

Lena shrugged. "I don't know. Guess I forgot. But, listen, she's going to be in Rochester for the rest of the summer, so that's good news, huh?"

Rebekah didn't bother to answer.

Aunt Jo rose from the table and went to the fridge for the pitcher of lemonade. "Anyone want some more?"

Lena held up her empty glass. "I do."

"Beka?"

"No thanks." Her glass was still almost full. Her stomach had only just settled enough that she thought she could drink. The kitchen was cozy now with the scent of baking bread. Rebekah felt the tension ease, the heaviness lift.

"Okay," Lena said, "now that that's settled, on to the next problem."

"Oh? What's that?" Aunt Jo returned the pitcher to the fridge and sat back down at the table. She looked at Lena expectantly.

"Do you know if Mom's seeing someone?"

"Seeing someone?"

"Yeah. A male type. You know."

A frown creased her aunt's brow. "She hasn't told me she is. Why?"

"She's acting all happy all of a sudden, the way she gets when she's seeing someone."

"And that's a bad thing?"

"Well, you know."

Aunt Jo laughed. "No, Lena. The only thing I know is that you don't like it whenever your mom gets into a relationship with someone."

"I just don't want her to get hurt."

"I think you just want her for yourself."

"That's not true."

"Oh, come on, Lena. You're never happy when she pays attention to someone other than you. If she's seeing someone, then I say good for her. And don't you even think about interfering."

Lena raised her brows.

Her aunt laughed again. "Yes, you, Lena. For Pete's sake, let her have some happiness in her life. Heaven knows it's about time."

Aunt Jo and Lena went on volleying, but Rebekah's mind drifted off to other things. She wasn't completely convinced she and Lena hadn't caused the accident, but what did it matter, as long as Jessica was going to be all right? She'd try to let it go for now, try to enjoy the rest of the summer with David.

But from now on, she would be careful. She didn't want trouble. She just wanted to be happy. And to be loved. Just exactly what most people wanted. That wasn't asking too much, was it?

CHAPTER THIRTY-SIX

John moved quickly up the narrow stairway and into the church foyer. He was about to cross the threshold of the front doors when he heard somebody call his name. He stopped, hesitated, turned around.

Pamela stood there in a white linen dress, her dark hair pulled up off her neck in a loose knot at the back of her head. Her sun-darkened skin shone like bronze in the dimly lighted foyer, and in spite of the humid heat of the night, she looked cool and stylish. John, well aware of how she looked, had just spent the past hour trying to avoid her.

"You know," she said, "you're allowed to say hello to me just like everyone else." Her voice was even, but her lower lip hinted at a pout.

Drops of sweat formed between John's shoulder blades and trickled down his back. "Hello, Pamela," he said quietly.

She seemed to sigh at that. She took a step toward him. "It's pretty obvious, John, that you've been ignoring me these past couple of weeks since . . ."

She didn't have to say it. He knew. Since the Fourth of July.

He looked beyond her shoulder to see whether anyone else was coming up from the A.A. meeting in the basement. He suspected the coffee and donuts would keep them downstairs for a while. "Let's go outside," he said.

He moved out the door and down the steps, with Pamela close behind. He stepped around the side of the church to the parking lot and stopped at her convertible. She joined him, standing uncomfortably close as she leaned against the driver's-side door.

"You aren't sorry, are you?" she asked uneasily, her large eyes searching his face.

He ran a hand through his hair, rubbed his temple a moment. "Listen, I . . . I don't know what to say. . . . I—"

"You *are* sorry, then. You wish it'd never happened."

"No. I mean . . ."

"What, John? Tell me."

His eyes darted nervously around the parking lot. He wondered whether Pamela could hear the pounding of his heart, that sledgehammer beating rhythmically against his chest. "Pamela, you know I'm married," he pleaded.

"And?"

"Well?"

"John, listen—"

"No, what I did—"

"You don't love her. You can't love her."

"I've got to think of my family."

"Let's go somewhere and talk."

"No, I . . . look, I'm sorry. Let's call it a mistake—"

"It wasn't a mistake." Her expression was stony, but her eyes suddenly shimmered with tears. "Please, John—"

She was interrupted when her cell phone rang. With an exasperated sigh, she unzipped her handbag and fumbled around for the phone. When she found it, she read the incoming number. "It's my daughter," she murmured. She pushed a button and in a brighter voice said, "Hello, sweetheart. . . . Yes, I'm just about to leave. . . . Well, yes, I guess that's all right, as long as it's all right with Sara's mother. . . . Okay then, I'll see you in the morning. . . . Yes, all right. Love you." She lowered the phone from her ear and pressed the off button. She kept her eyes down, seeming to need a moment to collect herself. Then with a wistful smile, she said, "Look, I got your picture tonight, during the meeting."

John drew in a sharp breath. "What?"

"Your picture, see?"

She turned the phone in his direction, but John took a step back. "Are you crazy? Erase it."

"Don't worry, John, no one's going to see—"

"Erase it, Pamela."

"I just wanted to have . . ." She didn't finish. She made a small taut line of her mouth, as though to keep herself from saying something she might regret. Then, with a lift of her shoulders, she relented. "All right." She pushed a button, closed the phone.

"Is it gone?"

She nodded.

An awkward silence settled over them. John told himself to do what he had to do and then go home.

"Pamela, I really think—"

"John," she interrupted quickly. Her tears were gone, her face expectant. "My daughter is spending the night at her friend's house. Come over for a while, just to talk."

"No, I—"

"Just to talk, I promise. Just for a little while, John. Please."

Where was everyone? John wondered. Why didn't someone come out of the church and give him a means of escape? He watched the steps. No one came.

He turned back to Pamela. He opened his mouth, closed it, shook his head. Finally he said, "Look, Pamela, what is it that you want from me?"

"Just a chance," she said. "That's all. Just a chance."

She opened the car door and slid in behind the wheel. She looked up at him with her lovely, inescapable eyes. "Are you coming?" she asked.

He thought of Andrea, wondered briefly how he would explain his not coming home after the meeting. But then, he knew he'd think of something, if he needed to, if she asked.

With only a slightly hesitant gait, he moved around the car, opened the passenger-side door, and got in.

CHAPTER THIRTY-SEVEN

"Hey, Dad?"

"Yeah, Billy?"

"Why'd you ask Uncle Owen if you could work the dishwasher instead of bussing tables?"

Billy gnawed on an ear of corn and waited for

his dad to answer. He'd been puzzling since the day before when he overheard his dad talking with Uncle Owen at the restaurant.

His father chewed slowly. He appeared to be thinking about something. Then he said, "Just for a change."

The whole family was seated around the table on the screened-in porch, eating a rare meal together on an evening when no one had to work. Dad had cooked hamburgers on the grill, and Mom had boiled huge ears of corn and whipped up a batch of Billy's favorite potato salad.

Billy dropped the corn back onto his plate and wiped the butter off his face with a napkin. "Don't you like bussing tables, Dad?"

"Oh sure, Billy," his dad responded quickly. "Sure I do. It's not that."

"Bet you just want to work the sprayer, huh?"

Dad laughed lightly, shook his head.

"But Uncle Owen said no, right?"

His dad was busy stabbing a chunk of potato. "He said he needs me more on the floor right now."

"I'm glad, because I'd miss you if you were stuck back in the kitchen."

"When I get big," Phoebe said, "I'm going to work at the restaurant too."

"That's great, Phoeb!" Billy said. "You'll love it."

"Wow, Phoeb," Rebekah cut in, "don't dream

too big. I mean, just because other girls your age want to be rock stars—"

"That's enough, Beka," Mom said. "Phoebe can work at the restaurant if she wants. It's a perfectly respectable place to work."

"That's what I love about this family, a bunch of overachievers, not a single loser in the lot."

"Beka—"

Rebekah shrugged, looked at the ceiling, took another bite of hamburger.

"The restaurant is a good place to work," Billy told her.

"Whatever."

"How come you're always in a bad mood?"

"How come you're such an idiot?"

"Beka!" Mom yelled.

"Can I be excused, Mom?"

"No. Apologize to your brother."

"He should apologize to me."

"Beka, I'm not going to tell you again."

Rebekah narrowed her eyes. "Sorry," she huffed.

"It's okay, Beka," Billy said. "You're excused for being stupid."

"Mom!"

"Quiet, Beka! You too, Billy. Not another word."

Billy looked at Phoebe and smiled, then picked up the ear of corn and nibbled from one end down to the other.

No one spoke for the next few minutes until Phoebe suddenly looked up and said, "Daddy?"

"Yes, sweetheart?"

"In one month I'm going to first grade."

"I know, honey. Isn't that exciting?"

Phoebe nodded and went back to eating.

"And then," Mom said, "I won't have any children at home during the day. The cottage will seem so empty."

Rebekah laughed. "And that's a bad thing?"

"Well, it's just that I'll miss you all when you're in school."

"Miss us? You should enjoy being able to walk around this old shack without bumping into people."

"It's not a shack, Beka," Billy argued.

"It is to me."

"Granted it's small," Dad said, "but we can be thankful we have a roof over our heads. Anyway, it's not forever."

"Yeah?" Rebekah taunted. "So where we going?"

"I don't know yet. In the meantime, let's make do the best we can."

Billy wiped his mouth again with his crumpled napkin. "I know how to make the place bigger."

"You do?" his mother asked.

"Sure." Billy nodded.

His father looked at him. "So fill us in."

"It's easy. Remember the story about the man

whose house was too small? He asked the wise man what he should do. The wise man said, 'Put a chicken in your house.' So he did."

"And the house seemed even smaller!" Phoebe joined in. "So he went back to the wise man—"

"—and he told him to put another animal in the house—"

"A goat!"

"Yeah, I guess a goat. So he did. But that didn't help either. So he went back to the wise man—"

"—and he told him to put a horse and a cow and a donkey or something in his house—"

"Yeah, a whole bunch more animals."

Billy took a bite of potato salad and chewed thoughtfully.

"So what happened?" his mother asked.

Billy pointed to his mouth. Mom nodded. When he'd swallowed, he said, "He lived like that for a while until he thought he'd go crazy."

"And then the wise man told him to take all the animals out of the house," Phoebe said.

"Yeah, yeah," Rebekah muttered, "so then with the animals gone, the place suddenly seemed huge, like it was a mansion or something. Well, we're not doing any of that mess around here."

"I know, Beka, but I'm just saying, sometimes things look bad, but then something happens, and you realize things are really pretty good."

"That makes no sense."

Billy started to argue, but Dad cut in. "Yeah it does. It makes sense."

"It means," Mom said, "you should just be thankful for what you have."

"Yeah, right. Name one person you know who's like that."

"Beka," Billy said, "why can't *you* just be thankful for what you have?"

"Because that's how people end up with nothing."

Billy squinted at Rebekah. He shook his head slowly.

Phoebe said, "Well, I like the cottage, and I never want to leave."

"I'm glad you're happy here, Phoebe," Dad said.

"She only likes it," Rebekah pointed out, "because she's never lived anywhere else. She's never lived in a real house."

"This is a real house," Billy countered.

"Give me a break. It was built to be a summer cottage—"

"But now it's a real—"

"Kids! Can't we be together for five minutes without fighting?" Mom's face was flushed, and she actually rapped on the table with her knuckles.

Billy looked at her, then at his dad, then at his sisters. For a long while, no one spoke. Then forks clanged against plates as everyone went back to eating.

It was Phoebe who broke the silence. "I wish we could get a goat," she said dreamily.

Billy thought about that. He smiled, his whole face brightening. "I wish we could get a whole bunch of goats. Then I wouldn't have to cut the grass."

"Yeah," Rebekah said, "and I wish the two of you *were* goats so I wouldn't have to put up with you."

To Billy's surprise, Phoebe giggled. "You're silly, Beka," she said.

Dad laid down his fork and lifted his napkin to the table. "I wish I could make all your wishes come true," he said, "though I for one wouldn't want to be the father of a couple of goats."

Billy and Phoebe laughed, and Dad joined in. Rebekah grimaced and looked at the ceiling. Mom didn't laugh, or smile, or even move. When the porch was quiet again, she said, "Well, you know what I wish?"

"What, Mom?" Billy asked.

She sighed loudly before answering. "I wish that none of us had any need for wishes."

Billy wasn't sure he understood, but he nodded anyway, then reached across the table for another ear of corn.

CHAPTER THIRTY-EIGHT

An August moon glowed overhead like a lantern, casting shadows across the road. Few cars traveled this way at this time of night. Most cottages were dark, save for a light on the porch or a lamppost at the end of the drive. The woods on the far side of the road were as black as an empty stage, though they pulsed with the chirping of crickets and the occasional flutter of wings. That and the crunching of gravel underfoot were the only muted sounds of this midnight journey.

John didn't need a flashlight; the way was easy and becoming easier every time he walked it.

He took a deep breath, felt his lungs expand with the cool night air. He slowed his steps, suddenly remembering.

"John?"

"Yes, Andrea?"

"Are you all right?"

"Of course. Why?"

"You look tired. Aren't you sleeping well?"

"I'm fine."

His feet grew heavy. He stopped. Throwing his head back, he looked up fully at the star-pocked sky.

What was he doing out here in the middle of the night, walking alone down a deserted road?

"Dad?"

"What is it, Beka?"

"Do you think there's evil in the world?"

Surely there was, but what was evil and what was good? That was what he was beginning to wonder.

He started up again, moving slowly. In a few more steps he came alongside a cottage where someone leaned against the back porch railing, smoking a cigarette. He smelled the smoke, saw the small round circle of fire lift and brighten as the man inhaled. From across the dark yard he sensed a pair of eyes watching him, wondering. Who would be out walking at this time of night? And why?

John hurried on. It wasn't far now. Still, there was time to change his mind, turn around, go back home.

He thrust his hands into his pockets and kept walking.

It had rankled him, the look on Andrea's face, the concern in her voice. *"Are you all right?"* As soon as the words left her mouth, he'd felt the anger rise in his chest. *Leave me alone,* he'd wanted to say. But he didn't say it. Just tried to brush her off.

He was on his way to that small grassy grove at the edge of the cemetery behind Grace Chapel. It wasn't ideal, but it was the only place they could think of to meet when her daughter was home. They'd met there three times now.

Tonight would be the fourth.

The first time they'd been amused at the empty bottles lying scattered among the gravestones, remnants of an earlier gathering. The bottles hadn't been there long. They still carried the scent of liquor.

I'll have to tell Larry to clean this place up, John had thought. And then he'd laughed at himself. How would he explain to Larry that he'd found the empty bottles when he had laid himself down among them in the graveyard?

Reaching the church, he stopped again, looked up at the light shining above the double front doors. He'd tried. God knew he'd tried, didn't He? Surely God had seen the turmoil, heard the pleas, watched as he'd lain awake staring at his wife and praying for strength.

But when Pamela spoke of a future together, he thought maybe there was something to be gained. And maybe it was good. Maybe it was even meant to be.

Around the back of the church he found her waiting among the shadows at the edge of the trees.

"John?"

"It's me, Pamela."

"Oh!" She sounded relieved. "I thought you might not come. I thought you'd changed your mind."

"No. I'm here now."

She moved toward him, and he took her in his arms.

CHAPTER THIRTY-NINE

Andrea pushed open the door to Selene's Hair Salon, even though the Closed sign hung in the front window. She knew the door would be unlocked; Selene was waiting for her.

Holding Phoebe by the hand, she stepped into the salon, where she was greeted by the all-too-familiar scent of hairspray and perming solution. This was where she had spent her time while John was away, answering the phone, cleaning up, doing work her sister-in-law didn't really need her to do but for which she was paid a small sum anyway. Selene had urged her to go to cosmetology school, learn to cut hair, have a trade under her belt, just in case. . . . Andrea said that wasn't necessary. John would be coming home.

Selene sat at the front desk, chewing absently on the end of a pencil as she frowned over her appointment book. The front strands of her frosted hair were held back from her face by a wide gold-colored clip at the top of her head. She looked up as Andrea and Phoebe approached, and her brown eyes widened. "Hey there!" she said. "I see you made it."

"Yeah." Andrea sighed but managed a smile. "It's been a long day."

"Hi, Aunt Selene," Phoebe said cheerfully. "What color are they today?"

Selene held up one hand to show off her acrylic nails. "Pistol Packin' Pink."

"Oh, nice!"

"Thanks, honey. And what have you got there? One of those pretty little picture thingies?"

"It's a kaleidoscope." Phoebe held it up for her aunt to see.

"Oh yeah. I used to have one when I was a kid, but I can never remember what they're called."

"Can I sit in Jennifer's chair while you do Mommy's hair?"

"Sure, sweetie. Just don't play with her scissors, all right?"

Phoebe wandered over to the salon chair at the back of the shop and climbed up into it. She put the kaleidoscope to her eye, held it up to the light, and started slowly turning the end.

Andrea glanced up at the clock. It was almost seven. "You the last one here?" she asked.

Selene nodded and stood. "Everyone's gone on home for the day."

"Well, thanks for fitting me in like this. Sorry I couldn't get in this afternoon."

"No problem, honey. You get that tire fixed?"

Andrea nodded. "More or less. It's patched. At least it's holding air."

"You take it down to Charlie's place?"

"Yes, but Charlie was busy with somebody's Lexus. He had some young kid patch my tire. I hope it lasts awhile."

"It should, unless you're planning any cross-country trips."

Andrea chuckled. "No. Not anytime soon."

"Well, listen, you ready for that trim? You want a shampoo first?"

"Yeah, let's wash it," Andrea said as she moved toward the row of sinks.

"You want to try a different cut this time?"

"No. Nothing special. Just trim it up." She settled into the padded chair and leaned her head back over the sink. Selene turned on the sprayer, adjusted the water temperature, held the hose against Andrea's scalp.

"Too hot?" Selene asked.

"No. It's good."

Andrea tried to relax under the flow of warm water. Selene lathered up a handful of shampoo, then rubbed the soap vigorously into Andrea's hair, using her square-edged nails to massage her scalp. Andrea remembered how once in a while, to help Selene, she had washed the hair of some of the customers. She didn't like it, especially if the customer was a man. She had never told Selene that, though. She did whatever she'd been asked to do.

Selene cut off the water, then squirted a small pool of conditioner into one hand. Andrea watched as Selene briefly rubbed her palms together, then flinched and squinted as the hands came down on her head again, working the conditioner through each strand of hair.

"Am I pulling?" Selene asked.

"No. You're all right."

Another blast of warm water, followed by a stiff white towel wrapped tightly around her head. Andrea held the head dressing in place with one hand as Selene led her to the salon chair closest to the front window. Selene then snapped open a plastic cape, tied it around Andrea's neck like a bib, and removed the towel.

"So listen," Selene said quietly as she worked a comb through the knotted hair, "how's it going otherwise?"

"Things are all right."

"Just all right?"

"Well, you know. I worry a lot."

"About what?"

"Well, everything."

"Can you narrow it down?"

"Well, I worry about Beka, for one."

"What? You mean the drinking?"

"That and other things. Mostly that right now, I guess."

"She's a good kid, Andrea. She's going to turn out all right."

"That's what I always thought too, till that night . . ." Andrea glanced over at Phoebe to see if she was listening. But Phoebe was busy with the kaleidoscope and wasn't paying attention to the women two chairs down the row.

"Listen," Selene said, "as if all kids don't drink once in a while."

"I never did."

"You were the exception, then, not the rule."

"Maybe."

"I don't like the boys drinking either, but while we try to put limits on them, I figure I can't stop them completely. I mean, really, you know? Kids are kids. They're going to sow their wild oats, and while they're doing that we'll worry about them, just like our folks worried about us. But we survived, didn't we?"

"I wish I could be as laid-back as you are, Selene."

Selene laughed lightly, waved a hand. "Worrying just makes you grow old faster."

"I'm already old."

"Old, nothing. You're not even forty."

"Yeah, but most of the time I look sixty and feel eighty. I guess I've had a lot to worry about."

"Well, listen, hon, I don't know how old you feel, but you don't look sixty, so you can just shut up about that."

Andrea looked at herself in the mirror, then glanced up at Selene's reflection and offered her a crooked smile. "Well, thanks, Selene. I don't mean to complain."

"Honey, if you can't talk to me, who can you talk to?"

Andrea thought about that and realized she didn't have an answer.

"Has Beka done it since?" Selene asked.

"Been out drinking, you mean? Not that I know of. But then, apparently there've been a lot of things I don't know about."

"Yeah, so welcome to parenthood."

Andrea laughed. "I've been a parent longer than you have."

"Yeah, but you lucked out the first time around. You got Billy."

Andrea nodded slowly. "Yeah, I did luck out, didn't I? You're the only person who would think so, though. You and Owen."

"And her," Selene added, nodding toward Phoebe. "Those two are a pair."

Glancing at Phoebe, Andrea said, "She loves her big brother."

"No question there."

"But you know, she's really warmed up to John these last couple of months. When he first came home she wanted nothing to do with him—"

"Yeah, I remember."

"But now he's Daddy."

"So I've noticed. He won her over, huh?"

Andrea nodded again as she watched Selene gather up her bangs with a comb.

"Hold your head still, honey," Selene said, "or you're going to end up with a Mohawk."

"Oh." Andrea stopped nodding. "Sorry."

"Of course, that might make John stand up and take notice, huh?"

Andrea didn't respond.

"So," Selene went on, "speaking of John, how are things?"

"Well, you know. Things are all right, I guess."

"Now that's a real positive answer."

Andrea shrugged.

"Not exactly a second honeymoon, huh?" Selene asked casually.

"Oh, Selene." Andrea looked up toward the ceiling and sighed.

"Okay, forget I asked."

"Well, it's—"

"Listen, honey, you don't have to explain anything to me. I know John. I know his type."

"His type?"

"I could have told you nothing would change when he came back."

"You *did* tell me that, Selene. More than once."

"And I was right, wasn't I? I'm sorry, honey, and I wish it weren't so, because I know how you were hoping things would be different."

"Well, at least he came back."

"Yeah, at least he did that much."

"And he's working."

"Thanks to Owen."

"Yes, thanks to Owen, but at least John's sticking with the job. He's trying real hard with the kids, and he's not drinking. That's something."

"Well, praise the Lord and alleluia."

"Oh, Selene." Andrea sighed again.

Selene only laughed. "I don't mean any disrespect, honey. You've got a point. The man's trying."

"It's hard . . . you know, coming back after being away so long."

"It's something of an adjustment. I can't disagree with that. Say, watch out, kiddo," Selene called down to Phoebe. "Spin too much there, you're going to make yourself sick."

Phoebe had the salon chair going around in circles while she held on with both hands.

"I can't stop, Aunt Selene!" she cried, her face a rotating beacon of glee.

"Well, you rascal." Selene stepped to the chair and put out a hand to stop it. "There. Now find something else to do. I'm almost done with your mom."

She returned to Andrea and eyed her hair pensively. "Short enough?" she asked.

"I think so."

"So what else is on your mind?"

"Huh?"

"I know you, honey. You're worried about more than just Beka. You might as well tell me what it is."

"Honestly, Selene, you know me better than my own mother."

"You're an open book, Andrea, far as I'm concerned. So tell me what's bothering you."

"It's . . . well, it's just that John's so . . . I don't know. Restless, I guess."

"What do you mean, restless?"

"He's worried. He's not sleeping well."

"What's he worried about?"

"I don't know. Everything, I guess."

"I've always admired the way you zero right in on things, Andrea."

Andrea dropped her gaze to her lap. She pulled a hand from beneath the cape and absently brushed away the snippets of hair cascading down the front. "Lately," she said, "I wake up at one or two in the morning, and he's not in bed yet. Last night it was even later than that. I think it was almost three o'clock before he came to bed."

"So where is he?"

"Downstairs watching TV. Or out walking."

"Out walking?"

"He says it helps to clear his mind if he goes for a walk."

"In the middle of the night?"

Andrea didn't like the expression on Selene's face as it reflected back at her from the mirror. "He's not going out drinking, if that's what you think."

"That's not what I'm thinking."

"Then what are you thinking?"

Selene hesitated. "I don't know. What are you thinking?"

Andrea frowned, shook her head. "I don't know

what to think. He has a lot on his mind, but he won't talk to me about any of it. I ask him if he's all right, and he says he's fine, though I know he isn't."

"And you don't find it strange that he's . . . walking around somewhere . . . in the middle of the night?"

"It's only happened a few times—"

"Andrea, honey." Selene glanced over at Phoebe, then said quietly, "Did it ever occur to you that at that hour of the night he might be doing something other than walking around clearing his head?"

"Like what?"

Selene let go a small gasp of exasperation. "Like—well, like seeing someone."

"Seeing someone?"

"A woman, Andrea. Don't you get it?"

"Where would he find a woman around here?"

"Oh my stars, hon. This isn't Siberia! There are women living on Conesus Lake, you know."

Andrea thought a moment, then shook her head. "I don't know, Selene, I mean, he really hasn't been home all that long."

"Long enough. Oh, honey, don't be naïve."

Her jaw tightening, Andrea looked long and hard at her sister-in-law's reflection. Finally she said, "I don't think I'm being naïve, Selene. I mean, he's either home or at work or at A.A. meetings. I always know where he is."

"Except for at night when he isn't in bed. Really, Andrea, think about it. You know the man's history. If he's cheating on you, it wouldn't be the first time. Oh, honey, don't you wonder?"

She hadn't wondered. Not about another woman. Not until this moment. She felt her stomach drop, pulling her heart along with it. She looked up quickly at Selene's reflection. "What should I do?"

"You've got to confront him. Ask him straight out if he's having an affair."

"And if he is?"

"Well, Andrea, you know what I've said all along. But since you won't listen to me, I've decided I can't help you there. Only you can answer that question."

Hours later, at two-thirty in the morning, Andrea pondered the answer to that question as she gazed at the solitary strip of moonlight falling across what was once again John's empty bed.

CHAPTER FORTY

After a long silence John sensed Pamela rising from the cool ground. He lay on his back with his eyes closed, his right arm thrown over his face like a shield.

"John?"

A moment passed. Then, "Yeah?"

"I have to get going."

He tried to nod, but he wasn't sure he succeeded.

She sounded irritated when she said, "Are you leaving or staying here?"

He didn't know. He couldn't give her an answer.

"John?" She kneeled down beside him and lifted his arm from his face. Reluctantly he opened his eyes. Her features were soft in the moonlight, but her voice held a sharp edge. "What are you doing?"

"I'm not doing anything."

"Aren't you going home?"

"I guess not right now."

"Well, I have to go. Don't fall asleep here. It won't look good if Larry finds you here in the morning."

He wondered briefly whether she was joking, then decided she wasn't.

"I won't fall asleep," he said.

"Why don't you go home?"

"I will in a minute."

She looked at him askew. "What's the matter?"

"Nothing."

A heavy silence settled between them.

At length she said, "I'll see you again, won't I?"

She didn't give him time to answer but leaned over and kissed him. His arm rose up and encircled her. He didn't want her to go. He wished they had never come.

"I'll see you again, Pamela."

"When?"

"Soon."

He knew his answer didn't satisfy her, but she rose anyway, dusting the earth off her bare knees and off the hem of her summer dress.

In another moment he heard her car start up in the parking lot, then turn onto Lake Road. Finally the purr of the engine faded into the distance.

When he couldn't hear the car anymore, he rolled over and pressed his forehead to the ground. He clenched one hand into a fist and pounded the grass. Each stroke kept pace with the repeated cry, "Oh, God. Oh, God. Oh, God."

The night offered no response. John didn't expect one. He exhausted his plea and lay silently on the cool earth beneath the distant moon and the uncaring stars.

He told himself to get up and go home, but he felt too heavy to move. His own body was too much for him.

"Dear God, help me," he whispered.

He waited, but the words fell back on him, drifting out of the sky like flakes of ash. They had nowhere to go. The door to heaven was bolted now, hurled shut and locked and double-locked.

Slam.

Click.

Click.

The moon was swallowed up by a cloud. John lay in the dark among the dead, his moist breath like dew on the brow of the slumbering grass.

CHAPTER FORTY-ONE

"John?"

"Yes, Andrea?"

"You were up late again last night."

John settled his nearly full mug of coffee in the sink. To Andrea, he appeared to be moving in slow motion. "I couldn't sleep," he said.

She waited for him to look at her. He kept his eyes on the mug.

Her heart pounded, stealing the air from her lungs. She tried to steady herself, not wanting to show her fear. "Why can't you sleep?"

He glanced at her, looked away. "What's that?"

She tried to speak more loudly. "I said, why can't you sleep?"

He shook his head. "I don't know. I have a lot to think about, I guess." He glanced at his watch and moved toward the door.

"Where are you going?"

"I'm going down to talk to Larry. I want to catch him before Billy and I leave for work."

She hesitated. She didn't want to sound like she was prying. Finally she asked, "Why do you have to talk to Larry?"

"Well," he shrugged. "I need a sponsor. I'm supposed to have a sponsor for A.A., and I've been putting it off. I thought Larry could help."

"I see."

He shrugged again, pushed open the screen door that led out to the side porch. "I'll be back soon."

She took a step forward. "John?"

"Yeah?"

He was anxious to leave. She could see that. "Are you—"

He waited. His eyes grew small. "What, Andrea?"

"Are you . . . um—"

His hand gripped the door handle more tightly. She looked at his hand, his face, his eyes.

"Are you going to ask Larry to be your sponsor?"

He hesitated, then said, "I think so. Why?"

"No reason. I was just wondering."

They gazed at each other in silence a moment. She didn't need to ask what Selene had told her to ask. He would only deny what she already knew. She had seen that look in his eyes more than once before.

"Well," she said, "I'll tell Billy you'll be back in time to catch the bus."

He nodded.

She watched him walk down the drive and disappear down Lake Road.

She thought it was a bitter thing to keep losing the same man over and over again. There really had to be a final time. She had to find the strength somewhere to make sure this was it.

CHAPTER FORTY-TWO

"So, John, you're troubled." Larry Gunther's face held a pained expression, but his eyes were kind. He appeared to study John intently. "You've done something you don't like to think about."

John dropped his gaze. "Yeah." He tried to laugh, but it came out a defeated sigh. "How'd you guess?"

"I don't have to guess, my friend. I've been a pastor a long time. I've been human even longer than that."

Larry leaned back in his desk chair and put a finger to his lips thoughtfully. John braced himself, glanced up, looked back down at his clasped hands. He'd shown up unannounced, found Larry alone in his office tediously two-finger typing a sermon on an outdated computer. Pastor Larry had welcomed the interruption.

"Do you want to tell me about it?" Larry asked.

John felt a twinge of nausea at the thought. For a brief moment he was sorry he'd come. He hadn't intended to, didn't know he was going to until he was drinking coffee in the kitchen and Andrea showed up. When he saw her, he knew he had to do something. He didn't know whether Larry would be at the church or not, but he headed down the road anyway, his own sense of shame the shoes that brought him.

Biding his time, John said, "Did you know there are empty liquor bottles scattered around the cemetery?"

Larry nodded, offered a wan smile. "Kids. It adds to the excitement to drink in the backyard of a church."

Rebekah, John realized with a start. This was where she came to party. And this was where he came—

"It keeps the janitor and me busy, gathering them all up and throwing them away," Larry went on. "The town's sanitation workers must think this is quite the happening church."

Larry chuckled quietly and looked at John.

John cleared his throat, clasped his hands together more tightly. He knew Pastor Larry was waiting for a confession of sorts. He had to say something, to explain why he had come. "Listen, Larry, I've—" He felt his throat grow tight again, his eyes well up. That was the last thing he wanted.

"Take your time," Larry said gently.

Drawing in a deep breath, John tried again. "I've cheated on my wife, Larry."

Silence. "I see," he finally said.

"My daughter was right."

"Right about what, John?"

John fidgeted uncomfortably. "I don't know if you know where I've been the past few years."

"Yes. It's all right. Billy told me. He's very proud of you, you know."

John's brow furrowed deeply as he looked up at Larry. "Yeah? For what?"

"He's your son, John. He loves you."

"You can love someone without being proud of him."

"He told me how you came to the Lord in prison."

"Oh." John sniffed sarcastically. "Well, he can stop being proud now. Like I said, my daughter was right."

Larry raised his eyebrows and waited.

"My first night home she said it wouldn't last. She said prison conversions never last."

"And it hasn't?"

"I've tried, Larry. But things were easier in prison than they are out here."

He watched as Larry leaned forward again and rested his arms on his desk. "Did you know," the pastor asked, "that few people believe in sin anymore. Did you know that?"

John shook his head slowly, his eyes narrowing. He wasn't sure what he had come for, but he knew he wasn't looking for a theological discussion.

"People don't like the idea of sin so—poof!" Larry threw his hands in the air to simulate something going up in smoke. "It's gone. We don't have to deal with it."

"Uh-huh," John said dully. "Okay. Well, look, Larry, I've messed up. I've . . ."

"Sinned?"

"Yeah. I guess I have."

"So you believe in sin?"

"Well, sure. I mean, maybe other people don't, but I do. How could I not?"

"And what about forgiveness? You don't think you can be forgiven?"

John looked directly into the pastor's eyes. "I guess I don't know what to think anymore. I'm not out of prison three months, and I've ruined everything. Me, with my big-shot ideas of making a new life, living for God." He shook his head again, ran a hand through his tangled hair. "Well, I can't do it."

"Of course not."

"What's that?"

"I said, of course not."

John stared quizzically at Larry, who was pensively drumming the desk with his fingers. He waited, wondering what was to come. Abruptly Larry silenced his fingers and said, "I think, John, you misunderstand the meaning of grace."

The two men looked at each other. After a long moment, John replied, "That may be, Larry. I'm not a reverend like you. All I know is, once God was with me and now He isn't."

"Are you saying He left?"

"How could He stay?" John shook his head. "I just can't do it, Larry. I can't keep it up, living like that. The alcohol—that's nothing. I don't want it. But the other . . ."

Another heavy silence descended over the room. Larry sat motionless, his eyes piercing. When he seemed quite sure that he had John's attention, he said carefully, " 'Of all man's clotted clay, the dingiest clot.' "

John shifted in the chair. He swallowed the annoyance that threatened to latch on to his next words. "I'm afraid I'm not following you. Is this about the whiskey priest?"

"No, it's about a great poet."

John's knee had started pumping; he laid a hand on it to stifle the piston. "Okay," he said.

"Francis Thompson. Ever hear of him?"

"I don't think so."

"He wrote some of the most beautiful descriptions of God's glory ever written. He's best known for a poem called 'The Hound of Heaven.' "

John shrugged, shook his head.

"It's the story of Thompson's own life, how he tried to outrun God. He spent years running, and during much of that time he was a homeless tramp, addicted to opium, which was the popular drug back in his day. People drank it as laudanum." Larry paused, shrugged. "It was as common as beer and cheaper too."

When Larry didn't go on, John said, "Well, I'm going to assume God caught up with him at some point."

"Oh yes. God has a way of doing that, doesn't He?"

"Uh-huh. So this guy kicked his addiction and went on to become some great writer? Is that what you're trying to say?"

"No, John, that's not what happened. He did stop using for a while. Then he became an occasional user. Finally he became permanently re-addicted. He remained addicted right up to his death at the age of forty-seven or so. He died of what they think was a combination of tuberculosis and laudanum poisoning."

John thought a moment, cleared his throat. "Well, that's not a pretty story, then, is it?"

"No, it isn't."

"I have a feeling you're not finished, though."

"No, I'm not. I have a question for you. Do you think, after all those years of pursuing Francis, God just up and left him because the man messed up?"

John thought a moment. "Maybe not. I don't know."

Larry shook his head. "I believe God stayed with him, inspired him, used him even. A dozen years ago, I was a whiskey priest. I'd lost my church, lost my livelihood, very nearly lost my family. While I was in rehab, I came across this book." He reached for a paperback book that lay on his desk, just beyond his right hand. "That was the first time I read this poem. Listen to these lines, John."

Larry opened the book to a page marked with a

scrap of paper. He looked up at John, back at the page, and began to read.

"And human love needs human meriting:
How hast thou merited—
Of all man's clotted clay the dingiest clot?
Alack, thou knowest not
How little worthy of any love thou art!
Whom wilt thou find to love ignoble thee
Save Me, save only Me?"

John's jaw tightened. He didn't speak.

"When I read those lines, I understood two things. First, like Francis, I knew I was about the dingiest clot of clay ever to sprout legs and walk the earth." He paused and smiled at John. "And second, I knew for the first time that God loved me."

John looked up sharply. "But you were a pastor, Larry."

"You'd be surprised what pastors don't know."

"Well, if you were preaching sermons and you didn't even know God loved you, what did you know?"

"Apparently not much. Certainly not the one essential thing, the heart of the Gospel. It was something Francis came to know, something that he came to experience—the paradox of grace."

John nodded, though he wasn't sure he fully understood.

Larry leaned forward again, held John's eye. "Now listen to me, John. Here's the paradox. We can fully embrace God's love only when we recognize how completely unworthy of it we are."

John sat in an uneasy silence, thinking about what Larry had just said. He wanted to take it in, but it seemed to hover on the far side of an impenetrable glass. At length he said, "You ever struggle, Larry?"

"I'm struggling right now, friend. I'd give just about anything for a drink. It's been twelve years since I had one, and the urge is still there."

John rubbed at his forehead. "With me, like I said, it's not the drink. It's . . . listen, Larry, you're married, right?"

"More than thirty years."

"You still love your wife?"

"She stayed with me even when I put her through every sort of misery imaginable. How could I not love her?"

John nodded, took a deep breath. "This . . . this woman, I'm thinking maybe I could make a life with her someday. It could be a good life—"

"But she's not your wife."

"No, but—"

"But she's beautiful, and she makes you happy."

John looked at the floor. "Yeah." He nodded. "She's beautiful. And when I'm with her—yes, I'm happy."

Larry leaned forward, held John's gaze. "Listen, John, let me tell you something. Not everything that's beautiful is good. Take it from someone who knows."

"But—"

"You'd be a fool to give up everything you have at home."

"Yeah. I know that, but . . ."

"What is it, John?"

"Andrea and I, we're just sort of—" he stopped, searching for the word—"roommates, I guess."

"Roommates?"

"Yeah."

"So whose idea was that?"

"Well, I don't think it was anybody's idea. It just sort of happened."

"Things like that don't just happen."

"No? Well, I don't know how to explain it, then."

"John, do you love your wife?"

Pause. "She's a good woman, Larry. . . ."

"But do you love her?"

John didn't answer.

"You know, John, you don't have to be in love with your wife to love her."

"I guess I'm not following."

"What do you share in common? What interests her? What makes her happy? Do you know?"

John thought a moment, shrugged. "I guess I don't know."

"Uh-huh. So you think she's not worth knowing."

"No, I . . ." John stopped, dropped his defenses. Larry was right and John knew it.

"There's one thing you need to understand," Larry said. "We love because God first loved us, even in the face of all our unloveliness." He paused. He seemed to want to give John time to think about that. Then he said, "Go home and love your wife, John."

"I'm afraid I can't find the strength in myself to do that, Larry."

Pastor Larry leaned forward, smiling tenderly. "That's good, my friend," he said. "Now we're getting somewhere."

CHAPTER FORTY-THREE

Billy stepped through the kitchen to the break room at the back of the restaurant. "Dad?"

"Huh!"

Billy bit back a laugh when his dad jumped. "Sorry, Dad. I didn't mean to scare you."

"That's all right, Billy."

"What are you doing?"

"Just reading the paper."

"It looked like you were asleep."

"Oh. Well, I might have dozed off. What time is it?"

"That's what I came to tell you. Uncle Owen says it's time for you to go back to work."

When his father looked up quickly at the clock, Billy thought he heard him swear under his breath.

"Don't worry, Dad," Billy said, "there's hardly anybody out there eating right now. I checked your tables. You're okay for now."

His father nodded, folded up the paper. "Thanks, Billy."

"You tired, Dad?"

"Yeah, I guess I am."

"You need more sleep."

"Yeah. I guess so."

Billy fidgeted. Needing a moment to think, he started tying knots into the strings of his apron. "Something bothering you, Dad?" he asked.

His father gave him a weary smile. "No. Nothing, really."

"You're looking in the paper for another job, aren't you?"

"Well, I don't really expect to find anything right now. But someday I'll want to move on."

"Listen, Dad, if it's money, I'll work more here. I'll give you half my paycheck."

Dad shook his head. "I appreciate that, son. More than I can say. But I don't want you to do that."

"Well, okay. If you change your mind, let me know."

His father tried to smile again, then pushed the chair back from the table and stood.

"Dad?"

"Yes, Billy?"

Billy looked at his apron strings, then worked at untying the knots. "There's something else, isn't there?" he asked. "Something wrong?"

"No, I—"

"I'm a grown-up now, Dad. I'm not a kid. I want to help."

His father looked at him a moment, then came and put a hand on his shoulder. "The best thing you can do for me is just go on being who you are."

"But, Dad," Billy protested, "that isn't much."

"No, Billy," Dad said. "It's everything. I'm proud of you, son."

Billy smiled. "I'm proud of you too, Dad."

His father squeezed his shoulder, glanced at the clock again, walked off toward the kitchen.

Billy hoped he had made his father feel better. But something about the look on his face when he turned away left Billy wondering.

CHAPTER FORTY-FOUR

"I don't get it, Lena," Rebekah said. "What's with you, anyway? I haven't seen you this mad since Jason Holloway called you a Satan worshiper over the school's PA system."

Lena scowled even as her jaw worked and her cheeks bulged with popcorn. The two girls sat on a padded bench in the theater lobby, waiting for David and Jim to meet them for the Saturday afternoon matinee.

"I mean, listen," Rebekah went on, "the guys are actually spending some money on us, like this is a real date or something. It's a red-letter day. You should be happy."

Huffing loudly, Lena said, "It's not our guys I'm mad at. At least not today."

"So, what? I mean, I was kind of looking forward to this afternoon, you know, and here you're acting like—"

"Listen, Beka, this is serious."

"Well, it might help if you tell me what it is."

Lena's face grew pinched as her eyes narrowed. "It's that guy."

"What guy?"

"The guy my mom's seeing."

"Who is he?"

"I don't know."

"What do you mean you don't know?"

"I haven't met him."

"You haven't?"

Lena shook her head. She chewed on another handful of popcorn, took a long drink of her Diet Mountain Dew.

"Has your mom told you anything about him?"

"She hasn't said a word."

"She hasn't told you she's seeing someone?"

"I asked her flat out, and she denied it."

"Why would she do that?"

"He's probably married."

"Oh, good grief, Lena. He probably isn't even there. I mean, you haven't seen him, and your mom says she's not seeing anyone, so why are you so convinced she is?"

"Because she's acting like a crazed teeny-bopper, the way she always acts when she's seeing someone."

"Maybe she's just happy."

"What about?"

"Well, I don't know. Whatever grown-ups get happy about."

"She's only happy when there's a man in her life."

With a long sigh Rebekah relented. "Okay, so what if there is? Is that so bad?"

"I don't like it."

"You know, sometimes I think you're really warped. I mean, who wouldn't want her own mother to be happy?"

Lena looked directly at Rebekah. "He's just using her like all the other men."

With a lift of her brows, Rebekah countered, "Well, I don't know how you can say that when you haven't even met him."

"That's the thing, Beka. Don't you get it? She doesn't bring him home and introduce him to me. She sneaks around behind my back."

Rebekah laughed out loud at that. "You sound

283

like you're the mother and she's the daughter. She *is* an adult, you know. She can do what she wants."

Her friend shook her head sharply. "She doesn't know how to take care of herself. She lets herself be used."

"I don't know, Lena. I mean, really, I think it just comes down to you wanting your mom all to yourself."

"That's not true."

"Yes it is. Every time she dates someone, you get mad."

"I wouldn't get mad if she dated someone decent."

"And how do you know this guy—if he's really there—isn't decent?"

"I just know, is all. And I've got to do something about it."

"Yeah? Like what?"

"Get rid of him. The way I got rid of the others."

"How?"

Lena paused at that, then turned fully to Rebekah. "Cast a spell with me, Beka," she pleaded.

"You're crazy."

"Come on. It's—"

"Listen, 'Do no harm,' remember?"

"I'm not doing any harm. I'm taking care of my mother."

"And don't forget the Rule of Three. Whatever energy you throw out comes back at you times three."

"You don't have to quote the rules to me, Beka. I'm the one who taught you everything you know."

"Yeah, and maybe you still have some learning to do yourself. Aunt Jo said she doesn't want you casting any spells until you're ready."

"I'm more ready than she thinks. I know what I'm doing. So are you with me or not?"

Rebekah hesitated. She bided her time by gazing across the theater lobby at the ticket window. No sign of the guys. Her jaw tightened in annoyance.

She was still trying to think of an answer when Lena said quietly, "You know, Beka, I thought you were my friend."

Turning back angrily, Rebekah said, "Listen, Lena, don't pull that one on me. Just because I don't want to throw some sort of hex on this guy doesn't mean I'm not your friend."

"I'm not throwing a hex on anybody. You're looking at it all wrong. I just want to put a wall of protection around my mom, to keep the wrong people away. That's all. Nothing bad."

"Well, don't you think you ought to at least meet this guy first? I mean, who knows? You might like him."

"I don't need to meet him to know I don't like him."

"Now that's just about the dumbest thing I ever heard. Honest, Lena, sometimes I think you've got a screw loose somewhere."

"Why? Because I want to take care of my mom?"

"No. Because you think she needs taking care of."

"You don't know my mother."

Rebekah shrugged. "I know her well enough to think she's not crazy like you are."

"Thanks a lot, Beka."

"Hey, look. There's the guys! It's about time they got here." Rebekah waved, trying to catch David's attention. He was pulling dollar bills out of his wallet and didn't notice. She started to rise, but Lena grabbed her elbow and pulled her back down.

"Listen, Beka, help me, won't you?"

Rebekah wiggled her elbow out of her friend's grip. "All right, all right, whatever. Though I really don't think your mother needs your help."

Lena's whole body relaxed as she smiled. "Thanks, Beka. I knew you wouldn't let me down."

"Whatever," Rebekah answered. She tried to stand up again, and this time succeeded. "Come on, let's meet the guys."

Chapter Forty-five

*The movie—a comedy—*and supper at a nearby bistro put Lena in a better mood, and afterward Rebekah stayed the night with her, half hoping that by morning she'd have forgotten about the whole spell thing. Thoughts of Jessica Faulkner still bothered her, and Rebekah wasn't sure how much deeper she wanted to go with the Craft.

Lena's good mood didn't last the night, though, and she woke up with the words "Let's do it" on her lips.

Rebekah knew exactly what she meant. She thought briefly of arguing but knew it was useless. With a tired shrug of her shoulders and the suggestion, "Let's at least eat breakfast first," she gave in.

Now the two girls sat cross-legged on the floor while Lena arranged candles, herbs, holy water, and crystals on the cedar chest she used as an altar. It sat right out in the middle of her room, not in the closet like Rebekah's altar at home. Lena's mother knew what it was, of course. After all, Aunt Jo was her mother's sister. Lena's mother didn't practice the Craft herself but didn't care if Lena did. *"Whatever works; whatever makes you happy."* That's what Lena's mother said, though usually with a sigh and a wave of her hand.

Whatever, Rebekah thought. That left a person with a whole universe full of choices. Maybe everything worked; maybe nothing worked. Maybe it took a whole lifetime to find out what made a person happy. Maybe some people never found it, no matter how many times they rummaged through the huge cosmic grab bag of possibilities. Rebekah didn't want to be one of those people. She hoped she could reach in the bag and pull out the one thing that worked for her, the one thing that could always make her happy.

The Craft was what made Lena happy, but Rebekah thought she was in it for all the wrong reasons. She wasn't like Aunt Jo, who really did want to do good, who really did want to be at peace with herself and the world. Lena's only goal was to use her powers and energy to get what she wanted for herself.

"Okay, I think we're almost ready," Lena said. She read silently a moment from a spiral notebook on her lap. When she finished, she shut the book and laid it beside her on the floor.

Rebekah eyed the cover. Written there in large letters were the words "Property of Lena Barrett. Keep out." As if anyone cared to read it. Even her own mother wasn't interested in Lena's Book of Shadows. Even as they were about to call on the powers of the universe on her behalf, the woman was downstairs drinking coffee, unconcerned about the two of them and what they might be doing to amuse themselves on a Sunday morning. She had stumbled into the kitchen a half hour earlier, just as the girls were rummaging through the spice rack, looking for basil and rosemary. She was still in her robe, her hair was a mess, and her skin was pasty and drawn. She moved around wide-eyed, as though trying to see without glasses, and she didn't bother to respond when Rebekah said hello to her. Instead, she poured herself a cup of black coffee, set it before her on the kitchen table, and sat staring into it like the thing was a crystal ball instead of a steaming cup of caffeine. Rebekah knew a hangover when she saw one. So where was the giddy teenager Lena had been complaining about, the one they were supposed to be saving from herself on the grounds that she was too happy? Lena's mother was no picture of love-induced happiness, or any kind of happiness, as far as Rebekah was concerned.

"Now, this is the spell you did before, right?" she asked her friend.

Lena nodded. "Yeah."

"And what is it?"

"It's a combination of stuff. I made it up."

"But what's it do?"

"All it does is put up a wall of protection around Mom. And it keeps the guys from coming back. That's it."

"And you're sure it's not going to hurt anybody?"

An impatient sigh. "Of course I'm sure."

"You still haven't told me what happened to the other guys."

"Like I said, they just stopped coming around."

The two girls looked at each other for a long moment. Finally Rebekah shrugged. "All right."

"Oh, one more thing." Lena dug into the pocket of her jeans and pulled out her cell phone. She placed it at the center of the altar, beside a framed photograph of her mother. "Okay, all I need you to do is concentrate on that picture of Mom. Just keep imagining a huge stone wall going up around her so nothing bad can touch her. All right?"

Rebekah nodded. She stared at the photograph on the altar. The woman was beautiful, far more beautiful than Lena, but wow—what rotten luck. Married and divorced how many times? Couldn't keep a man in spite of her looks. Maybe because she had a daughter who kept interfering. Or maybe because she had about a thousand years of bad karma to work off, which from the way she looked this morning, she still wasn't doing a very good job of.

Rebekah was vaguely aware of the scent of candles, of Lena standing up, taking small steps around her circle, chanting something. Rebekah went on staring at the photograph. Man, she didn't want to end up like this lady. Alone. Unhappy. Drunk much of the time. Lena never talked about that part of their lives, but Rebekah knew the woman was an alcoholic. There was enough booze in the cupboards downstairs to keep several frat houses happy, and the only person around to drink it was Lena's mother. And Lena. And Lena's friends.

Rebekah jumped when Lena suddenly snapped, "Are you concentrating?"

"Yeah, I'm concentrating."

"I need you to send out all your positive energy."

"I know, I know. I'm doing it."

Rebekah wished Lena would hurry up and finish. They hadn't had much breakfast, and she was hoping they could go out and grab some lunch somewhere. *Let's just get rid of this guy and go get something to eat,* she thought. She didn't know who he was, and she didn't much care at this point what the universe did with him, if Lena would just hurry up so they could grab a hamburger and some fries.

Several minutes dragged by. Rebekah felt sleepy. She stifled a yawn. Her stomach growled. She tried to picture a wall going up around Lena's mother, stone by stone, but her mind kept drifting.

Finally Lena said, "Okay, I'm done. That should do it."

"Yeah? You think there's, like, some sort of force shield protecting your mom now? Like a wall of energy or something?"

"Uh-huh. Something like that."

"So what do you think is going to happen to the guy?"

"I think he's going to go away."

"Since you've never seen him, how are you going to know when he's not there?"

Lena squinted in disgust. "Very funny, Beka."

Rebekah laughed. "Listen, I'm starving," she said. "Let's go get something to eat."

"Okay. Where do you want to go?"

"I don't care."

"Your uncle's place?"

Rebekah shook her head. "No, not there."

"Why? Your dad working? You know I want to meet him. I've never met an ex-con before. At least not that I know of."

"You'll meet him someday. No loss if you don't. Anyway, he and Billy don't work on Sundays. Why don't we go to Dairy Queen? We can get some ice cream for dessert."

"Sure, all right." Lena reached for her phone on the altar and started to tuck it back into her pocket.

Rebekah looked at it curiously. "So what's with the phone?"

"Oh, I forgot to tell you. I've got a picture of the guy."

Rebekah looked up sharply. "I thought you said you've never seen him."

"I haven't."

"So how'd you get his picture?"

"I found it on Mom's phone, so I sent it to mine. Want to see what the loser looks like?"

"Sure. I guess."

Lena opened the cell and pushed a few buttons. "This is him," she said dryly. "And now he can kiss himself good-bye."

Rebekah took the phone, turned it until she could see the face of the man they had just cast up to the mercy of the universe. She blinked, frowned, leaned one way and then another to see whether the face would change. But no matter which way she turned the phone, the face was the same.

"What's the matter?" Lena asked. "The battery dead or something? Can't you see it?"

Rebekah let out a small cry then, like a kitten snatched from its mother. She wanted to scream, but the wind had been knocked out of her.

"What's the matter?" Lena asked again. "You look like you're going to throw up. You sick or something? Hey, you'll break the phone, throwing it like that. Beka . . . hey, Beka, wait a minute! What—"

But Rebekah was already making her way down the stairs and through the kitchen where Lena's mother, Mrs. Jarvis, was asleep with her forehead pressed to the table, the fingers of her right hand curled loosely around a bottle of scotch.

CHAPTER FORTY-SIX

As the family pulled up to the cottage after church, John noticed Rebekah's car wasn't there.

"Beka's still not home," he remarked. "Did she say what time she'd be back?"

He looked over at Andrea, who was shifting the Volvo into park. She shook her head. "No telling. She doesn't have to be at work until four o'clock. Other than that, I don't know what her plans are."

"Shouldn't she let us know?"

"She will. She'll call, when she thinks about it. Otherwise, she'll probably show up around three o'clock to shower and get ready to go."

"What do you know about this friend she's with? Lena?"

"She's a nice girl. You'll like her."

"If I ever meet her. Anyway, I want to talk to Rebekah about not driving the car too much until we can have some work done on it. I'm sure it needs a new battery, and we ought to have the fluids changed, maybe have the tires rotated, and—"

Billy interrupted from the backseat, muttering, "Why are we just sitting here? I'm starving."

"You're always starving, Billy," Phoebe chided.

"What's for lunch, Mom?"

"I've got pork chops thawing in the fridge," Andrea said. "I guess I'd better get to work."

All four doors of the sedan opened at once as the family piled out. John stood, stretched. He wished he had enough money in his pocket to suggest they go out to eat. They could eat for free at Laughter's Luncheonette, but he sure didn't want to go there. He wished he could blow fifty dollars taking his family to Denny's or Applebee's, but that was going to have to wait until he was something other than a busboy.

He stepped toward the cottage, thinking about pork chops. Before he was halfway across the drive, Rebekah's car pulled off the road and came to a sudden stop.

"Hey, there's Beka," Billy announced. "She must have heard us talking about lunch!"

John chuckled, but the amusement slid off his face as he watched his daughter get out of the car, slam the door, and stomp toward him. Then, before he could even react, she was pounding his chest with her fists, screaming, "I hate you! I hate you!"

He heard Andrea call out their daughter's name, heard his other children give off puzzled cries, but their voices were drowned by Rebekah's screams and the flailing fists that hammered him again and again. He finally caught her wrists and held on tightly, though he was surprised by her strength as she struggled in his grip.

"Beka, what are you doing?" he demanded.

He searched her face; her mottled skin was

moist with tears. Strands of hair clung to her cheeks. As he tightened his grip, she relaxed her arms but resorted to kicking his shins. He fought the temptation to push her away, to throw her to the ground.

"Stop it, Beka," he yelled. "Stop kicking!"

Then Andrea was there, shaking the girl by the shoulders. "Beka, are you crazy? What are you doing? Stop! Stop it now!"

With that, Rebekah seemed to lose her momentum, like a child's toy winding down. Her chest heaved as she struggled to catch her breath. Her eyes shifted and blinked, then settled on him. Fresh tears streamed down her face.

As their eyes met, a groundswell of love rose up in John for his daughter. The feeling was so intense it left him lightheaded. "Beka, sweetheart—" he began, but she interrupted him.

"Let go of me."

He loosened his grip but didn't let go. She swore at him. "I said, let go."

"Are you done hitting me?"

She looked away.

He let go of her wrists, took one step back.

She turned and ran.

"Beka!" he shouted.

Andrea made a move to go after her, but John laid a hand on her shoulder. "Let me go," he said. "I'm the one she's angry with."

By the time he reached the road, she was

already a good stretch ahead of him. Vaguely aware of the next-door neighbors watching from their back porch, he sprinted after his daughter. He loosened his tie as he ran, fumbled to undo the top button of his shirt so he could breathe easier. The smooth soles of his loafers beat the blacktop but offered little traction over the occasional gravel in the road. Twice he stumbled, but he pushed on, his eyes fixed on the figure in the road ahead of him. He speeded up as he saw the distance between them growing shorter. Finally he came up from behind and threw his arms around her. She struggled, tripped, almost fell over, but John found his own footing and held her up.

"Beka, stop," he said quietly. "Just stop. Please. Settle down."

She squirmed another moment before giving up. The two of them stood there by the side of the road in a twisted embrace, winded, red-faced, defeated. She cried openly.

"If I let you go, will you talk to me?"

She nodded.

He slowly let go. He waited.

Finally, moving slowly, Rebekah turned around to face him. When she spoke, he had to strain to hear. "You're cheating on Mom."

He thought—hoped—he had heard wrong. When he didn't respond, she said it again, louder this time. "You're cheating on Mom."

"What?" He staggered backward, as though he'd been punched in the gut.

"You're having an affair with Mrs. Jarvis—"

"No, I—"

"How could you do it?"

"Beka, I—"

"Don't touch me!"

"Listen to me—"

"I hate you!"

John shut his eyes, nodded. He didn't speak.

"How can you cheat on Mom?" she asked again. "With my best friend's mother?"

He opened his eyes, tried to focus on his daughter's face. "What did you say?"

"Mrs. Jarvis—she's Lena's mother. Lena knew her mom was seeing someone but . . . how could it be you?" The look in Rebekah's eyes spoke of betrayal.

"Rebekah," John said firmly, "who told you this?"

"No one had to tell me. She has your picture on her phone. Lena's mother has your picture on her phone."

John felt his jaw tighten as anger surged through him. She had lied when she said she erased it. His mind worked frantically, looking for a way out, finally spotting a small window he might wiggle himself through. "Well," he said, "yeah, we go to the same meetings and for what-ever reason she took my picture there. That doesn't mean I'm having an affair with the woman."

Rebekah looked at him hard. "But you are, aren't you?"

"Beka," he whispered.

"You're having an affair with her, aren't you?"

His breath left him, and his legs felt weak. "Yes," he admitted. "I'm sorry, Beka. I'm so sorry."

He reached into the pocket of his trousers and felt the handkerchief that Andrea insisted belonged there. He dug it out, looked at it, couldn't help thinking of how it had been cleaned and ironed and neatly folded. That was what brought tears to John's eyes—the thought that, in spite of everything, Andrea had simply gone on cooking his meals, making his bed, folding his handkerchiefs.

He offered the handkerchief to Rebekah. She resisted a moment, sniffed hard, and then gave in. She took it and blew her nose, wiped her eyes. John wiped at his own eyes with the palm of his hand. A minivan approached, slowed down as it passed them, then sped up again.

John nodded toward the church, empty now after the morning service. "Let's go on up to the church, find a place we can talk."

For several minutes they walked in silence, both staring straight ahead. When they reached the church, John tried the front doors and found them locked. They settled on the concrete steps, hard and sun-warmed, though still partially shaded by the trees in the front lot.

While John searched for words, Rebekah said, "You're going to leave us again." It was a statement, not a question.

John took a deep breath, let it out slowly. "No, Beka, no. I'm not going to leave you."

"How can you not, now that you have someone else?"

"Listen, I've tried to end it. I've—"

"Why'd you start, Dad? Why'd you ever see her in the first place?"

"Because I'm human. And I'm weak. And I always seem to end up doing things that hurt people—the people I love."

"You don't love Mom."

John swallowed hard, set his jaw. "Honey, I've tried."

"Yeah, well, I've always known you had to get married because of Billy."

"Yes." He turned to look at his daughter. "That's true."

"Then everything—Billy and me and Phoebe, we're all just a mistake."

"No." He shook his head adamantly. "No, you were never a mistake. Never. You three—you were the best things I ever had. Especially you, Beka. When you came along, you brought something really good into my life for the first time."

She tilted her head back and looked up at the sky. One tear escaped the corner of her eye and rolled down her temple. She brushed it away. "Why didn't you just divorce Mom a long time ago, let her find someone else?"

"I offered, Beka. When I was in prison, I told her she should file for divorce, make a new life for herself. She didn't want to do it."

"She wanted to stay with you?"

"Believe it or not, yeah, she did."

"And then you came home and found someone else."

He drew in a sharp breath. "Look, Beka—"

"Do you love her?"

"Pamela? Lena's mom?"

Rebekah nodded.

"Yes," he said. Then, "No." Then, "Honey, I just don't know." Finally he said quietly, "You know what, Beka? I don't even know who she is."

For a long while neither spoke. John could hear the activity on the lake—the roar of outboard motors, laughter, the lilting cry of gulls. At length he said, "Listen, honey, I'm going to break it off."

"Forget it, Dad. It doesn't matter."

"It does matter. I'm going to break it off. I mean it. You're more important to me than she is."

Rebekah looked at him doubtfully. "Really?"

"Yes."

"We can never be like a real family, Dad."

"We can try. We have to try, Beka. It's what I want."

"Are you sure, or are you just saying that?"

"I'm sure. I've made a mess of things, but I want to try again. If that's what you want."

Rebekah turned away. John thought she might never answer, but she finally turned back and said, "Yeah, it's what I want. I don't want you and Mom to get divorced."

"We won't, honey."

"You promise?"

"I promise."

"You're going to break it off with Mrs. Jarvis?"

"Yes, Beka. I will. I promise."

She nodded. "I hope Mom never finds out about her."

"You know, Beka, your mother probably already knows."

"How?"

John sighed deeply. "Because she knows me. She knows who I am. But that's not the person I want to be anymore."

"Well, if you want to know what I think, I'm not so sure people can change. Not really. I mean, we are what we are."

"No. I thought that way once, but I think now— well, maybe we can change by letting ourselves be changed."

"Yeah? By what?"

"I don't know near enough about it, but it's

something called grace. I hear it can change you, if you let it. I'm going to hope I can let it."

"If you're talking about God, I'm not so sure about all that stuff."

"I know, honey. I know just how you feel. There was a time when it made no sense to me at all, and much of the time even now it doesn't make a whole lot of sense. But then again, there are moments when I get the feeling everything's all right, even in spite of how things look. I'm hanging my hat on those moments, trusting that's God telling me He's there."

She lifted her chin in a small nod. "So what are you going to do, Dad?"

"Like I said, I'm going to put an end to things . . . tell her it's over. And then I'll have to add it to the list of things I hope your mom will forgive me for."

Rebekah looked thoughtful. "I bet that's a pretty long list."

John smiled sadly, nodded. "You got that right, honey. From where I'm sitting I can hardly see the end of it." Several seconds passed before he added, "And, honey, I've got to ask you to forgive me too. I hope you will."

Her eyes grew small as she shrugged. "I'm not sure I'm ready to do that."

"Fair enough. Take your time. I'm willing to wait."

She looked at him, seemed to be studying him.

He returned her gaze, hoping she found in his face what she was looking for.

Then she said, "I think I want to go home now."

"All right." He stood, held out a hand to help her up. She accepted it, but as soon as she was standing, she pulled her hand away.

"I do love you, Beka," he said. "I want you to know that."

She looked away. "I know," she said, her voice small.

He hoped she would say she loved him back, but she didn't. He was going to have to wait for that too. For however long it took, he was willing to wait.

CHAPTER FORTY-SEVEN

She would have to get a lawyer, of course. Owen could recommend a good one. He'd already given her several names, years ago when John first went off to prison. She'd thrown the list away. She'd had no intention of filing for divorce.

Andrea leaned back in the overstuffed chair in the bedroom and closed the book on her lap. She'd read the same paragraph over and over, and she still didn't know what it was about. There would be no escaping into these pages tonight. She had too much on her mind, too many decisions to make.

She turned to the window and saw her own face reflected in the glass. How tired she looked, and faded. Life was passing, moving inexorably forward. Her children were growing up, and she was growing old. There was a time once when she thought life owed her something, but that was long ago.

She would let John go now. It would be best. For him. Maybe for her. She looked back across the years that he had been gone and realized, with a comforting sense of satisfaction, that she had survived. She would manage alone again, and without the hope of his ever coming back, it would be easier.

Andrea heard footsteps on the stairs and turned to see who it was. Billy paused halfway up and peered at her through the railing. "Hi, Mom," he said. "Is it okay if I come up?"

She smiled at her son. "Of course, Billy. What's the matter? Are you hungry?"

He shook his head as he moved up the stairs and across the room. "Naw, I'm not hungry. I just wanted to ask you something."

"All right."

He sat down on his father's bed and rested his chin in his hand. Then he said, "How come Beka was so mad this afternoon, Mom?"

"Well, I don't know, really. She's a teenager. She's full of emotion."

"Well, I'm a teenager too, but I don't act like

that. She's really mad at something. But I guess you don't want to tell me."

"It isn't that I don't want to tell you, Billy. It's just that—I honestly don't know. Dad wouldn't tell me what they talked about. He just said they had worked it out and everything was okay." She lifted her shoulders in a shrug. "So I didn't press it."

Billy looked thoughtful. He narrowed his eyes and drummed his fingers on his cheek. Andrea waited, giving him time to think. Finally he said, "I worry about Beka, Mom."

"I know, Billy. I do too."

"I wish . . . I wish I could . . . I'd like to help Beka feel better."

"That's awfully good of you, son. I wish I could make Beka happy too, but we have to let her work out some things on her own. That's how it is when you're growing up."

"Do you think when Beka's finished growing up she'll be happy?"

Andrea drew in a deep breath. "Let's hope she'll be happy then, Billy. Some people are when they get past the teen years. You know, they find themselves, they settle down and marry. . . ." Her voice trailed off as her thoughts wandered. But she pulled herself back and tried to smile at Billy. She hoped her unfinished answer had somehow satisfied him.

He was studying her intently. "Mom?" he asked.

"Yes?"

"Aren't you happy?"

"Oh! Well . . . ." She blinked several times, folded her hands together over the book in her lap. With false cheer, she said, "I have you, don't I?"

"Well, yeah." He spread his arms. "Here I am."

"Then I'm happy."

Billy smiled at that. But then he looked serious again and asked, "Do you think everyone in the family will ever be happy at the same time?"

Andrea hesitated. She reached out and patted Billy's hand. "Of course, Billy. Someday we'll all be happy at the same time."

Billy smiled again broadly. "That will be a good day, won't it, Mom?"

"Yes, Billy." She nodded. "That will be a very good day."

Billy stood then, bent over her, kissed her cheek.

"Good night, Mom."

"Good night, dear."

"Have sweet dreams."

"I'll dream about you, Billy, and what a nice young man you've grown up to be."

He grinned modestly, then brightened. "Oh, and sleep tight, don't let the bedbugs bite!"

"Okay." She smiled at him. "You too, son."

Andrea followed Billy with her eyes as he

stepped across the room and disappeared down the stairs.

As long as a part of him was still a child, she thought, he should still believe in happy endings.

CHAPTER FORTY-EIGHT

At the north end of the lake, the town of Conesus had long ago carved out a public park complete with swimming beach, picnic tables, grills, a playground, and numerous benches. The park was always busy on summer days, filled mostly with out-of-towners who came to the lake for sport but didn't own a cottage there. On any given afternoon, the beach might be cluttered with sun-bathers, so those headed out to swim had to walk gingerly, winding their way along paths created by the haphazard tangle of towels. On many occasions the picnic tables were full, and people resorted to spreading blankets on the ground like gypsies on the outskirts of a town. By evening, though, when dusk came, the crowds began to thin, and by nightfall the last cars were generally pulling out of the lot.

When John reached the park after eight o'clock on that final Monday night in August, a few stragglers remained—mostly couples, a family or two, one loner with long hair sitting cross-legged on the ground, strumming a guitar. John had walked four miles to get there, and after scanning the park, he thought he might have made the trip in vain.

But then he saw her. She was seated on the bench closest to the water, looking out. She wore a colorful silk scarf that was tied at the nape of her neck, and though the sun was setting, she hadn't yet removed her dark glasses. The frames were large, seemed to hide half her face. Perhaps that was what she wanted.

She didn't turn to look at him when, walking up beside her, he said, "Thank you for coming, Pamela."

She nodded, almost imperceptibly, but didn't speak.

"Well, I . . . I think you need to know that our daughters are friends."

"Yes," she said. "I know."

"And they know about . . . us. They saw the photo on your phone."

"You were right, John. I was a fool. I should have erased it."

"Well, I—"

"Lena and Beka aren't speaking to each other. They're very angry."

"Oh? Beka didn't tell me. I'm sorry to hear that."

"Don't worry. They'll make up eventually. They're more angry with me and you than they are with each other. Lena has made me very aware of her disapproval."

"I see."

She turned at last to look at him. He couldn't see her eyes behind the glasses. "You don't have to say what you came to say, John. In fact, I'd rather you didn't." Her mouth was small, her face drawn. She turned away again. "I have it memorized, every word by heart—"

"Pamela—"

"No, John. Please don't say it." He took a step toward her. "And please don't sit down. I couldn't bear it."

He waited, listened to the night sounds, the gulls, the young man strumming the guitar. "We can't keep going," he said at length.

"So we are at the end of the line."

"Yes."

A child laughed, incongruously. A car door slammed, and an engine started up. The intrusion of other lives sharpened the moment, nettling him. He tried to think of what to say next, but she spoke first.

"It's a shame, John. And there's really . . . there's no hope?"

"No. I'm sorry, Pamela."

"Are you? Sorry, I mean."

"Yes. God knows I wish . . . I don't want to hurt you."

"And yet you have chosen to leave, like all the rest."

Her words filled him with guilt, a sense that it

was wrong to be like all the rest. He should be different because he had a duty to her, some aberrant duty to stay and finish what he had begun. For a fraction of a second, he wondered whether he should reconsider. They could carve out some kind of a life, make each other happy. . . .

He drew back sharply then, rubbed his forehead with the palm of an open hand.

She was beautiful, and he wanted her, but there was something beyond all feeling and all appearances that he wanted more.

"Pamela, I'm sorry," he said again.

"Never mind. I don't need your apologies."

"I never should have—"

"Just go, John. Just leave me alone."

"Pamela, I want to ask you to forgive me."

He waited. He felt strangely light, as though he might fall apart before she answered.

When she spoke, her voice was low and even. "That, John, is one thing I will never do."

The words were a kick to the heart, but he gathered his strength, pulled himself together. "I think it best," he said, "that we try not to see each other at all. I'll find another A.A. meeting to attend."

"Don't bother. I'll leave. What's the use in all of it, anyway?"

"Well . . ."

She turned to look at him again. Her face was slowly sinking into the dark veil of night. "You're going back to your wife."

"Yes."

He took one step backward.

"You know, John, you don't realize what you are giving up. I could have loved you more than anyone has ever loved you."

John thought about that, shook his head. "No. I don't think so, Pamela."

He turned away then and started the long walk home in the dark.

CHAPTER FORTY-NINE

Rebekah rolled the car to a stop among a grove of trees on the Castle grounds. After turning off the engine, she stayed in the driver's seat, clutching the wheel. She looked up at the imposing stone structure. Most of its windows were boarded over, and the door facing the lake was a bulletin board for No Trespassing signs.

She almost hadn't come, probably wouldn't have come if she and Lena hadn't made up after the worst fight of their friendship. The explosion had happened on Sunday night, and after that Lena hadn't spoken to her for four days. But they'd made up on Friday, and now it was Saturday and time for the annual, unofficial big-bash-before-school-begins at the Castle.

Rebekah wondered whether Lena would go back to being mad at her once the party was over. After all, their fight had been over the man Lena's mom was seeing. Rebekah had to tell her who he was. She figured someday Lena was going to meet her dad, and then she'd know the truth anyway.

So she spilled the man's identity when Lena came to see her Sunday night at the amusement park. Rebekah was doling out prizes in the arcade when she admitted her reason for running out on Lena after they'd cast the spell that morning. As soon as she spoke, she realized she might have chosen a better place and time to make the confession to her friend.

At first there was an uncomfortably long silence, broken only when Lena's fist came down hard on top of the display case. A two-foot crack in the glass led to a volley of words and threats between the girls, which led to several kids screaming for their mothers, which eventually led to a security guard coming to break up the fight. Lena was escorted out of the park with the warning not to show her face there anytime soon.

That was Rebekah's last night on the job. She was given her final paycheck with the invitation not to reapply for employment the following summer.

It had not been a good day. Rebekah lost her job and her best friend and any respect she might have had for her father all in the span of twelve hours. For four days she simmered in a lonely pity party, made worse by the fact that even David was out of town for the week. The only break came on Tuesday afternoon when her father appeared in her bedroom doorway, leaned wearily against the doorframe, and said, "It's over." That was all he said, and then he was gone. For several minutes she felt triumphant, except she couldn't erase the image of her dad standing there looking defeated, as if he'd just been through some giant battle of his own. And who knew but maybe he had. And if so, he'd done it at least partly for her. That made her cry again.

On Friday Lena called and said they might as well make up. They couldn't blame each other for what their parents had done. Lena chalked it up to some sort of bad karma that had brought her mother together with Rebekah's father, but as long as those two had ended it, that was what mattered. "If Mom's ever going to end up in a good relationship," Lena said, "she's got to stop dating married men."

Rebekah was worried about the spell. "Can you undo it?" she'd asked.

Lena assured her it didn't need undoing since Rebekah's father had already dumped her mother. Together, Rebekah and Lena swore eternal silence about their parents' affair. If it ever blossomed on Conesus Lake's grapevine, it wouldn't be because of them.

Now dusk was just giving way to darkness as several more cars pulled up to the Castle. It was time for the blowout to begin.

All in all, though she'd looked forward to this since last year's party, Rebekah felt suddenly certain that she didn't want to be here now.

"Daddy, you're cheating!" Phoebe wailed.

John studied the Chinese checkers board on the kitchen table in front of him. "What'd I do?" he asked.

"You can't move your marble that way."

"I can't?"

"No, silly. Once you've made it home, you can't move back out again!"

"Oh, okay." John moved the offending marble back to where it was. "Well, you have to cut me some slack, Phoeb. I haven't played this game in decades."

"But everyone knows that, Daddy!"

"Well, I guess I'm not everyone. So let's see. How about if I move this one here instead. Is that better?"

Phoebe nodded. She pushed one of her own marbles forward with an index finger. John loved the child's hands, plump and dimpled. His child. He smiled at Phoebe and was lifting his hand to take a turn when he heard the Volvo turn off Lake Road. He looked out the window and saw the car limping down the drive.

"Uh-oh," he said.

"What's the matter, Daddy?"

John didn't answer. He watched the kitchen door expectantly, caught Andrea's look of frustration as soon as she came in. She dropped a small paper sack on the kitchen counter.

"Well, John," she said, "you won't believe it."

"I believe it."

"The tire's flat again."

"So I saw. How far did you drive with it like that? You can ruin the rim that way, you know."

"Everything was fine when I left the drugstore, but then I felt the bumping half a minute ago. The tire must have been leaking air as I went. I was almost home so I figured I'd just come on."

John sighed. "And you don't have a spare, right?"

Andrea shook her head. "No. There wasn't a spare in the car when Owen gave it to me."

"I wonder what he did with it."

"I have no idea."

"Well . . ." John thought a moment. "I suppose we need a whole new set of tires, just to be on the safe side."

"Probably so, I'm afraid."

"We'll just have to bite the bullet and do it. Do we have enough in savings to cover it, or do we have to put it on credit?"

"We'll have to put it on credit, I guess."

"All right. We'll have it towed tomorrow. While

we're getting the tires, we'll look into a new battery for Beka's car."

"When it rains, it pours," Andrea said.

"At least the toilet hasn't been clogged for a whole week," Phoebe piped up.

"We can be thankful for small blessings," John answered.

"Did Beka say what time she'd be home after the movie?" Andrea asked.

"Last I heard," John said, "she was going to spend the night at Lena's."

"I thought those two had a falling out."

John dropped his gaze and pretended to study the checkerboard. "Apparently they patched it up," he said. "You know how kids are."

"Where's Billy? I've got the nasal spray he wanted."

"Lying on his bed, I think."

"All right. I'll see to him, and then I'm going to go to bed myself pretty soon. It's been a long day."

"You go ahead. I'll take care of Phoebe."

"She should have her teeth brushed and be in bed by nine."

John glanced at the kitchen clock. "That gives me half an hour to beat her at Chinese checkers."

"Aw, Daddy! I can beat you with my eyes shut!"

"Oh yeah?"

"Yeah!"

317

"Well, then." John leaned over the checker-board, chuckling. "Bring it on."

Rebekah reached for the flashlight in the passenger seat but decided there was just enough light left for her to see the walkway to the Castle door. If she took the flashlight in with her, she'd most likely come out without it in the morning. Anyway, once she was inside, light shouldn't be a problem. Not if the usual lantern committee had done their job.

She opened the car door and swung her feet out to the ground; still, she hesitated. Morning seemed like a long way off. And the party wasn't officially over until the kids dragged themselves outside to watch the sun come up over the lake. She and Lena had made it last year—just barely—after a night of drinking. Sometime after daybreak Aunt Jo had come and peeled the two of them off the ground, taking them back to her place to sleep it off. Hours later, when they were sipping some sort of mixture of herbal tea at the kitchen table, Aunt Jo told them she admired their ode to nature, but they might have actually enjoyed the sunrise if they hadn't been simultaneously throwing up. "You're going to turn into your mother," Aunt Jo warned Lena. Rebekah remembered that now.

She stood up, shut the door, was about to step forward when a car approached and caught her in its headlights. She was momentarily blinded until the lights were turned off and the engine cut. The driver tapped playfully on the horn. Rebekah recognized the aging Chevy as Lena's.

Her friend got out and waved. Bypassing any other greeting, Lena said, "Hey, Bek, give me a hand, will you?"

She opened the car's hatchback to reveal a cardboard box filled with a variety of bottles. Contributing to any party was always easy for Lena.

"Come on," Lena said. "Let's get the show on the road."

John sat on the edge of the bed and tucked the sheet up around Phoebe's chin. He gently pushed the hair off her forehead and out of her eyes. "You're one mean checkers machine," he said, laughing softly.

"I told you I could beat you, Daddy."

"Yes, you did. Now it's time for you to shut those pretty eyes and go to sleep."

She sighed, her small chest rising and falling beneath the cool sheet. "All right. But can we play some more tomorrow?"

"You bet, honey."

"I'll beat you again."

"I'm sure you will. Now listen, go to sleep. And do you think you can stay here in your own bed all night?"

She moved her head slowly from side to side on the pillow.

"Does that mean no?" he asked.

"I like it in Billy's room," she answered. "And now it's extra nice because he has the nightlight."

"We can get you your own nightlight if that's what you need."

"It wouldn't be the same."

"Why not?"

"It wouldn't be Billy's."

He frowned, trying to understand her six-year-old logic. "Well, anyway, it's time to go to sleep now."

"But, Daddy, I haven't said my prayers."

"Oh. Okay, go ahead."

John shut his eyes and held her hand and listened as she recited her "Now I Lay Me" prayer. When she said amen, he echoed the word.

Leaning over to kiss her forehead, he said, "Good night, honey."

"Good night, Daddy." She shut her eyes, but just as quickly opened them again. "Daddy?"

"Yes, sweetheart?"

"Can you sing me a song to help me fall asleep?"

"Oh, well, I'm not much of a singer, but . . ."

"You can sing anything you want, Daddy, as long as it's a happy song."

"Hmm . . . all right."

He reached over and switched off the lamp on the bedside table. The bedroom door was open just enough to let in a swath of light from the kitchen. John gazed down at his daughter's serene young face, framed by blond ringlets. He was captured by the sense that she was a gift he didn't deserve, but one that he'd been given anyway.

He studied her for so long she finally asked, "What are you looking at, Daddy?"

"The face of an angel, I think."

She giggled. "Aren't you going to sing something?"

"I'm thinking," he replied. "I don't know very many songs, I'm afraid."

"You can make something up if you want. That's what Billy does sometimes."

"Well, I'm probably not as talented as Billy. So let's see. I guess you're too old for 'Rock-a-bye Baby'?"

She nodded.

"That's all right," he said. "I don't know all the words anyway."

He cocked his head, looked up toward the ceiling. His mind appeared a wasteland when it came to songs until he remembered what they always sang in prison at the end of chapel services.

"Okay," he said, "I think I've got one."

She shut her eyes and waited.

He shifted on the bed, cleared his throat quietly.

Then in a halting voice he sang, " 'Amazing grace, how sweet the sound, that saved a wretch like me. . . .' "

"Just grab a couple of bottles," Lena said. "I'll get some guy to help me with the rest."

Rebekah pulled a pint of scotch and another of vodka out of the box. Both bottles were half empty. "So," she said, "you don't think your mom will notice these are missing?"

Lena shrugged her bare shoulders. She wore a strapless tube top and a pair of black shorts, and even in the twilight Rebekah could see that her face was heavily made-up. Her eyes were dark with liner, and her mouth was as moist and plump as an overripe plum. "Mom isn't noticing much of anything right now."

Rebekah glanced away, shifting her weight from one foot to the other. "I'm sorry, Lena."

"She'll get over it. She always does."

"Yeah, but maybe . . ." Rebekah looked at her friend and tried to hold her gaze. "Well, I don't know. Maybe she should talk to somebody, get some sort of help."

"She doesn't need help. She just needs to actually find a decent guy, someone who isn't just out to use her."

Rebekah stiffened. "Listen, Lena, we've already been all through that. What I'm saying is, maybe your mom needs to stop drinking so much."

"And maybe you need to mind your own business," Lena shot back.

For a moment Rebekah was tempted to put the bottles down, get back in her own car, and leave. She told herself it would be easy. She could just go home and tell her parents she wasn't feeling well and had decided not to spend the night at Lena's after all. But before she could make a move, Lena said, "Listen, Beka, I'm sorry. Let's just drop it, okay? Come on." She nodded toward the Castle. "Let's get inside."

The front door had been padlocked once, but that was years ago. After the original lock was jimmied and tossed, no one had ever replaced it. No one knew exactly who owned the Castle now, though the story around Conesus Lake was that a check for the property taxes arrived every year from someplace in New Mexico. Several times during the summer a crew of workers showed up with riding lawnmowers and tree-trimming equipment to take care of the grounds. The hum of the mowers and the buzz of the chainsaw carried easily across the water to the Sheldons' cottage on the other side. Whenever these caretakers came, Rebekah's mother stood on their porch watching and listening. She shook her head at the commotion and wondered aloud why anyone would keep up the lawn while the house itself was simply allowed to fall apart. She said the place ought to be torn down and the property divided up and sold to people who actually wanted to live on the lake. Which was just like a grown-up, Rebekah thought. Leave it to her mother to want to get rid of one of the few places in Conesus that held any interest at all for the teenagers.

At least that's how she'd felt about it last year. This year, when Lena pushed open the front door, Rebekah felt something pull at her nerves, the way a violinist plucks at a string. She didn't want to go inside. Just the creaking of the door alone filled her with dread. But she could hardly back out now.

Just inside the door, on a small table in the generous entryway, a Coleman lantern hissed out a circle of light and gave off the stench of kerosene. Beyond that, about twenty feet away, another lantern glowed, and then another. The girls knew the drill. That path of light led the way to the kitchen, where they'd find the doorway to the party. Rebekah and Lena followed the lanterns through the still-furnished parlor and beyond that, a library with shelves that didn't stop until they reached the ceiling. Arthur P. King, the original owner of the house, had either been well-read or had wanted to look as though he was. The air inside the rooms was damp and heavy and smelled of mold and stagnant water.

The kitchen reeked of something else, something putrid, like an animal had got stuck in the drainpipe and died. Rebekah stepped lightly and shuddered to think of what must live in this so-called Castle. When King Arthur exited the place by drowning, all sorts of animals probably moved in. What was there to stop them? Squirrels, spiders, rats, snakes—they were probably all neighbors somewhere within the walls of this huge place. Why hadn't she thought about that last year? Or maybe she had, briefly—though as the night wore on she had no doubt cared less and less about the wildlife. She had probably cared less and less about anything at all.

Laughter broke through the front door as another group of kids spilled into the entryway. "The party can start now," someone hollered. "We're here!"

"Idiots," Lena whispered.

Another voice called out, "Yeah, we brought the coke."

More laughter. Rebekah sneered. "They brought Coke, and they think they're the life of the party?"

Lena turned to look at her. In the glow of lantern light her face showed disbelief. "They're talking about cocaine, stupid."

"Cocaine?" Rebekah stopped short in the middle of the kitchen. "You think they brought cocaine?"

Lena shrugged. "Who knows. More likely it's crushed aspirin. They probably can't wait to watch the first person snort a line of Excedrin up their nose."

Rebekah grimaced at the thought. "So what if it really is cocaine, and what if this is the year the police finally decide to bust the party?"

"They won't, Beka. They never do. Come on."

"But maybe they will. How do you know they won't?"

"You've never had to deal with the Conesus police, have you?"

"No. Have you?"

"Let's just say they're a bunch of morons who don't know their head from a hole in the ground, and on top of that, they're not above making a little extra money."

"What do you mean? Someone bribed them?"

Before Lena could answer, the coke-carrying crowd of half a dozen guys stumbled into the kitchen. One of them shot the beam of a flashlight directly into Rebekah's eyes. "Hey, girls!" the figure behind the flashlight yelled. "Ready to party?"

"Let's roll," Lena responded, and before she knew it, Rebekah found herself following the crowd down the stairs leading to the spacious underground room known as the Dungeon. With its packed-dirt floor and its walls of sweating fieldstone, the name seemed appropriate. Instead of chains and torture racks, though, the room was originally filled with rows of wine racks, several of which remained. Some even contained dusty bottles, though the corks were missing and the contents long gone. The parties at the Castle were now strictly BYOB—Bring Your Own Bottle—which was why the partiers never came empty-handed.

The place was already a busy port of young bodies swimming in and out of the shadows cast by a ring of lanterns. Cigarette smoke hovered over the crowd like fog. Strange computerized music rolled out of an open laptop and seemed to wrap itself around everything in sight, so that even arms and legs appeared bound by its slow staccato beat. It was unlike anything Rebekah had ever heard, and she felt the rhythm of it worming itself into her brain like some sort of parasite.

"Hey, guys," Lena called out, "here, take these bottles, will you?"

Two guys jumped at the request, taking the bottles from them. "And listen," Lena went on, "I need someone to carry in a box from my car. Can one of you do that?"

One of them volunteered, and Lena disappeared back up the stairs to lead the guy to her car.

Rebekah was left alone, but not for long. To her relief David stepped out of the crowd and greeted her with a kiss. "Hey, babe, you got here."

"Yeah."

"I missed you this week."

"Me too. You have a good trip?"

He shrugged. "Yeah, it was all right."

She didn't even know where he'd gone. He hadn't told her. She assumed he was off visiting relatives somewhere before school started.

"So what'd I miss?" he said. "Anything cool happen while I was gone?"

Rebekah shrugged casually. "No, same old stuff."

"Yeah, figures. So do your parents think you're at Lena's for the night?"

Rebekah nodded. She liked the way she felt with David's arm around her, and she relaxed for the first time since parking her car among the grove of trees outside. David would make sure everything was all right.

"Good, good. Cool," he said. "So we've got all night."

"Yeah." Rebekah smiled. "All night. Is Jim here?"

"Yeah, he's here somewhere. What about Lena?"

"She's gone out with some guy to bring in some stuff from her car."

"Good stuff, I hope."

"Straight from her mother's own stash."

David laughed. "Everyone needs a mother like that, huh?"

"Yeah." Rebekah shrugged. "Yeah, I guess so."

"So listen, Bek. We're going to try something new tonight."

"We are?"

"Uh-huh." He nodded, looked around the room. Rebekah thought of the coke. "I'm not sure I want to do anything like that."

David snickered. "You don't even know what it is."

"Yeah I do."

"No, I bet you don't. I just learned about it from my cousin a few days ago. Believe me, you'll love it. It's over the top. But first things first, huh? How about a drink?"

Rebekah drew in a deep breath. Maybe a drink would help.

David took her hand and led her across the room to an impossibly long table where bottles of booze were laid out like a glassy-eyed field of dreams.

Phoebe breathed softly and evenly. John stopped singing, waited, listened to the child draw in air, let it out. He stood slowly, so as not to wake her.

He looked down at the face illumined by the dim light from the kitchen. How could it be that she was his?

His heart ached with love and with a fierce determination. He wasn't going to make a mess of things with this child, no matter what. Now that he had her, he was keeping her, and he intended to give her a childhood worth cherishing. As far as the family as a whole was concerned, he knew there was plenty of work ahead of him. He still had messes to untangle with Andrea and Beka, but he was determined to smooth them out, to make amends for his mistakes, to ask forgiveness as many times as forgiveness was needed. Love covered a multitude of sins, even his.

He bent down and gently kissed the child's warm cheek. She stirred, sighed, rolled over. As he moved quietly across the room, he heard a tiny voice call out from the bed, "I love you, Daddy."

"I love you too, Phoebe."

He stepped into the kitchen and turned out the light.

The air in the Dungeon was beginning to be stifling. By now, Rebekah thought, the entire teen population of Conesus had succeeded in squeezing themselves into this one subterranean room. The only kids missing were the losers, the geeks, and the loners. Nearly everyone else she knew from school was at the Castle, along with plenty of people she didn't know. Not only were kids milling around, they were also crowded onto lawn chairs, bean bags, throw pillows, even several couches that had been dragged down from upstairs by partiers from years past. Rebekah was beginning to feel claustrophobic from the press of bodies around her. Maybe the police were willing to play dumb, but she wondered whether any parents might wise up and bust the party.

She surprised herself with the thought that she hoped somebody would. She hoped someone would come and blow the whistle, cutting short this whole end-of-summer blowout before something bad happened. She couldn't shake the feeling of dread that grew heavier as the night wore on. Outwardly she talked with friends, she laughed, she danced with David to the strange beat of the music. Inwardly she was on edge, as though she were inching up the steepest incline of a roller coaster and she was just about to reach the crest before the fall.

She nursed her fifth gin and tonic. The second, third, and fourth she had discreetly dumped out onto the floor. David kept bringing her more in large red plastic cups. But she didn't want to get wasted. She wanted to keep her head on straight. She was watching everyone, watching the crowd's slow descent from sobriety to tipsiness to flat-out drunk. The deeper they sank, the louder they got and the more they laughed. But after all, that was the point, wasn't it? To laugh all the way to that place of feeling no pain.

Rebekah had been there many times before, but she wasn't going back tonight. Not this time. Something was about to happen, and she was waiting for it. She didn't know what it was, but she knew it was coming. She could feel it.

She jumped when someone laid a hand on her shoulder. It was only Lena, who leaned in close and shouted over the music and the din of the crowd, "Hey, Beka, Jim and I are going up to the library for a while. We heard there's something going on up there."

Jim laughed. "Yeah, it's a meeting of the book club. Want to come?"

Rebekah ignored Jim. "What's going on?" she asked Lena.

"Someone brought something I want to try."

"It's not coke, is it?"

"No, no, no." Lena shook her head. Her eyes were beginning to glaze, and her breath was heavy with alcohol. "There are better ways to get high than to burn out the lining of your nose. I'd rather pop a pill. It's so much easier."

"What are you talking about?"

Lena leaned even closer. "It's Ecstasy. Want to try it?"

Rebekah drew back. "I don't think so. I—"

"Oh, come on, Bek. You won't believe the rush."

"How do you know? You've tried it before?"

Lena glanced at Jim, then back at Rebekah. "Sure. Once or twice."

"What's up?" David, who'd just returned from refilling his cup, shot the question at Jim and Lena.

"They've got some hug drug upstairs," Jim said. "Want a hit?"

"Ecstasy?" David asked.

Jim nodded.

"Who brought it?"

"Dan Bradley," Jim said.

"No lie." David's eyes widened. "Chief Bradley's son?"

Jim nodded again.

"What'd he do?" David asked. "Raid the evidence room?"

"I don't know," Jim said. "Who cares, as long as he's got it."

Rebekah kneaded her forehead with the fingertips of one hand. The son of the chief of police brought street drugs? *Everything's crazy,* she thought. Lena, Jim, this party, the whole world— nothing made sense. And she didn't know whether it was because the world really was senseless, or because her own mind was breaking up into fearful little pieces. *What's wrong with me?* she wondered.

She felt as though she were finally living out one of the recurring nightmares of this past year, the dream that something evil was moving toward her and she couldn't run away or even move. Half asleep and half awake, she lay helpless on the bed, pinned down by something she couldn't see, though she heard it breathing just above her in the dark.

"Listen, I don't think so," David said. Rebekah looked up and saw him wave a hand, as though to brush away Jim's offer. "Not tonight. Maybe next time, though, huh?"

Jim, looking cocky, said, "Your loss. Lena and I are out of here."

Rebekah grabbed Lena's hand. "You're coming back down, aren't you?"

"I don't know," Lena said. "Maybe. It depends."

"On what?" Rebekah asked, but Lena pulled her hand away, and in another moment she was lost to the crowd.

David drew her close, and Rebekah leaned hard against him.

She sighed deeply. At least she was safe here, her forehead pressed against David's shoulder. The drink in her hand—that she could get rid of. She wanted to stay straight and to stay close to David. He would make sure everything was all right.

She felt herself cradled in his arms for a moment, until he lifted her chin and said loudly over the music, "Well, babe, now that everyone's got a buzz on, time for a little Space Monkey."

"Space Monkey?"

"Come on."

He took her hand, and they wormed through the crush of bodies until David found who he was looking for. "Hey, Chase," he shouted, "ready for a little Airplane Ride?"

Chase smiled, nodded. Rebekah recognized him from the basketball team at Conesus High.

Girls fawned all over him for his golden-boy looks and his athletic ability, but he was also a bookish guy who worked as the sports editor for the school newspaper. He was known for his ranting editorials on the use of steroids in professional sports, and the faculty had set him up as a youthful front-runner in the zero-tolerance-for-drugs campaign.

At the moment he was drinking vodka straight from the bottle. "Let's do it," he said.

Rebekah watched as David and Chase rolled some kids off a couple of large pillows, claiming the cushions for themselves. The evicted kids protested until David said something, and they nodded. They cleared some space so that Chase could stand between the pillows, one in front of him, one behind. The bottle of vodka had disappeared.

Chase leaned forward and put his hands on his knees. Then he started breathing deeply and quickly while the kids around him cheered him on. Rebekah sensed the presence of the dream being just beyond her shoulder. The cup she was holding dropped from her hand and landed on the floor, splattering her drink everywhere. No one seemed to notice. Everyone close by was focused on Chase, who had straightened up and was holding his breath. David came from behind, wrapped both arms around Chase's chest and squeezed. Rebekah stood motionless, her heart beating out the seconds until Chase went limp and David let him fall to the floor. He rolled, stopped, lifted one hand to his head, then rolled some more. When he opened his eyes, he laughed loudly and pounded the floor with a fist.

One of the girls jumped up and yelled, "There's another way to do it. Watch!"

Rebekah took a step backward. She didn't want to watch, but she couldn't turn away. She knew the girl. Her name was Nadine. They'd briefly been lab partners in chemistry last year. Nadine pulled another girl up from the floor and told her to stand against the wall. She lifted her hands to either side of the girl's neck.

Now Rebekah understood. This was the Choking Game. She'd heard about it but had never seen it done. She'd looked it up once on the Internet, a search that landed her on a site that listed the names of the kids who had died playing. Cut off the oxygen to the brain long enough, you get a high. Cut it off too long, and that's it.

Rebekah took another step backward. "Dad," she whispered, surprised at herself for speaking the word aloud. But she said it again. "Dad." He had stood in the doorway, looking heavy and tired. *"It's over,"* he'd said. It must have taken all of his strength to end it. But that was the thing. He had done it.

She patted the pocket of her shorts, felt the

bulge of her car keys. In her mind she calculated the distance between herself and the stairs leading out of the Dungeon. The staircase wasn't far away. It was just a matter of pushing through the crowd to get there.

She turned, but even as she was turning, someone grabbed her hand and held it tight. She looked up into David's smiling face.

"Time to fly," he said.

John had just begun to sink gently into sleep when he was jolted awake by the telephone. He rolled toward the night table between the beds, noted drowsily the time on the clock—just past midnight—and picked up the cordless receiver in time to cut short the second ring.

Hoping it was a wrong number, he asked tentatively, "Yes? Hello?"

"Dad?"

He was wide awake now. "Beka? What's the matter?"

"I—"

He waited, but she didn't finish. She was weeping uncontrollably. John sat up, threw his legs over the side of the bed. Andrea was awake now too, watching him intently. "What is it?" she whispered.

He raised a hand. "Beka, sweetheart, pull yourself together and tell me what's wrong. Are you hurt?"

He heard her take a deep breath and then let the air out in a wrenching sigh.

"Daddy." She sounded far away, years away, as if she were a little girl again. "Can you come get me? My car won't start."

John frowned, rubbed the side of his brow with his free hand. "Of course I'll come get you but—"

"My car has a flat," Andrea reminded him, speaking softly. "Let me talk to her."

He held up his index finger this time. "Just a minute, Andrea," he said, speaking over the mouthpiece. Then into the phone, he said, "Honey, you're at Lena's, right?" Ironically, he knew exactly how to get to Lena's house. He could be there in just a few minutes.

He heard her sniff loudly. "No, Dad, no." More sobbing. "I'm at the party. At the Castle."

"At the Castle?"

John looked up and met Andrea's gaze. He should have known. Andrea had never been, but John remembered only too well those end-of-summer gatherings at the Castle.

John and Andrea both looked toward the window. Out there, across the lake, somewhere on the other side was their daughter. John stood and walked to the window. The night was calm. He heard the gentle lapping of the lake on the shore, the tapping of the boats against the dock. The night sounds stood in sharp contrast to the pounding of his own heart against his ribs. Never

338

in his life had he felt a fear quite like this, not even when the cell door slammed shut behind him for the first time.

Andrea came up behind him. "She's been drinking, hasn't she?"

That wasn't what mattered, not right now. All that mattered was that he reach her and bring her home.

"Beka, where exactly are you?"

He heard her sniff. "In my car," she said, her voice rising. "It won't start. Dad, I didn't like what they were doing in there. I ran out. I just want to come home, and now my car won't start."

"I know, honey. Listen, do you have a flashlight in the car?"

"Yeah."

"Okay. Here's what I want you to do. Take the flashlight and go down by the shore and wave it back and forth slowly, in a small arc. Just keep waving it, okay?"

"Why, Dad?"

"I can't drive over to get you because your mother's car has a flat. But Billy and I will come in the motorboat—"

Andrea pulled on his arm so hard the phone came away from his ear. "John, don't!" she cried. "I'll call Owen. He can drive over and get her."

John tensed. "Beka, hold on just a minute." Putting his hand over the mouthpiece, he said, "No, Andrea, we're not calling Owen. Not this time."

"But why not, John?" Andrea asked, wide-eyed.

"Because Beka is my daughter, and I'm going to go get her and bring her home."

"But you can't go out in the boat in the middle of the night. It's not legal. Don't be a fool!"

"Listen, Andrea," John said evenly. "I appreciate what Owen did for this family while I was gone. But I'm not gone anymore. I'm here and this is my family, and I'm going to take care of all of you. Do you understand? Now, it's one mile across. One mile. Billy and I can be over and back in ten minutes."

Andrea's lips trembled, but she didn't speak. John looked at her until footfalls on the stairs pulled his eyes past her shoulder. Then Billy's head appeared beyond the railings of the banister. "Mom, Dad, what's going on?"

"Get dressed, Billy," John said. "We're going out in the motorboat."

"We are? Right now?"

John nodded tersely.

"But, Dad, you can't be on the water after dark."

John ignored him. He lifted the phone to his ear. "Beka, honey, you there? Okay, listen, wait in the car for about five minutes, then go on down to the shore and start waving the flashlight. I'm going to hang up this phone now, but we'll call you back on Billy's phone, all right? We'll stay on the line with you until we get there. Okay, honey . . . don't be afraid. We'll call you right back, and we'll be there in just a few minutes. I'm going to hang up now, but Billy will call you right back. . . . Yes, it's all right. Don't cry. Hang up so Billy can call you on his cell. Bye, honey."

He pressed the off button on the phone. "All right, Billy," he said. "Let's go."

Andrea opened the door between the kitchen and the bedroom just far enough to peek in and check on Phoebe. Still sleeping. She quietly withdrew and shut the door.

She moved across the kitchen to the refrigerator, stepping softly on the cheap foam of the beach sandals she wore as summer slippers. The flashlight she was looking for clung to the side of the refrigerator by a magnet. She peeled it off and pushed the rubber-coated button that turned on the bulb. The beam settled on the face of the clock above the stove. 12:25 A.M. For a moment her feet refused to move as she considered what they were doing, the danger of it, and the stupidity. Why didn't they just call Owen? He could run over and get Beka and be back in his own bed in half an hour. But no, John had to play the hero, and he had to take Billy with him.

Andrea shut her eyes, clenched her teeth. *Dear God,* she thought, *if you've never done anything for me before, please do something for me now.*

"Andrea, did you find the flashlight?" John asked, calling softly from the front room.

She opened her eyes. She flashed the beam toward him as her reply. John and Billy, both in shorts, T-shirts, and their work Reeboks, stood illumined in the circle of light.

"Okay," John said. "Let's get moving."

Outside, a wave of cool air washed over them as they walked across the yard and down the steps to the dock. John spoke quietly into Billy's phone, assuring Beka they were coming. Billy eased himself down into the boat and took his position by the motor. John followed, settling in the front of the boat.

"We'll be there in just a few minutes," John said into the phone.

Andrea felt an increase in the wind, felt the hem of her cotton robe dance about her legs like an open tent flap. Overhead, the moon disappeared behind a cloud, then reappeared. A thousand stars winked at her through a thin veil of scattered clouds.

"There's Beka," Billy said, pointing toward the Castle. The whole lake was rimmed with lights— porch lights, streetlamps, the occasional cottage window. But directly across the lake was a wide expanse of darkness in which one small light moved rhythmically back and forth along the shore.

"We see you, honey," John told Rebekah. "We're in the boat now. We're on our way."

John looked up at Andrea. "You do the same on this side, Andrea. Just wave the flashlight till we get back. Got it?"

Andrea nodded. She tried to swallow her fear, but it stuck like a bitter pill at the back of her throat.

"Start that motor, Billy," John said.

Billy nodded importantly, turned toward the motor, and pulled the cord. Nothing happened. He tried again.

Nothing.

"All right, Billy," John said. "Don't pull too hard. Just a good swift jerk should do it."

"I'm trying, Dad."

"I know you are, son."

Billy stood over the motor, breathed in, pulled the cord. In the silence that followed he said, "Remember, I told you. It doesn't always start right away."

"Do you want me to give it a try?"

"No, Dad. I know what I'm doing. I know this motor, and you don't."

"Okay. Give it another pull when you're ready."

Andrea tried to keep quiet. She looked across the lake at the one small pendulum of light swinging on the shore. Her daughter, alone in the dark, waiting for rescue by a couple of knights in shining armor who couldn't get their horse saddled and running.

"John—"

"Just a minute, Andrea. Okay, Billy, give it a sec, then try again."

"John, I really think . . ."

But he wasn't listening.

A minute passed, then two, as Billy pulled the cord again and again. Finally John slapped the rim of the boat with an open hand. "It's not going to start!" he yelled. "Doesn't anything work around here?"

"I'll keep trying, Dad!"

John stood up, steadied himself as the boat rocked slowly from side to side. "It's no use. It's not going to start."

Andrea saw her chance. "I'll go call Owen."

"Nobody's calling Owen," John shot back. He climbed out of the motorboat onto the dock. "Beka is my daughter, and I'm going to get her."

"But, John—"

He pushed past her and leapt into the rowboat tied up on the other side of the dock.

"What are you doing?" Andrea asked.

"Getting my daughter."

"You can't—"

She didn't finish. She watched helplessly as John untied the rope anchoring the boat to the dock. She turned back to the motorboat, where Billy continued pulling the cord. At the sight of him, a memory flashed through her mind: Billy the ten-year-old child, up half the night, alternately attempting to tie his shoes and pounding

344

the floor with his fists. No matter how she coaxed and finally begged, she couldn't persuade him to give up and try again in the morning. It was after one o'clock when, with his shoes still on his feet, he fell exhausted into bed. But the shoes were tied.

"Billy!" she cried. "Hand me one of those life jackets." She waited, hand extended. He didn't turn from the motor. "Billy, give me a life jacket now!"

John had settled onto the middle bench of the rowboat and was slipping the oars into the locks.

"Billy!"

Billy froze as though her voice had finally cut through his concentration. He turned a scowling face at her, picked up a life jacket from the floor of the boat, and tossed it at her.

She caught it, turned, and passed it off to John. "Here," she pleaded, "put this on."

He reached for it, slid it around his neck, left it untied. "I'll be back in twenty," he said.

Andrea watched as the oars sliced the surface of the lake. The paddles momentarily disappeared, then shot up again like harried wings. The beads of water rolling down the paddle edges flashed like shiny gems in the beam of her flashlight.

Just as John passed the end of the dock, Andrea thought she felt a drop of rain.

"Hello?" Rebekah whispered into the phone. "Where are you guys?"

She sat crouched on her haunches by the shore of the lake, instinctively trying to make herself small. She looked behind her, first to the right, then to the left. She was afraid someone would stumble out of the Castle and find her. She didn't want to be found. She just wanted to go home.

She shivered in the cool air. "Dad?" she called, a little louder now. "Billy? Will somebody please answer me?"

She pressed the phone against her ear, listening intently. Her mother's voice reached her, sounding far away, calling Billy's name.

"Mom?" She pressed her lips together to stop them from trembling as tears rolled down her cheeks. "Will somebody please tell me what's going on?"

No one answered. Rebekah looked over her shoulder again. She shifted her position on the pebbled shore. Her legs had begun to ache. She realized she had stopped swinging the flashlight. Sighing, she started again.

"Mom? Dad? Billy?"

No one answered.

Billy's fist met the motor with a deep thud. "Come on, you stupid thing!" he cried, his voice high-pitched with frustration.

"Billy, never mind. Dad's already headed out in the rowboat."

"But, Mom . . ." Billy squeezed his small eyes shut and clenched both fists at his sides.

"It's all right, Billy. Really. You tried really hard. But there's something wrong with the motor, and it's just not going to start."

Billy's doughy fist slammed once more against the top of the motor.

Andrea looked out over the lake, saw the small light waving on the other side. "Listen, Billy," she said. "I know you want to help, and there's something you can do. We need to wave the flashlight the way Beka's doing. That will help Dad find his way home once he's got Beka. Come on. You can wave the flashlight."

Billy looked up at her then with eyes that glistened in the peripheral glow of the flashlight.

Andrea pretended she didn't see the tears. She held out a hand to her son. "Come on, Billy. It's important that you wave the light."

He would need a few minutes to concede defeat. Andrea waited.

John figured he was halfway across the lake now, right in the middle of the dark water, sandwiched between the two swinging lights. He willed himself not to think of the murky depths below, the black depths that had so frightened him as a boy. *Just keep rowing,* he told himself. *Concentrate on reaching Beka.*

Oars in, pull, oars out, swing back. In, pull, out,

swing back. The small vessel lurched forward. John's heart pumped, his breath was rapid and shallow. He was out of shape and already tiring. When was the last time he had rowed a boat? So many years ago, he couldn't remember.

In, out, pull, swing back.

He would be there in just another couple of minutes. Maybe Beka could see him now, slicing his way through the glassy lake.

He stopped, looked over his shoulder, adjusted the boat slightly to line up with the light. He was more than halfway there.

Suddenly he remembered Billy's phone. He had had it in his hand in the motorboat. He must have dropped it when he was climbing out. He hoped Billy had found it by now and was on the line with Beka, assuring her that Dad was coming.

In, pull, out, swing back.

The wind was picking up again, and it seemed to be working against him. Maybe it would be in their favor on the way back. Head winds now, tail winds home.

John looked overhead while trying not to break his rhythm. The night sky's array of lights grew dimmer as the low-lying clouds grew thicker, eclipsing the stars. But John knew he'd be all right as long as he was guided by the flashlights on either side of the lake.

In the next moment he seemed to pass over an invisible line that said he was safe. He could feel it in his gut. The depths had receded, and the floor of the lake was tilting upward now, the water becoming shallower with every stroke. He was almost there. Yes, there was Beka, waving her long arms triumphantly, signaling him to shore. He might have pulled up to the Castle's dock had it not rotted away long ago. Only a few of the supporting poles remained, sticking up out of the water, useful only as perches for gulls. John kept rowing until the ribs of the boat rubbed up against the lake's sandy bottom, bringing him to an abrupt stop. He breathed out a sigh of relief, settled the oars in the boat, and stepped out. Holding the boat with one hand, he embraced his daughter with his free arm as she waded out to meet him.

"Are you all right?" he asked.

"Yeah," she nodded. "I'm just—I thought you were coming in the motorboat."

"It wouldn't start."

"I was scared, Dad."

"It's all right, honey. You're safe now."

He helped her into the boat and then climbed in after her.

"Is there a life jacket under your seat?" he asked.

She looked, shook her head no. He took off the one he was wearing and tossed it to her.

She started to protest. "No, Dad. You keep it—"

"Put it on, Beka," he interrupted. "Let's get going."

• • •

Rebekah wanted to say she was sorry, but she couldn't find the words. She would probably end up grounded again. That was all right. She didn't want to see David for a long time anyway. Maybe never. She wasn't even sure about her friendship with Lena. If she wasn't allowed to talk with anyone for a month, what would it matter?

She looked off into the distance, thinking how strange it was to be in the middle of the lake in the middle of the night. How big and empty it was without the usual boats and jet skis and swimmers. Just a wide, lonely patch of black that she and her dad were moving across in small, uneven strokes. No sign even of one of those Coast Guard Auxiliary patrol boats that buzzed all over the lake on summer days. They were off duty now, assuming no one would be crazy enough to be out in a boat at this hour. Especially since it was against the law.

"Dad?"

"Yeah, Beka?"

"If they catch us out here, what'll happen to you?"

"What do you mean?"

"Will they send you back to prison?"

"For this? No."

"Are you sure?"

"Yeah."

But he didn't sound sure. Rebekah was

ashamed to think her dad had had to come out and get her like this. Ashamed and yet glad that he was there and more grateful than she could say.

"Dad?"

"Yeah, Beka?"

"I really just want to go home."

Her father sat outside the glow of her flashlight, but still she was able to see the puzzled look on his face.

"That's where I'm headed," he said.

She shook her head, looked beyond his shoulder to the light swinging at the end of their dock. "No. I mean, go back to Rochester. Maybe even live in the neighborhood where we used to live when I was a kid."

He pulled on the oars a couple of times before saying, "Would you like that?"

"Yeah, I would."

"Well, I'd like that too. But I'm not sure it's going to happen anytime soon."

She nodded, dropped her eyes. "I've pretty much made a mess of everything here, I guess."

"Well, I wouldn't say that, Beka."

"I would. I've made a huge mess of everything," she said again.

"Hmm, maybe so," he replied, "but there's such a thing as second chances, you know."

She shrugged but didn't respond. She watched him pull on the oars. He was rowing slowly, as though they were out for pleasure.

"So why'd you leave the party?" he asked.

"They were doing some things I didn't want to do."

"Then I'm proud of you, Beka."

"You shouldn't be. I shouldn't have gone in the first place."

He laughed lightly. "Listen, honey, you're talking to someone who's been there. We all end up doing things we shouldn't do. That doesn't mean we're stuck there. You did the right thing in leaving."

She thought a moment. "Yeah, I guess so."

"I hate to be the snitch, but soon as we get home we'll call the police. Get them over there before anyone gets hurt."

"Lena said someone bribed the police so they wouldn't break up the party."

He laughed again. "I doubt that. But if that's the case, I'll call the mayor. We'll get someone over there."

By now they were halfway across the lake. The flashlight on the other side was drawing closer. Rebekah could see the dark outline of someone on the dock, her mother, probably. She shrank at the thought of facing her. Of course Mom was mad. She would probably start yelling as soon as Rebekah was within hearing range.

Rebekah lifted her gaze to the sky beyond the cottage. It may have been her imagination, but the night seemed to be growing darker. The stars above the western horizon were gone, as if someone had flipped a switch and turned them off. She dropped the beam of the flashlight to the water then and watched curiously as the lake's calm surface suddenly wrinkled. Small trails opened up and snaked toward the boat, followed by a wall of wind. Rebekah gasped, clutched the rim of the boat with her free hand while shining the flashlight toward her father. His face, caught in the light, was frozen and pale. He had stopped rowing. Both dripping oars hung suspended over the water.

"Dad?"

Before he could answer, the sky rumbled like a crumbling dam, dropping rain and hail over the lake. The water lashed back like a wild animal, kicking against the onslaught, churning out waves that beat against the boat. Thunder exploded around them while lightning jabbed at the shore.

Rebekah screamed. She batted her eyes against the torrent of cold rain and shivered as small pebbles of hail pelted her skin. She dropped the flashlight and held on to the boat with both hands as it thrashed about in the water.

She watched in disbelief as her father rose from his seat, reaching for an oar that had slipped from his hand. Even before he'd fully extended his arm, though, the oar was gone. He was still standing when another blast of wind slammed the boat. Rebekah screamed again, shutting her eyes against the wind and the rain and the terror. When she dared to open them, she was alone in the boat. She inhaled sharply, trying to make sense of what was happening.

"Dad!" she screamed. "Dad!"

But there was only wind and rain. And an empty seat. And one oar still held in its oarlock with no one to row it.

Odd how quiet it was beneath the surface of the lake, while overhead—only inches away—a storm raged. Wind. Thunder. Lightning. The lightning alone could stop his heart in a flash, if the water didn't fill his lungs first.

But he wasn't going to let the lake take him. Not without a fight. He had so much he needed to do. So many things he wanted to say. Still, the water was stronger than he could ever have imagined, and he felt himself held in a grip that was determined to pull him under.

Oh, God, help. . . .

His feet were bound by the weight of his shoes. He kicked his legs as though in slow motion. He used his arms to part the water over his head, to make a way out. He thought of only one thing: air. He was angry now, angrier than the lake, angry enough to break through the surface.

He could breathe! He ate the air hungrily while thrashing his arms. The rain had lessened, but the wind was still strong and the water still choppy. The waves slapped his face, threatened to drown him.

"Dad!"

Beka! Where was she? Where was the boat? He filled his lungs, gathered his strength. "I'm here! Here!" He waved an arm toward the sound of her voice.

Dear God, help me. . . .

"Dad!"

"Beka! Beka!"

"Grab the oar, Dad! Grab the oar!"

By the pale light of the moon, he saw it. He saw Beka in the boat, leaning over, thrusting the oar in his direction. He reached for it, but she was drifting, the boat was drifting.

"Dad, the life jacket! Catch it!"

He saw it fly from the boat in a narrow arc, land somewhere on the water. He flailed his arms, felt for it. It wasn't there.

A wave pushed him under. There was that eerie silence again. He wasn't going to give in to the silence.

He pulled himself up, into the air. He was tiring quickly now. He saw lights at the edge of the lake; he saw the moon, some stars. He couldn't see the boat.

Oh, God, don't let me die. . . .

"Dad! Daddy!"

Dear God, Beka! Please God, save Beka!

He hadn't done what he was supposed to do. He hadn't said all the things he was supposed to say. He hadn't listened long enough to make things right with the children, with Andrea. Certainly not with Andrea. He had waited too long for something that would never come now.

He swallowed water, felt himself sinking. He heard a buzzing in his brain, like a swarm of bees beneath his skull. Then the waters closed over his head, and everything was black.

CHAPTER FIFTY

The lake was sleeping now, like a child drained by a tantrum. Rebekah sat on the end of the dock, clutching her knees to her chest. A morning breeze sailed across the surface of the water. The air was a riot of birdsong. Gulls soared against a gray sky, dipped squawking toward the lake, rose skyward again.

As she shut her eyes and listened, she became aware of the gentle drumming of the motorboat against the dock. It was a solitary player in the morning song, now that the rowboat was lost. The storm had carried it off, whirling, without oars, helpless. No doubt it would wash up on shore somewhere, sometime. In a day or two they could search for it, haul it home. Maybe they would. Probably they wouldn't.

She wasn't sure she would ever go out in a boat

again. How could she, without remembering? For the rest of her life she would feel the rain and the wind and the hail. For as long as she lived, she would see her father struggling, his arms flailing. She would see him disappear beneath the surface of the water, reappear thrashing and gasping for breath, go under again.

Rebekah breathed deeply, as though to take in the air that her father's lungs had needed. She heard again her own screams—*"Dad! Daddy!"*— as she saw him struggling to stay afloat. She thought of how she had tossed him the life jacket; she saw him reaching for it. But then there was only the jacket floating uselessly on the heaving waves.

The dock beneath her creaked softly. Someone was coming. Rebekah slowly let out her breath before turning her head to look. There was her mother in a blue cotton dress, her hair drawn back into a clip.

"What are you doing out here so early, Beka?" she asked. She didn't sit but crossed her arms and looked out over the lake.

"Thinking."

"Did you get any sleep at all?"

"Not much."

Her mother sighed. "Are you all right?"

Rebekah was quiet a moment. "I just don't know why he did it." She had her eyes fixed on the Castle on the far side of the lake.

"You mean why he insisted on taking the boat?"

"That, and . . . why he gave me the life jacket. Why did he have to give me the life jacket?"

"Because he loves you, of course."

A weighty silence fell over them. Finally Rebekah said, "Dad and I both could have drowned, and it would have been my fault."

"It would have been your father's fault—"

"No, Mom." Rebekah shook her head sharply. "I never should have gone to the party. Then nobody would have been out in the boat."

"Well, it doesn't matter now, does it? What's done is done."

"But Dad was never a good swimmer, you know."

"Yes, I know that."

"He shouldn't have been out on the lake."

"He wouldn't listen to me. I tried to get him to call Owen, but he wouldn't. He had to get you himself."

Rebekah turned and looked up at her mother. "You know, Mom," she said, "I don't think I can ever really be mad at him again."

Her mother's face lighted up as she laughed. "Don't count on it."

"No, really, Mom. I mean, not like I was mad before. He was afraid of the water, but he was still willing to come and get me. He was even willing to . . ."

"To die saving you?"

Rebekah nodded. When she spoke, it was little more than a whisper. "Yeah. I've been thinking . . . I want to tell him . . ."

"Tell him what, Beka?"

"So many things. That I'm glad he came home, first of all. He didn't have to, did he? I mean, after prison. He could have gone somewhere else and started a different life, but he came back to us."

"Yes," her mother conceded. "He didn't have to, but he did come home."

"I guess I wish I could go back to that first day and, you know, welcome him home a little bit nicer."

"Well, it's not too late, you know." Mom nodded back toward the cottage. Rebekah followed with her eyes. Her dad, in dark shorts and white undershirt, stood on the porch steps. He lifted a hand, moved forward across the lawn and down the steep steps.

Rebekah rose to stand beside her mother as he approached.

When he reached them, he asked, "You two all right?"

Rebekah nodded.

Mom said, "Yes. We're all right. Some night, though, huh?"

"Yeah." Her father smiled sheepishly. "And some hero, huh?"

"But you are, Dad," Rebekah blurted. "You are to me."

He shook his head. "If it hadn't been for Billy's getting the motorboat started . . . He's the real hero."

"You both are, Dad."

He seemed not to hear. He was looking past her shoulder at something beyond her. "I never would have imagined Billy's doing something like that. But he has no fear of the water, does he? And anyway, he's all grown up now. He's still got that determined streak, thank God."

"Dad—"

"We'll have to make sure he knows how proud of him we are, maybe do something special for him."

"Dad?"

His eyes came to rest on her now. She locked onto his gaze to make sure he was listening.

"What is it, Beka?" His voice was gentle.

"I just wanted to say, well . . ." She glanced at her mom, back at her dad. "I'm glad you're home."

He blinked, looking puzzled. And then he seemed to hear the words and understand. He smiled. "Me too, Beka."

"Only, Dad?"

"Yeah?"

"What if the kids at school find out we were the ones who called the cops?"

Her father frowned. Then his face opened up as he shrugged. "I guess I'll just have to take you with me next time I do a dig in Peru. They'll never find us there."

Rebekah stiffened, chagrined by her old lie. But the feeling melted when she saw her father smile, heard him chuckle. Then they were laughing together.

"I don't get it," her mother said. "What's this about Peru?"

"Just a little inside joke, Mom."

"Oh. Well, then, while you're making your plans, I think I'll go up and make breakfast."

When she was gone, Dad said to Rebekah, "You hungry?"

"Starving."

He nodded toward the cottage. "Let's go set the table for your mother."

He held out an arm; she took it. Linked at the elbows, they moved along the dock toward shore.

"I hear Peru's nice this time of year," he said.

She pinched his arm and kept on walking.

CHAPTER FIFTY-ONE

"Tell me again, Billy!" Phoebe begged.

Billy laughed. "I've told you a hundred times today, Phoebe. You should be able to tell *me* the story by now."

"But I want to hear you tell it."

"Well, all right." He pretended to frown, though secretly he was happy that his little sister wanted to hear it again. She had followed him around all day like a shadow, wanting even more than usual to be with him. On top of that Dad had taken the whole family out to eat, not at Laughter's Luncheonette but at that nice restaurant on the edge of town where they'd never eaten before. Billy had asked if they could afford it, and Dad had answered, "You let me worry about that, son. This dinner is in your honor, and the guest of honor doesn't ask questions." Billy had felt like a real hero then. It was just about the best day of his life.

Now he and Phoebe were face-to-face in the bay window, Phoebe sitting cross-legged in her pajamas, waiting eagerly for Billy to start. "One more time," Billy told her, "and then you have to go to bed. Okay?"

"Okay." Phoebe nodded, and Billy smiled at the way her blond curls bobbed around her face.

"Well," he said, "you know how Beka's car died. She was stuck over there. You know, at the Castle."

"Uh-huh!"

"So she called Dad. 'Come get me!' But Mom's car had a flat. So Dad said, 'Billy, we're going in the boat!' He wanted me to drive."

Billy beamed while Phoebe's eyes danced in the artificial light of the lamp.

"But you couldn't get that old motor to start!" she piped up.

"That's right. I tried and tried. It wouldn't start. So Dad got in the rowboat, and Mom told me, 'Come on out of the motorboat.' She said, 'Shine the flashlight for Dad.'"

"But you wouldn't do it, would you, Billy?"

"No, I wouldn't!"

"Yup!"

"I hit the motor a couple of times with my hand." Billy made a fist and pointed to the fleshy part below his pinky finger. "Bam, bam! Sometimes that helps, you know."

"I bet you were mad, Billy."

"Well, yeah I was. Dad left in the rowboat. Mom swung the flashlight. I kept pulling the cord."

"And then what happened, Billy?"

"It started to rain. It rained like you never saw before. Just out of nowhere the rain was coming down and the wind was blowing"—Billy waved his arms—"and thunder was booming, and I almost fell out of the boat. Then Mom yelled, 'Get out of the boat!' She didn't want me to be hit by lightning in an aluminum boat. So I crawled up to the dock. And it rained real hard. I started to get scared. I prayed, 'God help us. God help us.' Just like that, Phoebe, because I didn't know what else to say."

Phoebe, wide-eyed, whispered, "I think He heard you."

"Yeah." Billy nodded. "He did. Because the rain slowed down. And I got back in the boat. Mom was yelling at me, but I did it anyway. I got in the boat and tried one more time. And this time the motor started."

"Oh my!" Phoebe clapped, then laced her hands together in anticipation.

"So I headed out, Phoeb. I headed to the Castle. But when I couldn't see the rowboat I got scared. Then I heard someone yelling. It sounded like Beka. I turned the boat around and headed toward the yelling. I thought it had to be Dad and Beka. Who else would be out on the lake at night like that, you know?"

A nod from Phoebe.

"But it wasn't Dad and Beka. It was just Beka. She was standing in the boat, and I saw her throw something into the lake."

"And what was it, Billy?"

"It was her life jacket. She was throwing away her life jacket, and I thought she was crazy. I didn't know why she'd do that."

"It was because Dad didn't have a life jacket on."

"That's right, Phoeb."

"He'd given her his."

"Yup, that's right."

"And he was out in the water drowning."

"Beka said she saw him go under."

"What happened after that, Billy?"

"Beka saw me. She screamed at me, and you know how she can scream."

A sympathetic nod this time.

"She said, 'Dad's drowned. Dad's drowned.' I didn't want to believe it." It didn't matter how many times Billy told Phoebe about last night. Every time he reached this part, tears came to his eyes. He blinked them back. "I was going real slow, and I pulled up alongside the rowboat the best I could. I put the motor on idle and helped Beka get in the motorboat. She was screaming and crying. I was scared we'd both fall overboard if she didn't stop. I made her sit down. I kneeled in front of her, and I put my hands on her shoulders and held on tight. She'd gone crazy, Phoebe. She kept saying she'd started the storm and killed Dad and it was all her fault. I shook her and told her to stop, but she kept screaming.

"I've never been so scared. Not ever," he whispered. He looked past Phoebe into the night, remembering.

"But what about the hand, Billy?" Phoebe prompted.

He turned his gaze back to his sister's eager face. "While Beka and I were crying and carrying on, the boat leaned way far over, and there was a hand holding on to the side!"

"It was Daddy!" Phoebe cried, clapping her hands again.

"Well, I didn't know at first what it was, but I

sure hoped it was Dad. I let go of Beka and reached over and grabbed that hand"—Billy grabbed the air—"and then another hand came up, and I grabbed it too, and then, Phoebe . . . then I was looking right into Dad's face."

"He was alive!"

"Yeah, he was. I yelled, 'Dad! Dad!' And you know what, Phoebe? I think he was kind of surprised to see me."

Phoebe lifted two small fists to her mouth and giggled. "He must have thought you'd walked on water like Jesus to come save him."

As many times as Billy had told her the story, she hadn't said that before. Billy stopped short, cocked his small head. "If I could walk on water, I would have, to save Dad. But all I did was start that dumb old motorboat."

"Oh no, Billy, you did more than that!" Phoebe shook her head hard. "You got right in the water with Dad and held on to him while Beka drove the boat home."

But Billy wasn't listening. He was looking past Phoebe again, toward the dark window. "You know, Phoeb, all day I've been feeling like I saved Dad."

"You *did* save Dad."

"Not without help."

"What do you mean, Billy?"

"Like you said, I can't walk on water."

"No, but you can swim real good."

Billy smiled at that. "Yeah," he said. "Thank God."

"Thank God," Phoebe echoed. "So then what happened?"

"Dad weighed a ton, and he was real tired. I tried to pull him into the boat, but I knew real fast I couldn't. He'd end up dumping us all out, and then we'd all be goners. So I got in the water."

"And what'd Beka say then?"

"She said, 'Billy, what are you doing? What are you doing in the water?'" He shrugged, grinning. "Well, what did she think I was doing? Taking a bath? Going scuba diving?"

Phoebe threw her head back and laughed loud and long. Billy liked that. Nothing sounded better than his little sister's laugh.

"I told her, 'I'm helping Dad hold the boat.'" I told her, 'Drive us home real slow.' So that's what we did, Phoeb."

"And Mom was still out there swinging the flashlight."

"Yup. In a few minutes we were at the dock. Dad and I walked to shore and fell over. Then Mom and Beka were there, and then we were all hugging and laughing and crying all at the same time. Like I told you before, I don't think I've ever been so happy in my whole life as I was right then."

He felt happy, just remembering. He looked at his sister and sighed in satisfaction. "So that's what happened, Phoeb."

Phoebe crossed her arms. "And I slept through the whole thing."

"Yup."

"Billy?"

"Yeah, Phoeb?"

"Thanks for saving Dad."

Billy nodded, smiled a little. "You're welcome."

"And Billy?"

"Yeah?"

"Next time you go save Dad, wake me up!"

CHAPTER FIFTY-TWO

Rebekah sat on the floor of her room, her Book of Shadows open on her lap. She read the words she had written in red ink at the beginning of the summer.

He came home today. He being the one who ruined my life. I hate him and I won't pretend to be nice to him, even though I know that's what Mom wants. Like we're one big happy family— yeah, right! I can't wait to turn eighteen and get out of here. I don't know how I'll stand it for the next two years, unless I can try and ignore these people and keep my head in something good and beautiful. That's why I need to keep up with practicing the Craft, like Aunt Jo says. She says I'll only find true peace when I recognize all is one and all is divine and even I am one

*with the goddess and the god. I can do any-
thing. If I listen to the goddess within me, she
will show me the way to peace.*

There was more, but Rebekah stopped there.
She had read enough. She slowly tore the page
out of the book and ripped it up, not stopping
until the words were broken into indecipherable
pieces on the floor at her feet.

The day her father came home she'd been given
a gift and had called it a curse. She didn't hate
him. She loved him and had loved him even then.
Part of her had known it, but the stronger part of
her had given in to anger and listened to the lies.

She pulled another page out of the notebook
and added it to the pile of shredded paper. And
then another and another. She didn't stop until
every used page in the book had followed the
first, drifting down like leaves dropping off a
vine.

When the storm started out on the lake, she
thought she had caused it—she and Lena. She
thought it was the universe responding to their
spell. But when Billy showed up and they all
reached the shore, she knew she'd had nothing
to do with any of it, and that no matter what
Lena wanted to believe, they couldn't bend the
universe to their will. They didn't have any such
power. In truth, she was smaller and weaker
than she ever might have believed. Rebekah
welcomed that thought with relief.

She pushed the pile of paper into the closet and threw what was left of the notebook on top of it. She'd clean up the mess tomorrow. Standing, she stretched her legs, then turned out the light on the bedside table.

The sun was long gone, and the room should have been dark, but a soft glow rose from the floor beneath the window. Thinking Phoebe must have been playing with a flashlight, Rebekah walked around the foot of the bed to turn it off.

But when she saw what was shining, she said aloud, "What's that doing in here?" Slowly she knelt in front of the light in the outlet, Billy's little lamb nightlight. It seemed the perfect picture of peace, the little lamb curled up sleeping in the glow of the light. No wonder kids liked the thing when they saw it on display down at the arcade. She could even understand why Billy wanted it. What kid wouldn't feel safe, drifting off to sleep while gazing at a picture like that? It gave a person the feeling that there really was peace in the world somewhere.

But then, Rebekah thought, maybe there was. And maybe it was even possible to find it.

Laughter drifted in from the front room, and Rebekah followed it to where Billy and Phoebe sat together in the bay window.

"Hey, Billy?"

"Yeah, Beka?"

"Your nightlight's in my room."

"I know. I put it there."

"Well, why? I mean, I thought you wanted it so bad."

"I did, and I'm going to take it back someday, but for now I want you to use it."

Rebekah cocked her head. "How come?"

"I thought it might help keep away the nightmares. With little lamb there, the room won't be so dark."

"But—" Rebekah started to protest, then stopped herself. "Are you sure, Billy?"

"I'm positive."

"Well . . ." Rebekah smiled and shrugged. "Okay. Thanks. But let me know when you want it back, okay?" She turned to Phoebe. "Time for you to go to bed, isn't it?"

The child nodded. "Billy was just about to sing me a good-night song."

"Oh yeah? How about if I tuck you in tonight?"

She saw Phoebe hesitate. "Will you sing me something?" the child asked doubtfully.

"Well," Rebekah paused, thought a moment, "yeah. I'll try to come up with something. Come on." She held out her arms to Phoebe. "I'll give you a lift."

Phoebe jumped up and fell into her sister's arms.

Rebekah started to turn away when Billy called her back. "Hey, Beka?"

"Yeah, Billy?"

"You have to sing a happy song, remember? We don't sing any sad songs around here."

Rebekah nodded. "Don't worry, Billy," she said. "I'll sing something happy."

"Okay. Good night, Phoebe."

"Good night, Billy."

"I love you, Phoeb."

"I love you too, Billy."

Rebekah turned again and started to step across the room when Billy's voice stopped her.

"Beka?"

She looked over her shoulder. "Yeah, Billy?"

"I love you too."

Rebekah felt something stir inside of her, something that resisted his words. But as she gazed at his open, childlike face, her resistance melted.

"I love you too, Billy," she said, and she knew that it was true.

Even as she spoke Rebekah heard her father's footsteps on the stairs. Then Phoebe called out, "Good night, Daddy! Beka's putting me to bed tonight."

He came to them, kissed them both tenderly on their foreheads. "Good night, girls. I love you both."

"We love you too, Daddy," Phoebe said. "Good night, Mommy!"

Their mother stood beyond the screen door, blowing kisses from the porch. "Good night, Phoebe. Sweet dreams."

"You don't have to tuck me in tonight, Mommy. Beka's going to do it."

"I can see that. Aren't you lucky?"

Rebekah felt Phoebe's arms tighten around her neck in a long hug. Rebekah squeezed back. "Come on, you," she said, "let's get you in bed. You have the nightlight to help you sleep now."

"And you have the nightlight too, Beka."

"Yeah, me too."

"And a happy song."

Rebekah laughed lightly. "Yeah, that too."

She kissed the child softly and carried her to their room.

CHAPTER FIFTY-THREE

After saying good-night, Andrea moved across the porch and looked out toward the lake. She had one finger pressed between the pages of a book to mark her place, though she was tired of reading beneath the dim wattage of the porch light. It didn't matter. She had been reading from a collection of poems, and she knew this one by heart.

> Downstairs I laugh, I sport and jest with all;
> But in my solitary room above
> I turn my face in silence to the wall;
> My heart is breaking for a little love.

Christina Rossetti died alone, never having married. Some lives refuse to become love stories. Andrea knew this by now. Still, when she read this poem, when Christina's voice rose up off the page and traveled through the years to live again in Andrea's mind, Andrea was strangely comforted. She was in the company of lonely women, and there were many. Some, she knew, gave in to despair. Others, like Christina, waited, believing that though they would never fall in love in this life, they would fall wholly into love in the next. At least that seemed to be what Christina meant in the final lines of her poem.

> Yet saith an angel: "Wait, and thou shalt prove
> True best is last, true life is born of death,
> O thou, heart-broken for a little love.
> Then love shall fill thy girth,
> And love make fat thy dearth,
> When new spring builds new heaven and
> clean new earth."

Andrea didn't know what she thought about that. *Wishful thinking,* the skeptics might say. *A kettle of false hope.* She might have agreed once, having been ambivalent about God all her life. But now she wasn't so sure.

Just last night, after the storm, she had kneeled beside John on the rocky shore. Rebekah was there, and Billy—all of them wet, cold, shivering, but they were alive. "Thank God," she had said. John had looked up then, had pressed a gentle hand against her cheek.

She lifted her fingers now to her face, felt again the warmth of his moist skin against her own. "Thank God," she'd said, and she had wanted there to be someone to receive her gratitude, someone who was not only watching over them from a distance, but who was right there with them on the rocky shore after the storm.

Maybe it was so, she thought. And maybe she had seen a miracle of sorts. Not just last night, when who knew but maybe the hand of God had been extended to them over the lake. But she was thinking too of tonight, of her children, the three of them calling out to each other, "I love you."

Something had come to this small cottage, bringing with it a measure of healing. She hoped that whatever it was, it would stay. There were so many broken places to be healed.

John didn't love her, but she wouldn't allow herself to give in to despair. He would never love her, and he would probably never be faithful. She knew that. But maybe his faithlessness didn't mean a loveless life, not while she had her children, not while there was the possibility of a loving God in heaven. She wanted to hope, the way the poet had hoped.

"Andrea? What are you doing?"

She gasped, startled, then looked back over her shoulder to find John standing in the doorway. He stepped fully onto the porch, the screen slamming behind him.

"I'm just—" What was she doing? She was trying to live without him, even though he was there. "I was reading, but it's grown too dark to read now."

"What are you reading?"

"Oh." She tried to laugh. "A book of poems. It's just something I've had a long time."

"You like poetry?"

"Some. There are some poems I like."

"That's interesting. I never knew that."

Andrea tilted her head. "Never knew what?"

"That you like poetry."

"Well, yes . . ." Her voice trailed off. Her breath grew shallow and her jaw tightened as she waited for him to speak.

"Andrea," he said at length. "We need to talk."

So that was it, she thought. He might have picked a better time, at the end of a different day, or at least when the children weren't home. She took a deep breath to steel herself. "Okay."

He nodded toward the glider. "Want to sit down?"

She did. Her legs had suddenly grown weak. She joined him on the glider, settled the small volume of poetry on her lap. She folded her hands and kept her eyes downcast. Her heart leapt wildly in her chest. It was one thing to know; it was something altogether different to hear the words.

It'll be all right, she told herself. *You'll manage. You always do.*

When at last John spoke, he said, "I need to ask you to forgive me."

She waited a moment, but when he didn't say anything more, she asked, "For what, John?"

He sighed heavily. "The list is so long, I hardly know where to begin."

She knew. She knew what was on that list, knew even better than John all the ways he had hurt her. But she said, "Whatever all of it is, none of it matters."

"It does matter, Andrea. All of it."

She tried to moisten her lips, but her tongue was dry. "Well, it's all right, then," she said quietly. "I forgive you."

"Don't say that yet, or it won't really mean anything. Hear me out, all right?"

She lifted her shoulders lightly. "Okay."

"You say you like poetry?"

"Yes. Some."

"Have you ever read a poem called 'The Hound of Heaven'?"

" 'The Hound of Heaven'?"

He nodded. She thought a moment, shook her head. "No, I don't think so. What's it about?"

"I'll tell you. But at the same time, I want to tell

you about what happened to me in prison. Can I do that?"

"I've been waiting all summer for you to tell me."

To her surprise he reached over and unclasped her hands, pulling one into his own. She had forgotten what that was like, the simple act of holding John's hand.

He said, "We're going to make this family work, Andrea."

"We are?"

"Yes. I'm determined."

"Then—" She was afraid to say it but forced herself. "Then you're not leaving me?"

"Leaving you?" He shook his head, slowly at first, then more emphatically. "No, Andrea, I'm not leaving you."

"But—"

"We have so much to talk about—"

"I thought maybe you wanted—"

"Andrea, hear me out. I've been a lousy husband and a not-so-good father, but that's going to change. You, me, the kids—we're going to be a family. I mean, a real family. Tonight was a good start, don't you think?"

"Well, yes." She was hesitant but willing to agree. "I mean, I never would have imagined all three of them together like that, getting along. Billy and Phoebe, yes, but Beka . . ." She shook her head. "I don't know how that happened."

"I think . . ." He paused a moment, seeming to weigh his words. Then he said, "I think it's called grace."

She went on shaking her head, her brow heavy. "I don't know what that is."

"That's what I want to tell you, the best I can."

He squeezed her hand. And when he did, she tried—she tried very hard—not to let the tears rise up, not to let them gather on the half-moon of each lower lid. But she couldn't hold them back. When they spilled over, she watched as John lifted his free hand to wipe them away.

"I'm sorry, John," she said.

"No, no, no, it's all right. Don't apologize." He let go of her hand and dug into the pocket of his shorts. He pulled out a neatly folded handkerchief and offered it to her. "You know, I can't believe you even stick a handkerchief into the pocket of my shorts, for crying out loud."

She smiled apologetically, then took the handkerchief, blew her nose, dabbed at her face. As she wiped away the tears, she found herself laughing—at herself, at the handkerchief, at the strange twists and turns of life.

"There. That's better," John said. He was smiling too. "You know what Billy says. We don't sing any sad songs around here. Only happy songs."

She shut her eyes, nodded, knew that she was opening the gift she had longed for on the day

John came home. Even the summer they were young and in love wasn't like this. Second chances were sweeter than the first.

"So in prison," John started, taking her hand again, "I was biding my time, trying not to be noticed, you know? I just wanted to do my time and get out. But someone found me there— chased me down, I guess you could say. . . ."

She nodded again, listening. The glider swayed gently as he talked. As the minutes ticked by, and then an hour, she felt something she hadn't felt in a long time. She thought it must be hope, but as he told his story, she realized that what filled her was something wholly unfamiliar, and she decided it just might be the first raw impression of grace.

She was content to sit and listen to John for as long as he wanted to talk, far into the night, if need be. She would be happy to stay right there until the whole night passed and dawn came seeping in through a crack in the horizon. It would be the first day of a life she'd never known before, and she would welcome it. For now, though, beyond the dim light of the porch and out beyond the dark sloping yard, a streak of moonlight glimmered like a golden road across the lake while a flock of gulls lifted from the shore and sailed like pilgrims toward the waiting stars.

Author's note

Sometime back in the 1920s my grandfather Harry Tatlock bought a cottage on Conesus Lake in upstate New York, not far from the family home in Rochester. I have photos of my mother as a very young girl there. My favorite is the one in which she's about four years old and she's standing on the dock with the lake behind her. She looks adorable in a cotton print dress, her smiling face framed by a floppy sunbonnet. Decades later she would return to the cottage for summer vacations with her husband and their three daughters. I am, of course, one of those girls, and my memories of that lakeside cottage are among the best of my childhood.

The setting re-created here is based largely on those long-ago impressions of Conesus Lake, mixed with more than a little poetic license. But that's a writer's prerogative, I think, and I hope those readers presently acquainted with the lake will be patient with my flights of fancy.

About the Author

Ann Tatlock is the author of the Christy Award–winning novel *All the Way Home*. She has also won the Midwest Independent Publishers Association "Book of the Year" award in fiction for both *All the Way Home* and *I'll Watch the Moon*. Ann lives with her husband, Bob, and their daughter, Laura, in Asheville, North Carolina.

Visit Ann's Web site: *www.anntatlock.com*

Center Point Publishing

600 Brooks Road ● PO Box 1
Thorndike ME 04986-0001 USA

(207) 568-3717

US & Canada:
1 800 929-9108
www.centerpointlargeprint.com